DEATH
TROOPERS

Books published by The Random House Publishing Group
are available at quantity discounts on bulk purchases for
premium, educational, fund-raising, and special sales use.
For details, please call 1-800-733-3000.

STAR WARS®
DEATH TROOPERS

JOE SCHREIBER

DEL REY • NEW YORK

Star Wars: Death Troopers is a work of fiction. Names, places, and incidents either are products of the author's imagination or are used fictitiously.

2010 Del Rey Mass Market Edition

Published in the United States by Del Rey, an imprint of Random House, a division of Random House LLC, a Penguin Random House Company, New York.

DEL REY and the HOUSE colophon are registered trademarks of Random House LLC.

Originally published in hardcover in the United States by Del Rey, an imprint of Random House, a division of Random House LLC, in 2009.

This book contains an excerpt from the forthcoming hardcover edition of *Star Wars: Red Harvest*. This excerpt has been set for this edition only and may not reflect the final content of the forthcoming novel.

ISBN 978-0-345-52081-4

Printed in the United States of America

www.starwars.com
www.delreybooks.com

10   9   8   7

To my children, J and V. Every day you amaze me.

Acknowledgments

First and foremost, I want to offer my heartfelt thanks to Keith Clayton and Erich Schoeneweiss at Del Rey for planting this demented seed and making it grow, with a particular shout-out to Erich's brother-in-law Andrew Goletz, who wrote the first outline for the project—the one that convinced everybody that it wasn't just a crazy fever-dream. Dave Stevenson is the greatest art director in the world, the man responsible for the awesome-beyond-awesome jacket that grabbed the Internet by the throat. Ali Kokmen, Christine Cabello, David Moench, and Joseph Scalora are all mad and wonderful marketing and publicity geniuses, and they've been over-the-top enthusiastic and supportive of this project from the beginning. And of course, Shelly Shapiro, you are the absolute bomb.

At Lucasfilm, I want to express my deep and heartfelt gratitude to Sue Rostoni and Leland Chee for giving this lowly boogeyman a free pass to roam about the *Star Wars* galaxy.

Thanks as always to my agent, Phyllis Westberg, for helping it all come together.

To Michael Ludy, my best friend from middle

school. Mike and I paid $2.50 to see *Return of the Jedi* the day that it opened and things have never been the same since.

On the topic of money, I want to thank everyone who has ever opened up his or her wallet and put down their hard-earned cash to buy my work. Simply speaking, without you, none of this would be possible. So thanks.

Finally, to Christina, who not only puts up with my mercurial author nonsense on a daily basis but put in the winning bid for a vintage 1979 Kenner Alien figure on eBay . . . pretty much making her the coolest wife ever.

THE STAR WARS NOVELS TIMELINE

BEFORE THE REPUBLIC
37,000-25,000 YEARS BEFORE
STAR WARS: A New Hope

c. 25,793 *YEARS BEFORE STAR WARS: A New Hope*

Dawn of the Jedi: Into the Void

OLD REPUBLIC
5000-67 YEARS BEFORE
STAR WARS: A New Hope

Lost Tribe of the Sith: The Collected
Stories

3954 *YEARS BEFORE STAR WARS: A New Hope*

The Old Republic: Revan

3650 *YEARS BEFORE STAR WARS: A New Hope*

The Old Republic: Deceived
Red Harvest
The Old Republic: Fatal Alliance
The Old Republic: Annihilation

1032 *YEARS BEFORE STAR WARS: A New Hope*

Knight Errant
Darth Bane: Path of Destruction
Darth Bane: Rule of Two
Darth Bane: Dynasty of Evil

RISE OF THE EMPIRE
67-0 YEARS BEFORE
STAR WARS: A New Hope

67 *YEARS BEFORE STAR WARS: A New Hope*

Darth Plagueis

33 *YEARS BEFORE STAR WARS: A New Hope*

Cloak of Deception
Darth Maul: Shadow Hunter
Maul: Lockdown

32 *YEARS BEFORE STAR WARS: A New Hope*

STAR WARS: EPISODE I
THE PHANTOM MENACE

Rogue Planet
Outbound Flight
The Approaching Storm

---

22 *YEARS BEFORE STAR WARS: A New Hope*

STAR WARS: EPISODE II
ATTACK OF THE CLONES

22-19 *YEARS BEFORE STAR WARS: A New Hope*

STAR WARS: THE CLONE
WARS

The Clone Wars: Wild Space
The Clone Wars: No Prisoners

Clone Wars Gambit
Stealth
Siege

Republic Commando
Hard Contact
Triple Zero
True Colors
Order 66

Shatterpoint
The Cestus Deception
MedStar I: Battle Surgeons
MedStar II: Jedi Healer
Jedi Trial
Yoda: Dark Rendezvous
Labyrinth of Evil

19 *YEARS BEFORE STAR WARS: A New Hope*

STAR WARS: EPISODE III
REVENGE OF THE SITH

Kenobi
Dark Lord: The Rise of Darth Vader
Imperial Commando 501st

Coruscant Nights
Jedi Twilight
Street of Shadows
Patterns of Force
The Last Jedi

10 *YEARS BEFORE STAR WARS: A New Hope*

The Han Solo Trilogy
The Paradise Snare
The Hutt Gambit
Rebel Dawn

The Adventures of Lando Calrissian
The Force Unleashed
The Han Solo Adventures
Death Troopers
The Force Unleashed II

THE STAR WARS NOVELS TIMELINE

**REBELLION
0–5 YEARS AFTER
*STAR WARS: A New Hope***

Death Star
Shadow Games

0

STAR WARS: EPISODE IV
A NEW HOPE

Tales from the Mos Eisley Cantina
Tales from the Empire
Tales from the New Republic
Scoundrels
Allegiance
Choices of One
Honor Among Thieves
Galaxies: The Ruins of Dantooine
Splinter of the Mind's Eye
Razor's Edge

3 YEARS AFTER STAR WARS: A New Hope

STAR WARS: EPISODE V
THE EMPIRE STRIKES BACK

Tales of the Bounty Hunters
Shadows of the Empire

4 YEARS AFTER STAR WARS: A New Hope

STAR WARS: EPISODE VI
THE RETURN OF THE JEDI

Tales from Jabba's Palace

The Bounty Hunter Wars
The Mandalorian Armor
Slave Ship
Hard Merchandise

The Truce at Bakura
Luke Skywalker and the Shadows of
Mindor

**NEW REPUBLIC
5–25 YEARS AFTER
*STAR WARS: A New Hope***

X-Wing
Rogue Squadron
Wedge's Gamble
The Krytos Trap
The Bacta War
Wraith Squadron
Iron Fist
Solo Command

The Courtship of Princess Leia
Tatooine Ghost

The Thrawn Trilogy
Heir to the Empire
Dark Force Rising
The Last Command

X-Wing: Isard's Revenge

The Jedi Academy Trilogy
Jedi Search
Dark Apprentice
Champions of the Force

I, Jedi
Children of the Jedi
Darksaber
Planet of Twilight
X-Wing: Starfighters of Adumar
The Crystal Star

The Black Fleet Crisis Trilogy
Before the Storm
Shield of Lies
Tyrant's Test

The New Rebellion

The Corellian Trilogy
Ambush at Corellia
Assault at Selonia
Showdown at Centerpoint

The Hand of Thrawn Duology
Specter of the Past
Vision of the Future

Scourge
Survivor's Quest

Dramatis Personae

Aur Myss; prisoner (Delphanian male)
Jareth Sartoris; captain of the guard, Imperial Prison
   Barge *Purge* (human male)
Kale Longo; teen prisoner (human male)
Trig Longo; teen prisoner (human male)
Waste; 2-1B surgical droid
Zahara Cody; chief medical officer, Imperial Prison
   Barge *Purge* (human female)

A long time ago in a galaxy far, far away . . .

1/Purge

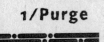

THE NIGHTS WERE THE WORST.

Even before his father's death, Trig Longo had come to dread the long hours after lockdown, the shadows and sounds and the chronically unstable gulf of silence that drew out in between them. Night after night he lay still on his bunk and stared up at the dripping durasteel ceiling of the cell in search of sleep or some acceptable substitute. Sometimes he would actually start to drift off, floating away in that comforting sensation of weightlessness, only to be rattled awake— heart pounding, throat tight, stomach muscles sprung and fluttering—by some shout or a cry, an inmate having a nightmare.

There was no shortage of nightmares aboard the Imperial Prison Barge *Purge*.

Trig didn't know exactly how many prisoners the *Purge* was currently carrying. He guessed maybe five hundred, human and otherwise, scraped from every corner of the galaxy, just as he and his family had been picked up eight standard weeks before. Sometimes the incoming shuttles returned almost empty; on other occasions they came packed with squabbling alien life-forms and alleged Rebel sympathizers of every stripe and species. There were assassins for hire and sociopaths the likes of which Trig had never seen, thin-lipped things that cackled and sneered in seditious languages that, to Trig's ears, were little more than clicks and hisses.

Every one of them seemed to harbor its own obscure appetites and personal grudges, personal histories blighted with shameful secrets and obscure vendettas. Being cautious became harder; soon you needed eyes in the back of your head—which some of them actually possessed. Two weeks earlier in the mess hall, Trig had noticed a tall, silent inmate sitting with its back to him but watching him nonetheless with a single raw-red eye in the back of its skull. Every day the red-eyed thing seemed to be sitting a little nearer. Then one day, without explanation, it was gone.

Except from his dreams.

Sighing, Trig levered himself up on his elbows and looked through the bars onto the corridor. Gen Pop had cycled down to minimum power for the night, edging the long gangway in permanent gray twilight. The Rodians in the cell across from his had gone to sleep or were feigning it. He forced himself to sit there, regulating his breathing, listening to the faint echoes of the convicts' uneasy groans and murmurs. Every so often a mouse droid or low-level maintenance unit, one of hundreds occupying the barge, would scramble by on some preprogrammed errand or another. And of course, below it all—low and not quite beneath the scope of hearing—was the omnipresent thrum of the barge's turbines gnashing endlessly through space.

For as long as they'd been aboard, Trig still hadn't

gotten used to that last sound, the way it shook the *Purge* to its framework, rising up through his legs and rattling his bones and nerves. There was no escaping it, the way it undermined every moment of life, as familiar as his own pulse.

Trig thought back to sitting in the infirmary just two weeks earlier, watching his father draw one last shaky breath, and the silence afterward as the medical droids disconnected the biomonitors from the old man's ruined body and prepared to haul it away. As the last of the monitors fell silent, he'd heard that low steady thunder of the engines, one more unnecessary reminder of where he was and where he was going. He remembered how that noise had made him feel lost and small and inescapably sad—some special form of artificial gravity that seemed to work directly against his heart.

He had known then, as he knew now, that it really only meant one thing, the ruthlessly grinding effort of the Empire consolidating its power.

Forget politics, his father had always said. *Just give 'em something they need, or they'll eat you alive.*

And now they'd been eaten alive anyway, despite the fact that they'd never been sympathizers, no more than low-level grifters scooped up on a routine Imperial sweep. The engines of tyranny ground on, bearing them forward across the galaxy toward some remote penal moon. Trig sensed that noise would continue, would carry on indefinitely, echoing right up until—

"Trig?"

It was Kale's voice behind him, unexpected, and Trig flinched a little at the sound of it. He looked back and saw his older brother gazing back at him, Kale's handsomely rumpled, sleep-slackened face just a ghostly three-quarter profile suspended in the cell's gloom. Kale looked like he was still only partly awake and unsure whether or not he was dreaming any of this.

"What's wrong?" Kale asked, a drowsy murmur that came out: *Wussrong?*

Trig cleared his throat. His voice had started changing recently, and he was acutely aware of how it broke high and low when he wasn't paying strict attention. "Nothing."

"You worried about tomorrow?"

"Me?" Trig snorted. "Come on."

" 'S okay if you are." Kale seemed to consider this and then uttered a bemused grunt. "You'd be crazy not to be."

"*You're* not scared," Trig said. "Dad would never have—"

"I'll go alone."

"No." The word snapped from his throat with almost painful angularity. "We need to stick together, that's what Dad said."

"You're only thirteen," Kale said. "Maybe you're not, you know . . ."

"Fourteen next month." Trig felt another flare of emotion at the mention of his age. "Old enough."

"You sure?"

"Positive."

"Well, sleep on it, see if you feel different in the morning . . ." Kale's enunciation was already beginning to go muddled as he slumped back down on his bunk, leaving Trig sitting up with his eyes still riveted to the long dark concourse outside the cell, Gen Pop, that had become their no-longer-new home.

Sleep on it, he thought, and in that exact moment, miraculously, as if by power of suggestion, sleep actually began to seem like a possibility. Trig lay back and let the heaviness of his own fatigue cover him like a blanket, superseding anxiety and fear. He tried to focus on the sound of Kale's breathing, deep and reassuring, in and out, in and out.

Then somewhere in the depths of the levels, an inhuman voice wailed. Trig sat up, caught his breath, and felt a chill tighten the skin of his shoulders, arms, and back, crawling over his flesh millimeter by millimeter, bristling the small hairs on the back of his neck. Over in his bunk the already sleeping Kale rolled over and grumbled something incoherent.

There was another scream, weaker this time. Trig told himself it was just one of the other convicts, just another nightmare rolling off the all-night assembly line of the nightmare factory.

But it hadn't sounded like a nightmare.

It sounded like a convict, whatever life-form it was, was under attack.

Or going crazy.

He sat perfectly still, squeezed his eyes tight, and waited for the pounding of his heart to slow down, just please slow down. But it didn't. He thought of the thing in the cafeteria, the disappeared inmate whose name he'd never know, watching him with its red staring eye. How many other eyes were on him that he never saw?

Sleep on it.

But he already knew there would be no more sleeping here tonight.

2/Meat Nest

∎∎∎∎:∎∎∎∎∎:∎∎∎

IN TRIG'S OLD LIFE, BACK ON CIMAROSA, BREAKFAST
had been the best meal of the day. Besides being an ex-
pert trafficker in contraband, a veteran fringe dweller
who cut countless deals with thieves, spies, and coun-
terfeiters, Von Longo had also been one of the galaxy's
greatest unrecognized breakfast chefs. *Eat a good meal
early,* Longo always told his boys. *You never know if
it's going to be your last.*

Here on the *Purge,* however, breakfast was rarely ed-
ible and sometimes actually seemed to shiver in the
steady vibrations as though still alive on the plate. This
morning Trig found himself gazing down at a pasty
mass of colorless goo spooned into shaved gristle, the
whole thing plastered together in sticky wads like some
kind of meat nest assembled by carnivorous flying in-
sects. He was still nudging the stuff listlessly around his
tray when Kale finally raised his eyebrows and peered
at him.

"You sleep at all last night?" Kale asked.

"A little."

"You're not eating."

"What, you mean this?" Trig poked at the contents

of the tray again and shuddered. "I'm not hungry," he said, and watched Kale shovel the last bite of his own breakfast into his mouth with disturbing gusto. "You think the food will be any better when we get to the detention moon?"

"Little brother, I think we'll be lucky if we don't end up on the menu."

Trig gave him a bleak look. "Don't give 'em any ideas."

"Hey, lighten up." Kale wiped his mouth on his sleeve and grinned. "Little guy like you, they'll probably just use you for an appetizer."

Trig put his fork down again with a snort to show that he got the joke. Although he couldn't have articulated it, his big brother's easygoing bravado—so obviously inherited from their old man—made him downright envious. Kale wasn't wired for fear. It just didn't stick to him somehow. The only thing that ever really seemed to trouble him was the prospect of not getting another helping of whatever the COO-2180s behind the lunch counter had been slopping onto the inmates' trays.

Out of nowhere, from the ridiculous to the sublime, Trig found himself thinking about his father again. Their final conversation hung in his memory with stinging vividness. Just before he'd passed away in the infirmary, the old man had reached up, clutched Trig's hand in both of his, and whispered, "Watch over your brother." Caught off-guard, Trig had just nodded and stammered out that he would, of course he would—but soon afterward he realized that his dad, in his final moments, must have been confused about which son he was talking to. There was no reason he'd ask Trig to

look after Kale. It would be like assigning the safe-
keeping of a wampa to a Kowakian monkey-lizard.

"What's wrong with you, anyway?" Kale asked from
across the table.

"I'm fine."

"Come on. 'Fess up."

Trig pushed the tray aside. "I don't see how they
can serve us this stuff day after day, that's all."

"Hey, that reminds me." As if on cue, Kale flicked
his eyes over at Trig's tray. "You gonna eat that?"

When the alarm shrilled out the end of the meal, he and
Kale stood up and slipped through the mess hall along
with the sea of other inmates. From overhead observation decks, a retinue of uniformed Imperial corrections
officers and armed stormtroopers stood watch, observ-
ing their passage into the common area with soulless
black eyes.

Down below, the prisoners sauntered in packs, muttering and laughing among themselves, deliberately
dragging out the process as much as possible to exploit
whatever small amount of leniency the guards granted
them. There was a sticky, smelly closeness to their un-
washed bodies, and Trig thought of the phrase *meat
nest* again, and felt a little nauseated. This whole place
was a meat nest.

Little by little, with studied casualness, he and Kale
slowed down, falling farther back from the crowd.
Although he didn't say a word, a subtle change had already worked its way through Kale's posture, straightening his spine and shoulders, a serene vigilance
moving over his face, supplanting the old insouciant

gleam. His eyes darted right and left now, never stopping anywhere for longer than a moment or two.

"You ready for this?" he asked, barely moving his lips.

"Sure," Trig said, nodding. "You?"

"Full on." Nothing about Kale's face seemed to indicate that he was speaking at all. "Remember when we get down there, it's gonna be close quarters. Whatever you do, always maintain eye contact. Don't look away for a second."

"Got it."

"And if anything starts to feel wrong about it, and I mean *anything* whatsoever, we just walk away." Now Kale did glance at his brother's face, perhaps catching a whiff of his apprehension. "I don't think Sixtus would try anything, but I can't vouch for Myss. Dad never trusted him."

"Maybe . . ." Trig started, and stopped himself. He realized that he was about to suggest calling off the whole deal, not because he was nervous—although he certainly was—but because Kale seemed to be having second thoughts, too.

"We can do this," Kale went on. "Dad taught us everything we need to know. The whole thing should take no more than a minute or two, and we'll be back out of there and back in full view. Any longer than that and it gets dangerous." He jerked his head around and looked hard at Trig. "And I go first. Clear?"

Trig nodded and felt a hand drop on his shoulder, stopping him in his tracks.

3/Where the Bad Air Goes

TRIG TURNED AND LOOKED UP AT THE FIGURE STAND-
ing in front of him.

"You." It was a piggy-eyed guard whose name he
didn't remember, peering back at him through a pair of
tinted, decidedly nonregulation optic shields. "What
are you doing all the way back here?"

Trig tried to answer but found his reply lodged somewhere just beneath his gullet. Kale stepped in, offering
up an easy, disarming smile. "Just walking, sir."

"Was I talking to you, convict?" the guard said, and
without waiting for an answer, pivoted his attention
back to Trig. "Well?"

"He's right, sir," Trig said. "We were just walking."

"What, you're too good to move along with the rest
of the scum?"

"We try to avoid scum whenever possible," Trig said,
and then added, "Sir."

The guard's eyes slitted behind the lenses. "You yanking me, convict?"

"No, sir."

" 'Cause the last maggot that yanked me's doing a
month in the hole."

"Understood, sir."

The guard glowered at him, twitching his head slightly to one side as if searching out some angle at which Trig's unblemished teenage face might somehow become threatening, or even make sense, amid this larger mass of incarcerated criminals. Watching his expression, Trig punished himself by imagining a glimmer of recognition in those squinty eyes, and for an instant he thought how bizarre it might be if the guard had said, *You're Von Longo's boys, aren't you? I heard what happened to your father. He was a good man.*

But of course no guard on this barge thought Longo had been a good man, or even bothered to learn his name, and now he was dead and already so completely forgotten that he might as well have never lived, and the guard just shook his head.

"Move along," the guard muttered, and walked away.

The moment they were out of earshot, Kale elbowed Trig in the shoulder.

"We try to avoid scum whenever possible?" A tiny grin dimpled the corners of Kale's mouth. "What, did you just make that up on the spot?"

Trig was unable to restrain a smile of his own. It felt liberating, probably because he couldn't remember the last time he'd allowed himself anything less than a troubled grimace. "You think he bought it?"

"I think *you* almost bought it." Kale reached up without looking over and tousled his fingers through Trig's hair. "Keep smarting off like that, convict, and you *will* be down in solitary with the real dangerous types."

"I hear there's a couple of hard guys down there now locked up tight," Trig said. "Could be our future customers."

Kale favored him with a glance of approval. "You've got a lot more of Dad in you than I thought," he said and, with one last look at the prisoners in front of them, nodded ever so slightly to the left. "Come on, follow me. And don't get crazy, okay?"

"Sure." Trig sensed Kale slowing his pace, dropping back several strides, scarcely enough to be noticed, and adjusted his step to match his brother's. Up ahead the main concourse broke off into three prongs, branching off into a series of lesser throughways that crisscrossed the detention levels at every imaginable vector and angle.

During his time aboard, Trig had made it his business to learn as much about the *Purge*'s layout as possible. Eavesdropping on conversations between guards and maintenance droids, he'd learned early on that there were six main detention levels, each one housing about twenty to thirty individual holding cells. Above that was the mess hall, followed by the admin offices, prison staff quarters, and the infirmary. Nobody talked much about solitary, down at the bottom of the barge—nor was there much speculation about the literally hundreds of meters of narrow access routes, sublevels, and dimly lit concourses that honeycombed every level.

Falling into single file, Kale and Trig slipped through an open gateway, striding along the damp prefab walls, down a flight of steps, deeper in the jaundiced subcutaneous bowels of Gen Pop. The air down here immediately became thicker, darker, and dramatically less breathable, on its way to an array of refurbished air scrubbers before circulating back through the barge.

"Well, well," a voice said. "The Longo brothers ride again."

Trig caught a quick breath, hoping it didn't sound like a gasp. In front of him, Kale froze, instinctively extending a hand behind him, and both of them peered into the open space that made up their immediate future. It took no extra time for Trig's vision to adjust. He could already make out the forms of several inmates, all members of the Delphanian Face Gang, and in front of them, Aur Myss.

Whether Myss's nearly vertical sneer was a genetic accident or the result of one of his legendary knife fights was a matter of perpetual speculation among the other inmates. Below the flattened suede accordion of his nose, a row of mismatched tribal piercings dangled from the drooping lower lip, collected like trophies from all the other crew leaders while Myss and his boss, Sixtus Cleft, had slowly consolidated the Face Gang's position as the *Purge*'s preeminent prison crew.

"You're right on time," Myss said, piercings jingling as he spoke.

Kale nodded. "We're always prompt."

"An admirable trait for a prison rat."

"That's why you chose to do business with us."

"One of many reasons," Myss said, "I'm sure."

Kale smiled. "Did you bring the payment?"

"Oh yes." Myss produced a sibilant gurgle that might have been laughter, and extended one spade-claw hand, pointing down at the empty floor in front of him. "It's right there in front of you. Don't you see it?"

Trig sensed, or perhaps only imagined, his older brother stiffening, preparing for trouble, and willed Kale to stay calm. It appeared to work. For the time being at least, Kale kept his posture erect and didn't look away, careful to keep his own voice steady and calm. "Is this some kind of a joke?"

"Perhaps." Myss looked at the Delphanian foot soldiers standing on either side of him, grinning and sniggering. "Maybe you just don't share our sense of humor."

"Our deal with Sixtus—"

"Sixtus is dead."

Kale stared at him. "What?"

"A terrible tragedy." Myss was almost whispering and the mushy sibilance in between words, Trig realized, was definitely laughter this time, accompanied by the faint metallic jingle of his piercings. "ICO Wembly found him in his cell this morning with his throat slashed. *I'm* the new skipper now." He stopped, and then his voice abruptly frosted over. "And alas, the terms of our deal have changed."

"You can't do that," Trig cut in, unable to hold back any longer. "Sixtus and our dad—"

"No, it's all right," Kale said, still not taking his eyes off Myss, and when he spoke again he sounded absolutely calm. "I'm just sorry things worked out this way."

Myss appeared genuinely curious. "Oh?"

"None of this is necessary." Kale's voice was so casual it was almost like listening to their father talk, that same mellifluous we-can-work-this-out inflection that had gotten them out of so many dicey exchanges in the past. "We've built a mutually beneficial relationship here, and it's crazy to jeopardize it with rash decisions."

"Rash decisions?"

Kale waved a hand in the air. "Of course we'll be happy to tell you where the blasters and power packs are hidden, free of charge. Take them with my compliments. Consider it my gift to you as the new leader of the Face Gang. And everyone walks out of here to do business another day."

"A generous proposal." Myss seemed to consider the idea for a long moment. "There's only one problem."

"What's that?"

Myss glanced at the Delphanian inmates slathering next to him on either side. "I already promised my men that they could kill you."

"I see." Kale hove up a dramatic sigh. "In that case, I guess we don't have a deal, huh?"

"No."

"I suppose there's only one thing left to do."

Aur Myss tilted his chin upward slightly. "And that would be?"

At first none of them moved, and Trig had no idea what was going to happen. Then, before he realized it, Kale's hand blurred forward, moving faster than Trig could even see, his fingers hooking down to rip the piercings out of Myss's face.

The Delphanian shrieked in surprise and pain and one of his hands flew up to cover his wounded, spurting lips and nose. Simultaneously the two inmates who had been flanking him burst forward in a rush, and Kale grabbed his brother's shoulder, spun him hard around, and thrust him back in the direction they'd come.

"*Run*," Kale shouted, and they did, Trig first, Kale behind him, both of them flying back up the corridor they'd just come down. Behind them the Delphanians' boots clanged off the metal floor, and Trig could hear them shouting, coming closer. There was no way he and his brother could possibly outrun them. And even if by some quirk of fate they did escape, Aur Myss would be waiting for them tomorrow and the next day and—

Rounding the bend, Trig almost collided with a guard standing directly in front of him. The ICO put up both hands in a reflexive warding-off gesture, and the sudden stop that kept Trig from slamming into him was followed an instant later by Kale hitting him from behind.

"What's going on here?" the guard asked.

"Nothing, sir, we just . . ." Trig started, and it occurred to him that there was no reason why the guards should be this far down the walkways to begin with.

And then, between the pounding rhythm of his own heart, he realized something else.

The *Purge* had fallen absolutely silent.

The vibrations that had unsettled him, broadcasting their emanations up through the bones of his feet, ankles, and knees, had gone completely still.

For the first time since he'd come aboard, the engines had stopped.

4/Medbay

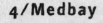

"Hey, Waste," Zahara Cody said. "Are we there yet?"

The 2-1B surgical droid looked up at her with a blank stare. It had been in the process of injecting a syringe of kolto into the left arm of the Dug inmate lying in the oversized medcenter bunk between them. Within seconds of receiving the injection, the Dug writhed and rolled up onto its back, twitching its lower legs beneath the sheet, then stiffened and lapsed into a very convincing state of rigor mortis.

"Congratulations," Zahara said, "you killed him. Looks like you saved the Empire another four hundred credits." Reaching over, she tapped the surgical droid on the shoulder. "Job well done. Way to be a team player."

The 2-1B looked at her in something like alarm. "But I didn't—"

"Let me do a quick test, just to confirm time of death." Zahara reached down and rolled the Dug sideways, pushing it over until it fell out of bed with a thud. Seconds later, the inmate sat up with a squeal of displeasure, scuttling back up to its bunk, where it glared at her balefully and muttered some black condemnatory oath under its breath.

"Looks like another miracle recovery," Zahara said, and smiled. "Another one of your many skills, apparently."

"A most irregular approach," Waste intoned, and something deep inside its torso cowling clicked and whirred. "Don't you think that given the patient's ongoing complaints we should run some additional tests?"

"Unless I'm mistaken, this particular patient's main complaint is with the food." Zahara glanced at the Dug. "And maybe one of the several different prison gangs that want his scalp for overdue loan payments. That's about right, isn't it, Tugnut?"

The Dug snarled and jerked one hand up in a gesture that transcended language barriers, then went back to faking its own death.

"Scramble up an orderly droid," Zahara said, "have him taken back to his cell." She looked back at the 2-1B. "You're aware, Waste, that you still haven't answered my initial question?"

"Excuse me?"

"Are we there yet?"

"Dr. Cody, if you're referring to our ETA at Detention Moon Gradient Seven—"

"The *Purge* is a prison barge, Waste. Where else would we be headed? Wild Space?" She waited patiently to see if the 2-1B was going to favor her with another of its flat, implacable glances. Throughout the last three months of working alongside the droid, Zahara Cody had come to think of herself as a connoisseur of such reactions, the way that some people collected rare pseudo-genetic polymorph species or trinkets from older, pre-Imperial cultures. "We've already dropped out of hyperspace. Our engines have been stopped for almost an hour now and we're just sitting here stock-still, so that can only mean one thing, right? We must be there."

"Actually, Doctor, my uplink to the navicomputer indicates that—"

"Hey, Doc," A blunt finger reached out from behind Zahara and prodded her somewhere in the vicinity of her lower spine. "We there yet?"

Zahara looked over at the Devaronian inmate sprawled languorously on his side on the bed behind her, then turned back at her surgical droid. "See, Waste? It's the question on everyone's lips."

"No, I'm serious, Doc," the Devaronian groaned, peering up at her from the depths of melancholy. His right horn had been snapped off midtrunk, giving his face a peculiarly lopsided look, and he poked himself in the abdomen and groaned. "One of my livers is going bad, I can feel it. Thinking maybe I caught something in the shower."

"May I offer a more likely diagnosis?" The 2-1B scurried eagerly around Zahara, already exchanging tools in its servogrips as the internal components of its diagnostic computer flickered beneath its torso sheath. "Liver damage in your species is not uncommon. In many cases your silver-based blood results in depleted oxygen due to the low-level addiction to the recreational use of—"

"Hey, interface." The Devaronian sat up, suddenly the robust picture of perfect health, and grabbed the 2-1B's pincer. "What are you saying about my species?"

"Easy, Gat, he doesn't mean anything by it." Zahara placed a hand on the inmate's wrist until he released the droid. Then, turning to the 2-1B: "Waste, why don't you go check out what's happening with the Trandoshan in B-seventeen, huh? His temp's up again and I don't like the last white counts I saw this morning. I doubt he'll make it through today."

"Oh, I concur." The droid brightened. "According to my programming at Rhinnal State Medical Academy—"

"Right. So I'll meet you later for afternoon rounds, all right?"

The 2-1B hesitated, seeming briefly to entertain the idea of objecting, then walked away clucking softly to itself in dismay. Zahara watched it go, its gangling legs and oversized feet passing between the rows of bunks that lined the infirmary on either side. Only half of those beds were full, but that was still more than she would have preferred. As chief medical officer on the *Purge,* she knew that at any given time a large percentage of her patients were dogging it, either prolonging their stay in medbay or faking it entirely to stay out of Gen Pop. But it had been a long trip and supplies were low. Even with the 2-1B, the prospect of a legitimate medical emergency—

"You okay, Doc?"

Looking down, she realized that the Devaronian was watching her from his bed, fidgeting nonchalantly with his broken horn.

"Sorry?"

"I said, you all right? You look a little, I dunno—"

"I'm fine, Gat, thanks."

"Hey." The inmate glanced off in the direction that

the surgical droid had gone. "That bucket of bolts won't hold it against me, you think?"

"Who, Waste?" She smiled. "Believe me, he's a paragon of scientific objectivity. Just throw some obscure symptoms at him and he'll be your best friend."

"You really think we're almost there?"

She shrugged. "I don't know. You know how it is. Nobody tells me anything."

"Right," the Devish said, and shook his head with a chuckle. Aboard the barge, there were a few phrases that circulated among Gen Pop endlessly: *Are we there yet?* and *They expect us to eat this stuff?* were chief among them, but *Nobody tells me anything* was also a big favorite. Over months of service, Zahara had adopted these phrases as well, much to the chagrin of the warden and many of the ICOs, most of whom held themselves up as an example of superior species.

Zahara knew what they said about her. Among the guards, no real effort was made to keep it subtle. Too much time spent down in the medbay with the scum and droids and the little rich girl had started to go native, preferring the company of inmates and synthetics to her own kind: corrections officers and stormtroopers. Most of the guards had stopped talking to her completely after the situation two weeks ago. She didn't suppose she blamed them. They were a notoriously tight-knit group and seemed to function with a groupthink that she found downright nauseating.

Even the inmates—her regulars, the ones she saw on a daily basis—had noticed a change in the way she'd started spending extra time training Waste—preparing the 2-1B not as her assistant anymore, but as her replacement. And although there hadn't been any official response from the warden, she could only assume that he'd received her resignation.

After all, she'd walked into his office and slammed it down on his desk.

There was no way she could keep working here.

Not after what happened with Von Longo.

Take a girl from a wealthy family of Corellian financiers and tell her she'll never have a care in the world. Ship her off to the best schools, tell her there's a spot waiting for her in the InterGalactic Banking Clan, all she has to do is not mess up. Keep her nose clean, uphold the highest standards of politics, culture, and good manners, and ignore the fact that compared with what she's used to, 99 percent of the galaxy is still hungry, sick, and uneducated. Embrace the Empire with its quaint lack of diplomatic subtlety and strive to overlook the increasingly uncomfortable squeeze of Lord Vader's ever-tightening fist.

Flash to fifteen years later. The girl, now a woman, decides to go to Rhinnal to study, of all things, medicine—that dirtiest of sciences, better left to droids, full of blood and pus and contagion, hardly what her parents had hoped for. But the decision is made to indulge her, based on the hope that this is just an idealistic whim and soon enough little Zahara will be back to take her rightful position at the family table. After all, she's young, she has plenty of time.

Except it doesn't play out that way. Two years into Rhinnal, Zahara meets a surgeon twice her age, a craggy veteran of hundreds of humanitarian missions beyond the Core Worlds, who opens her eyes to the true need of the galaxy around her. The mismatched love affair runs its course predictably enough but even after that part of it winds down, Zahara can't forget the picture he's painted for her, a mural of staggering need, beings whose desperation is utterly beyond her ken. He reminds her that the poor are out there in their countless millions, human and nonhuman alike, young ones dying of malnutrition and sickness, while the galaxy's upper echelons bask in self-induced oblivion. *You can either live with something like that,* the surgeon tells her, on what turns out to be one of their last nights together, *or you can't.*

And it turns out she can't. After being universally rejected by various aid groups because of her lack of experience, Zahara makes the decision to go to work for the Empire, which her family reluctantly accepts—at least it's a known entity—but in a capacity that leaves her parents speechless, stupefied, and outraged. No daughter of theirs is going to work on an Imperial prison barge. The indignity of it is beyond all scale.

Yet here I am, Zahara thought now, queen of her own miniature kingdom, after all, duchess of the empty bunks, and our lady of the perpetual stomachache. Involuntary lust-object of a hundred emotionally frustrated prison guards and deprived stormtroopers. Dispenser of medicine, charged with keeping the inmates of the Imperial Prison Barge *Purge* alive long enough to be permanently detained on some remote prison moon.

The irony, of course, was that in a standard week's time, or whenever they finally arrived at their destination, she would be going back to her father and mother—if not exactly hat-in-hand, then close enough.

Her mother would sniff and scowl, her brother would jeer, but her father would throw his arms around his little girl and after the acceptable amount of time had passed, her penance would be complete, and she would be welcomed back into the fold. And her time aboard the barge would become what they'd thought it would be all along, an adventure in her youth, a charming dinner anecdote for diplomats. *You'll never believe how our little girl decided to spend her youth . . .*

Looking through the medbay again, Zahara felt a thin tremor of uncertainty steal over her and willed it away. But like most aspects of her personality, it didn't go without a fight.

Instead, unbidden, the image of Von Longo floated back up into her memory, the man's bloody face trying to talk to her through the ventilator, clutching her hand in both of his, asking to see his boys one last time. Begging her to bring them to him so that he could speak to them in private. Moments later, the cloud of heavy menace emerged behind her back and she turned to see Jareth Sartoris, close enough that she could actually smell his skin, speaking through thin lips that hardly seemed to move.

Paying your respects, Doctor?

Longo had died later that day, and Zahara Cody decided that she had flown her last voyage with the *Purge* and the Empire. The next step would be contacting her parents and letting them know she was coming home. Luxurious clothing and fine crystal had never been her first choice, but at least she'd be able to sleep at night. And in the evenings she would sit down to dinner with the wealthy and proud and forget about what had happened with Von Longo and Jareth Sartoris.

Is this really what you want?

Zahara shook it off. In any case, she'd always assumed she'd have lots of time to think about it before the barge got where it was going.

Plenty of time to make up her mind.

Except now the engines had stopped—had been stopped for over an hour.

From across the infirmary, another voice, one of the other inmates, cried out, "Hey, Doc—are we there yet?"

This time, Zahara didn't answer.

5/Word

━━━:━━━━:━━━

JARETH SARTORIS MADE HIS WAY DOWN THE NARROW
gangway outside the guards' quarters, massaging his
temples as he walked. He had a headache, nothing
new there, but this one was something special, a vise
grip across his temporal lobes that made him feel like
he'd been gassed with some kind of low-grade neuro-
toxin in his sleep. The greasy smear of breakfast
down the back of his throat hadn't helped.

He'd been awake even before the warden's summons
came through. After working third shift last night, he'd
toppled into his bunk early this morning and lapsed
into restless unconsciousness, but two hours later the
abrupt silence had awakened him, the feeling of his
tightly coiled world spinning off its axis. They were
seven standard days out. So why had the engines fallen
silent? Sartoris had gotten dressed, grabbed some luke-
warm caf and a reheated bantha patty from the mess,
and headed down the hall toward the warden's office,
hoping to build up enough mindless momentum to
keep him going as far as he needed.

To his right the turbolift doors opened. Three other
guards—Vesek, Austin, and some pompadoured

newbie—came out, falling into step behind him. They had to walk single-file to fit comfortably down the hall. Sartoris didn't break stride or even glance back at them.

"Me and the guys, Cap," Austin's voice piped up, after a respectful pause, "we were, you know, wondering if you could shed a little light on what's going on."

Sartoris shook his head, still not looking back. "What's that?"

"I heard we blew out both thrusters completely," Vesek put in. "Word is we're just sitting here somewhere outside the Unknown Regions, waiting for a tow."

Austin sniggered. "Barge full of stranded convicts, I'm sure we're top priority for the Empire."

"Stang," Vesek said. "Maybe they'll just decide to leave us drifting out here, right?"

"Ask the rook." Austin poked the pompadoured guard walking in front of him. "Hey, Armitage, you think they'll rescue us?" He sniggered, not waiting for the kid to respond. "He'd probably like it. Suits his *artistic temperament,* right, Armitage?"

The newbie just ignored him and kept walking.

"How long did you spend on your hair this morning, rook? You hoping Dr. Cody's taken an interest?"

"All right." Sartoris snapped a glance up at them. "Belay that noise, understand?"

Nobody spoke the rest of the way to the warden's office.

Kloth's office had been tricked out to look larger than it actually was—light colors, holomurals, and a colossal rectilinear viewscreen facing out the star-strewn expanse—but Sartoris had always found the effect paradoxically oppressive. Some time ago, he'd noticed a blown voxel in the corner of the desert landscape above Kloth's desk, a missed stitch in the digital fabric. Ever since then, something about the second-hand technology seemed to be pushing in on him, and now his eyes always felt as if they were being tricked, lulled into a false sense of openness.

"First the bad news," Kloth said. He was standing in his usual position, hands clasped behind his back, looking out the viewscreen. "Our thrusters are seriously damaged—probably beyond repair. And as I'm sure you know, we're still seven standard days out from our destination."

One of the other guards, the rookie probably, let out a nearly inaudible groan. Sartoris only heard it because he was standing next to him.

"However," the warden continued. "There is a positive side."

Kloth turned slowly to face them. Upon first glance, his face was the usual blunt bureaucratic hatchet, slightly curved and angular upper lip, gray-rimmed eyes, and bluish silver bags of freshly shaven cheeks. Only after spending a certain amount of time with the man did you come to know the soft thing residing within that calculated outer shell, a spineless, gelatinous creature that exuded nothing so much as the tremulous anxiety of being drawn out and exposed.

"It seems the navicomputer has identified an Imperial vessel," Kloth said, "a Star Destroyer actually, within this same system. While our attempts to make contact have met with no reply, we do have enough power to make our approach."

He paused here, apparently in anticipation of applause or at least a round of relieved sighs, but Sartoris and the others just looked at him.

"A Destroyer?" Austin asked. "And they're not responding to our call?"

Kloth didn't answer for a moment. He touched his chin, fingering it thoughtfully, a pompous and disaffected gesture Sartoris had seen a thousand times and had come to loathe in his own special way. "There's more to it than that," he said. "According to our bioscans, there's only a handful of life-forms on board."

"How many's a handful?" Vesek wanted to know.

"Ten, perhaps twelve."

"Ten or twelve?" Vesek shook his head. "Sounds like a scanner issue. Destroyers can carry a crew of ten thousand or more."

"Thank you," Kloth said drily. "I'm well aware of the standard Imperial specs."

"Sorry, sir. It's just, either our equipment is undergoing some serious malfunction, or . . ."

"Or there's something else going on up there." It was the first time Sartoris had spoken in the office, and he was surprised at the hoarseness in his voice. "Something that we don't want any part of."

The others all turned to look at him. For what felt like a long time after that, no one spoke. Then the warden cleared his throat. "What are you saying, Captain?"

"There's no reason the Empire would just abandon

an entire Star Destroyer out here in the middle of nowhere without a good reason."

"He's right," Austin said. "Maybe—"

"Internal atmosphere diagnostics show no sign of any known toxin or contamination," Kloth said. "Of course it's always possible that our instruments are misreading how many life-forms are on board. We screen for numerous variables, electrical brain activity, pulse, motion, any number of those things could skew the reading. In any case . . ." He smiled—a wholly unconvincing dramatization that ought to have involved invisible wires and hooks on either side of his mouth. "The most critical factor is that we may be able to salvage equipment for our thrusters and get back on course before we're completely behind schedule. To that end, I'll be sending a scouting party up—Captain Sartoris, along with ICOs Austin, Vesek, and Armitage and the mechanical engineers, to see what they can salvage. We anticipate docking within the hour. Questions?"

There were none, and Kloth dismissed them in the usual fashion, by turning his back and letting them find their own way out. Sartoris was about to follow them when the warden's voice stopped him.

"Captain?"

Stopping in the doorway, Sartoris drew a breath and felt the ache in his head become a deeper, more impacted pounding, like a gargantuan infected tooth somewhere in his frontal sinus. The door closed behind him, and it was just the two of them in what felt like an increasingly shrunken space.

"Am I making a mistake, sending you up with these men?"

"Excuse me, sir?"

"*Sir.*" Kloth's smile rematerialized, a wisp of its former self. "Now, that's a word I haven't heard from you in a long time, Captain."

"We haven't seen each other much lately."

"I'm aware that this voyage has been particularly . . . challenging for you personally," Kloth said, and Sartoris found himself hoping fervently that the warden wouldn't start stroking his chin again. If he did, Sartoris wasn't sure he could rein in the urge to punch him straight in his pompous and disaffected face. "After what happened two weeks ago, in many ways I expected your resignation right alongside Dr. Cody's."

"Why?"

"She saw you kill an inmate in cold blood."

"It was her word against mine."

"Your antiquated interrogation techniques aren't appropriate anymore, Captain. You're costing the Empire more information than you're retrieving."

"All due respect, sir, Longo was a nobody, a grifter—"

"We'll never know now, will we?"

Sartoris felt his fists clenching at his sides until his nails burrowed into his palms, delivering stinging pain deep into the skin. "You want me off your boat, Warden? You just say the word."

"On the contrary. You may consider this mission an opportunity to redeem yourself. If not in my eyes, then certainly in the eyes of the Empire to which we both owe so very much. Is that understood?"

"Yes, sir."

Kloth turned and scrutinized him as if for any sign of sarcasm or mockery. In his decades of service, Jareth

Sartoris had been to the very edges of the galaxy, living under conditions he wouldn't wish on his worst enemy. He'd had to sleep in places and commit unspeakable deeds that he would've given entire body organs to forget. That simple *yes, sir* didn't taste any worse than any of the rest of it.

"So we're clear, then?" Kloth asked.

"Crystal," Sartoris replied, and when Kloth turned to show him his back, it wasn't a moment too soon. The warden's office was bigger than any other on the barge but it was still too small for Sartoris, and as the cooler air of the outer corridor hit him he realized he'd sweated through the armpits of his uniform completely.

6/Dead Boys

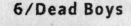

"YOU KEEP LOOKING OUT THERE," KALE SAID, "sooner or later you're going to see something you won't like."

"I already have." Trig was stationed in his usual spot in the detention cell, gazing through the bars. Across the hall, directly opposite them, the two Rodian inmates who'd been there ever since he and Kale and their father had been brought aboard stood glowering back at him. Sometimes they muttered to each other in a language Trig didn't recognize, gesturing at the brothers and making noises that sounded like laughter.

Now, though, they just stared at him.

At least two hours had passed since the *Purge* had gone into total lockdown. Trig wasn't sure when all this had happened. It was one of the first things the Empire took from you when they took your freedom: the sense of passing time. It was information you didn't deserve. As a result, Trig relied on his body to tell him when it was time to eat, sleep, and exercise.

Now it was telling him to be afraid.

The noise from the rest of the hall was louder than he expected. Standing here next to the bars, Trig could make out individual voices, prisoners bellowing in Basic and a thousand other languages, demanding to know why the barge had stopped and how much longer it was going to be until they got going again. The deviation from routine had left them restless and giddy. Someone was screaming for a drink of water, someone else wanted food—another voice shouted and spluttered with hysterical, gibbering laughter. There was a sonorous, deep-chested growl, probably a Wookiee, Trig thought, though for the most part the ones he'd seen on board kept to themselves unless threatened. Someone else kept hammering something metallic against the wall of their cell, a steady, methodical *wham-wham-wham*. You could go crazy listening to something like that, Trig thought; you could go right out of your mind.

"All right, that's enough!" a guard's voice broke in. "The next maggot that makes so much as a peep goes straight down to the hole!"

Silence for a moment, yawning . . . and then an anxious titter. It brought another, followed by a wild yodeling shriek, and the entire detention level erupted in an avalanche of chatter, louder than ever. Trig put his hands to his ears and turned back to the corridor. Then he jerked backward in surprise.

"Wembly," he said. "You startled me."

"Two dead boys," ICO Wembly said, with real regret. "And I liked you guys, too. Decent fellas. Not that it counts for much aboard this rotten bucket of garbage, but . . ." The guard sighed. He was a fat man in his late fifties, with a loosely knit face, veins on his nose, and lines cut deeply beneath his watery eyes—

eyes made for crying, a mouth made for laughter, shoulders made for shrugging, Wembly was a walking miracle of compulsive self-expression. "I sure am gonna miss you, tell you true."

"What are you talking about?" Kale asked.

There was a click, and a synthesized voice buzzed from somewhere behind Wembly's head. "You haven't heard? Aur Myss just put a ten-thousand-credit bounty on your heads."

Trig glanced at the BLX unit standing behind Wembly's shoulder. For some reason, the labor droid had adopted the guard, following him everywhere, and for reasons equally nebulous Wembly allowed it. As one of the senior corrections officers aboard the *Purge*, he was technically permitted a droid assistant, though Trig knew of no other guard, including Captain Sartoris himself, who actually tolerated one.

"Ten *thousand*?" Kale muttered from his bunk. "He's got that much?"

"Don't tell me you're shocked." Wembly looked pained and laced his hands over his formidable belly, almost dyspeptic with incredulity. "Please, don't tell me that. You yanked out half his face, what did you expect?"

"The ugly half." Kale flopped down on his bunk with a muffled groan. "I probably improved his looks."

"I very much doubt that to be true," the BLX interjected. "In my experience—"

Wembly cut the droid off without hesitation. "Improved his looks, huh? Make sure you explain that to him while his flunkies slit your throats." He glanced across the hall at the Rodian inmates staring through their bars, the intensity of their regard suddenly making more sense to Trig. He guessed that they were probably already spending that ten thousand credits.

"Hey, Wembly, you're a guard," he said. "Doesn't that mean you're supposed to guard us?"

"That's a good one, kid, make sure to write it down. In case you didn't notice, preventing you scofflaws from offing one another isn't exactly in our job description. The warden sees it as saving the Empire the trouble." He swung out one baggy hand at the rest of the detention level outside the cell. "As far as your colleagues out there are concerned, when we come out of lockdown, that's the dinner bell ringing on your sorry necks."

"And there's nothing you can do about it?" Trig asked.

"Hey, I'm warning you, aren't I?"

"Yes, that's right," the BLX echoed. "And at no small risk to our own well-being, either. If Captain Sartoris knew—"

"Listen," Wembly said, his tone shifting a little, lowering his voice to the very brink of an apology, "right now I've got bigger worries. We're getting ready to send a boarding party to this Star Destroyer. The warden's not saying anything, but—"

"Wait a second," Kale said. "Star Destroyer?"

"Navicomputer found one drifting out here, a derelict. We just docked. Kloth's sending a boarding party to scavenge parts. If they can't find anything to get the main thrusters running again, who knows how long we'll be sitting here?"

"That reminds me, sir," the BLX said, "if I'm not mistaken, I'm due for an oil bath this afternoon, if you can spare my assistance for an hour or two. If not, I can always—"

"Take your time," Wembly said drily, then turned back to Kale and Trig. "Listen, I've got to blow. Do me a favor and lay low awhile, huh? I'll do everything I can to keep you alive until we get where we're going."

Kale nodded. "Thanks," he said, but this time the gratitude sounded sincere. "I know you're walking a line just coming out here to see us. And we appreciate it, right, Trig?"

"Huh?" Trig looked up. "Oh, yeah. Right."

The guard shook his head and glanced back at Kale. "Keep an eye on this one, will you?"

"All the time."

Wembly pursed his lips. "I'll drop by again next time I feel like getting abused. If you live that long, which I doubt." He turned and waddled away humming under his breath, a wide-hipped man whose girth enjoyed its own unique relationship with the galaxy's greater gyroscopic nature. The BLX followed along obediently afterward. When guard and droid rounded the corner and disappeared, Trig turned to look straight out of the cell again.

Across the hall, the Rodians were still staring at him.

7/Destroyer

━━━■━■━■━━━

S<small>ARTORIS</small> <small>LED THE OTHERS UP THE STAIRS FROM THE</small> admin level to the barge's pilot station, walking across it up to the docking shaft. It was a cylinder that made his throat feel tight, particularly now that he was surrounded with nine men—Austin, Vesek, Armitage, along with four mechanical engineers and a pair of stormtroopers who'd swaggered in at the last second like they owned the place.

Kloth had sent the troopers along as an afterthought, ordering them to join the boarding party just before they'd started up. Sartoris wondered what had changed the warden's mind. If there *was* something aboard the Destroyer that they needed to worry about, two stormtroopers weren't going to help the situation much.

But there is *nothing to worry about up there,* Sartoris told himself, dropping the thought like a pebble into the deep well of his subconscious and waiting to hear some sort of telltale *plink* of response. The silence that came back wasn't particularly reassuring.

The tube lift carried them steadily upward, and

Sartoris watched the faint green lights strafe the faces of the other men, seeking any echo of his own apprehensions. But their expressions were pictures of bland neutrality, obedience as a rarefied psychological state. Sartoris supposed he ought to be thankful for guards that just followed orders as opposed to questioning them. He'd worked with both types in the past and had unfailingly preferred the company of the former—at least, strangely, until now, when some part of him could have appreciated a little back-and-forth about the nature of their destination.

It was Austin, predictably, who ultimately broke the silence. "What do you think happened up there, Cap, that there's only ten life-forms still on board?"

"Warden says zero contamination," Vesek said. "So it's gotta be a malfunction on our end."

"So how come they never acknowledged?"

"Maybe our communications suite got scrambled along with our bioscanners."

"Negative." One of the engineers, Greeley, shook his head. "Communications are five-by. Ditto the scanners. It all checks out." He flicked his eyes upward. "It's just a ghost ship, that's all."

Austin gave him a look. "What?"

"A derelict, you know—ships get scuttled, abandoned by the fleet, left behind. Empire doesn't like to talk about 'em, but they're out there."

"So where's the crew?"

"Evacuated," Greeley said. "Or . . ." He moistened his lips and tried to shrug it off. "Who knows?"

"Great." Vesek sighed. "A Destroyer that can't fly on its own and we're going aboard to scavenge parts.

This one's got Kloth's name written all over it." He rolled his eyes at Sartoris. "Is there a greater plan at work here, Captain, or we just winging this one?"

"When we get up there," Sartoris said, "I want two groups of five. Vesek, that means you, me, and Austin will go with Greeley—" He pointed at one of the engineers, and the second man standing next to him. "—and Blandings. The rest of you, Armitage, Quatermass, Phibes, stay with the troopers. We'll reconnoiter back at the docking shaft in an hour."

"You want one of us to go with you?" one of the stormtroopers asked.

"Why would I want that?"

The trooper brandished his blaster rifle. "Just in case."

Sartoris was aware of Vesek and Austin looking at him, awaiting his reply. "I think we'll be fine," he said. "Stay with Armitage's group and let me know what you find."

"What exactly *are* we looking for?" Austin asked.

"I've uploaded a list of the parts onto each of your datalinks along with a detailed layout of the Destroyer's concourse and maintenance levels. I don't have to tell you this is a big ship. Maintain strict com-link contact at all times. I don't want to be sending out search parties to look for my search parties. You follow?"

The platform stopped moving long enough for the hatch above them to unseal with a faint hydraulic hiss. Then it lifted the rest of the way up, into the landing bay.

*   *   *

At first nobody said a word.

Sartoris thought he'd been prepared for how big it would be, but after two solid months aboard the *Purge,* he was simply overwhelmed by what awaited him here. He'd never actually set foot on a Destroyer before, although he'd seen smaller Imperial warships and had assumed this would be like those, only bigger. But it wasn't. It was more like its own planet.

The docking shaft had delivered them into the durasteel cathedral of the Destroyer's cavernous main hangar, its vaulted ceilings and paneled walls soaring upward and outward in an ecstasy of forced perspective. As Sartoris stared down those long planes into some barely visible vanishing point, he reminded himself that he was looking at less than a tenth of the Destroyer's actual sixteen hundred meters. He needed to keep that figure in mind if he didn't want to spend his entire time aboard wrestling with the enormity of it.

He took in a deep breath—the cold air tasted like metal shavings and the sterile, out-of-the-box smell of long-chain polymers—and let it out. For a man with a horror of tight spaces, standing here should have been a tonic. But instead of relief he only felt some arcane new species of panic fluttering in the pit of his stomach, this time in reaction to the seemingly limitless rebate of pure space. He grunted at the absurdity of it. Apparently he'd gone from claustrophobia to ballroom syndrome in one quick leap, without any time to appreciate the difference.

"Ah, Cap?"

Sartoris didn't bother looking over. "What is it, Austin?"

"All due respect, sir, I think we're going to need more than an hour to look through all this."

"Stick to the plan," he said. "We'll start with an hour and check back then. Report anything out of the ordinary."

"Whole bloody place is out of the ordinary," Austin muttered, and one of the engineers, Greeley, he thought, let out a gruff chuckle.

"Come on," Sartoris said, "let's go. We're wasting time."

"Hold up a second, Cap." Vesek pointed off in the opposite direction. "What's all that? Over there?"

Sartoris looked behind him and saw several of what looked like smaller attack and landing craft scattered across the hangar floor. "Spacecraft," he said. "TIE fighters, from the look of them."

"Yeah, but those don't all look like TIEs, chief."

Sartoris took a closer look and saw that Vesek was right. There *were* TIE ships there, but there were also four or five other craft mixed in—long-range freighters and transport shuttles, along with something that could've been a type of modified Corellian corvette.

"Captured enemy spacecraft," Sartoris said, masking his uncertainty with impatience. "Who knows?" He snapped a glance at Greeley. "Any of them have the parts we need?"

"Probably not."

"Then—" He stopped.

They all saw it at the same time. Something across the bay was moving behind the TIE fighters, its shadow bulking forward, slanting across the deck toward them. Behind him he was aware of the troopers already going for their blasters.

"What's that?" Austin whispered.

"No life-forms registering in the loading bay," Greeley said, voice trembling slightly. "I don't—"

"Hold it." Sartoris raised one hand without glancing back at them. "Wait here."

He took a step forward, wading deeper into the near silence, tilting his head to get a better look across the poorly lit hangar. His heart was beating too hard—he could feel it in his neck and wrists—and when he tried to swallow, his throat refused to cooperate. It was like trying to swallow a mouthful of sand. Only through sheer willpower was he able to avoid coughing.

Standing motionless, Sartoris narrowed his eyes at the things lurking in the shadows behind the TIE fighters. There were several of them, he realized now, stooping forward with gangling, flat-handed limbs, the familiar whine of servos accompanying their steady up-and-down gestures.

"Captain," one of the guards murmured behind him, "are they . . ."

Sartoris exhaled, and drew in a fresh breath. "Binary loadlifters," he said. "Still going about their routines."

Even as he said it, one of the CLL units stepped fully into view, facing them dully for a moment before pivoting and stomping back to the stack of crates rising up behind it. Moving the same stack from one side of the hangar to the other, Sartoris thought, back and forth endlessly.

He heard someone in the boarding party let out a sigh and a nervous chuckle. Sartoris didn't bother acknowledging it. It would have been too much like acknowledging his own sense of relief.

"We've wasted enough time," he said. "Let's move out."

They found the hovercraft on the far side of the hangar. It was the standard utility model, a balky thing with grappling servo-mech arms fore and aft, built for transporting fuel cells, but when they all climbed in, the thing sank to the floor. A pair of startled MSE droids skittered out from underneath, squealing anxiously, and disappeared into the gloom.

"Overloaded," Vesek said with just-our-luck exasperation. "Looks like we're hoofing it."

At first it wasn't bad. To get to the lower maintenance levels, they had to walk down a series of wide and silent corridors through the Destroyer's midsection, until they found their way to the cavernous storage bays beneath the primary power generator.

"Karking strange place," Austin muttered, his voice sounding alone down the long tunnel. "What do you think happened?"

"Who knows," Vesek said. "Whatever it is, the faster we're shut of it, the happier I'll be."

"Heard *that*."

"I'll tell you one thing, I'd hate to be anywhere near Lord Vader when he finds out they abandoned ship. How much you think it costs to replace a Destroyer?"

Austin snorted. "More credits than you and I'll ever see."

"I ever tell you I saw him in person once?"

"Who, Vader?"

Vesek nodded. "My transport was due for a routine inspection. All of a sudden my CO's having a major sphincter moment, scrambling us up to the flight deck, all spit and polish, making sure everything's extra shiny. Next thing I know, we're lined up in the hangar and his transport's landing and there he is."

"What's he like in person?"

Vesek considered. "Tall."

"Yeah?"

"And you feel something when you look at him. Like, I don't know . . . Cold inside." Vesek shuddered. "Kind of the way it feels in here, actually."

"All right," Sartoris said, "let's can the banter."

Ultimately the request for quiet turned out to be unnecessary. By the time they were amidships, the conversation had dried up completely and the men had lapsed into a glum and pensive silence.

Sartoris was deep in one of the lower maintenance levels when he realized that he simply wasn't going to get used to being here.

He and Vesek were loitering in one of the secondary corridors while the engineers dug through a power substation on the other side of the open hatchway. He could hear them in there, picking through parts and tossing them back. The other guard, Austin, had gone wandering through an adjacent series of interconnected chambers, rhapsodizing about how they seemed to go on forever, and Sartoris was forced to agree with him.

The vacancy of the Destroyer was both disorienting and nerve-racking—they had already walked almost a kilometer of wide-open uninhabited gangways to get here, rounding each corner half expecting to find the last survivor staggering toward them, cackling. So far all they'd encountered was a menagerie of mouse droids and janitorial units, cleaning and installer droids, all going about their business as if nothing had changed. One of them—a protocol droid, a 3PO unit—had almost gotten blasted when it wandered out in front of the troopers with its hands in the air, babbling senselessly.

Sartoris kept thinking about what the engineer, Greeley, had said about ghost ships. Although the power was on, lights and instrument panels fully activated, there was no trace of any crew or the missing ten thousand troopers that should have been here. There was only silence, stillness, and emptiness, creaking softly around them in the void of space.

"You find everything we need in there?" Sartoris called, hearing his voice roll down the hallway afterward. The engineers didn't answer. He glanced at Vesek. "You check in with the other group?"

"Not lately."

"See if you can get them to acknowledge. I want to be out of here soon."

Nodding, the other guard thumbed his comlink. "Armitage, this is Vesek, do you copy?"

There was no response, just a crackle of static.

"Armitage, this is ICO Vesek—can you hear me? Where are you guys?"

They both waited, far too long, it seemed to Sartoris, and this time Armitage's voice did respond, but it was faint, fading in and out. "... *med lab* ... *quadrant sevente* ..."

"I didn't copy, Armitage. Say again."

"... *in* ... *vat* ..." The rest was gone in a foaming tide of white noise. Vesek shook his head and looked at Sartoris.

"We're picking up a lot of interference from some-where on the Destroyer."

The captain nodded and walked over to pound on the bulkhead next to the hatchway. "Greeley, how much longer?" He stuck his head in, stopped, and looked more closely.

The engineers were gone.

Except for a seemingly random pile of integrated components and upended packaging cartons scat-tered across the floor, the chamber was completely empty—or at least it appeared to be. Sartoris felt a single pinhead of sweat rising to the surface beneath his left armpit and trickling down. The room felt too warm, air molecules compressed too closely together. "Greeley? Blandings?"

There was no answer. A pellet-sized bubble of some-thing, maybe fear, worked its way down his throat un-til it came to rest under his sternum. *They're dead in there,* a voice inside him gibbered. *Whatever wiped out the crew, it got them, too. It's already too late.*

Idiocy, of course, there was no sign of violence here or attack, but—

"Right here," Greeley said, rising up from behind one of the cartons, where he was followed in short or-der by Blandings. "Got the last of it." He held up a slender stalk of electronic equipment not much longer than his finger and put it in the box he'd found. "Let's roll."

"That's it?" Sartoris hoped his voice sounded stead-ier than he felt.

"Affirmative. Primary tuning shim for a Series Four thruster, *Thrive* class. Tests positive. We're a go."

"You're sure?"

Greeley gave him a long-suffering look reserved for those who questioned his judgment of such minutiae. "Yeah, Captain. I'm pretty sure."

"Okay, all right." Sartoris turned. "Austin?"

"Sir?" The guard's voice came back from far up the corridor, more distant than Sartoris had imagined. How far away had the man wandered? Sartoris felt his anger returning, plowing over him in a red wave.

"Get back here now, we're moving out."

"Yeah, but sir . . ." Austin still hadn't come back into the hallway. "You gotta see this, it's unbelievable, I . . ." The words broke off with a series of short, sharp coughs, and Austin finally emerged, shaking his head and covering his mouth. Eventually he got his breath and stopped coughing, but by then they were already on their way back to the main hangar, and Jareth Sartoris never found out what ICO Austin had seen back there.

8/Lung Windows

ARMITAGE WAS AN ARTIST.

Back home on Faro, he'd delighted his younger brothers and sisters with countless airpaint murals, but his talent was largely wasted in Imperial Corrections— if anything, his co-workers requested countless renderings of the female form, or worse, machinery, their beloved speeders and flitters from back home. Armitage hated drawing machines. It was enough to put him off art altogether . . . and that was saying something for a kid who'd once dreamed of attending the Pan-Galactic Arts Conservatory on Miele Nova.

Once he glimpsed what was in the Destroyer's Bio-Lab 177, however, he knew he had to paint it.

He'd broken away from the troopers and the engineers, Phibes and Quatermass, down at the other end of the corridor, ostensibly to check the supply dump on sublevel twelve, happy for any excuse to get away from them. How long were you expected to stand around complaining about the mess hall food and speculating which body part Zahara Cody washed first when she took a shower? And if he *didn't* participate in this enlightened conversation, the troopers and guards started heckling him, asking what was wrong with him, didn't he like working here? Maybe he'd be happier helping the Rebels plan another of their cowardly attacks on the Empire?

Checking out the bio-lab, no matter how boring it turned out to be, would have to be an improvement on that.

But the bio-lab *wasn't* boring.

The first thing Armitage noticed as he'd stepped through the hatchway was the vat. In many ways it was the only thing he saw, because after that he simply stopped looking. Its contents were simply too overwhelming and—in a bizarre way—too beautiful to get past.

The vat itself was huge, wall-sized, filled with some sort of clear bubbling gel. Suspended inside were dozens of oddly shaped pink organisms with wires and tubes running from them to a bank of humming equipment stacked beside the tank. Armitage, who had already stopped in his tracks, could only regard them in wonderment. From a distance the pink things looked like an unlikely hybrid of flowers, peeled fruit, and some species of embryonic winged animal whose like he'd never seen—they resembled a flock of tiny, skinned angels.

Then he came closer and realized what he was looking at.

They were sets of human lungs.

If he felt any tremor of disgust, it flicked through him so fleetingly that he scarcely noticed, and was supplanted immediately by a deeper and more fulfilling sense of artistic fascination. In each set, the entire respiratory tract had been carefully winnowed out to preserve the trachea and, above it, the larynx and all the more delicate organs of sound. Tubes were pumping oxygen into the lungs, causing them to expand and contract in their clear liquid bath.

Armitage realized they were all breathing together.

He counted thirty-three pairs of lungs in the vat before he gave up and stopped counting. Each was tagged with numbers and dates, part of some abandoned scientific experiment whose nature he could only guess at.

Some of the lungs were different. Their pink surface had gone a mottled gray in places, the muscle wall thickened with what looked like gray scar tissue. Armitage moved closer—he was no longer aware of himself at all now—and stared at them. Were they breathing more rapidly, or was that just his imagination? And was *he* breathing with them? It felt as though he'd been drawn into the larger, almost hypnotic tidal rhythm of their movement.

As always, when faced with something so innately striking, his first wish was to paint it, to capture what he saw in front of him. Not just the lung bath—*not a bad name for a painting,* he thought—but the emotion he'd felt when he'd realized what he'd been looking at. Awe. Shock. And ultimately a kind of unconscious familiarity, like something he'd once glimpsed in a dream.

He watched them sucking oxygen through tubes, and realized they were breathing more quickly and deeply. Somewhere on the other side of the vat, a machine beeped, and beeped again. Looking at them more closely, Armitage noticed for the first time the sets of rubber tubes that came braiding out of the lungs themselves. They seemed to be pumping some kind of thick gray fluid to a group of black tanks on the far side of the lab.

Lights flickered over the distant shoals of monitoring equipment on the other side of the vat. The lungs swelled and shrank, swelled and shrank, faster and faster.

Suddenly, at full inspiration, they stopped.

And, as one, they screamed through the tubes.

It was a high buzzing shriek that rose up and then sloped down, and it sent Armitage staggering backward with its intensity. Never in his life had he heard such a scream. He covered his ears, ducked his head, not wanting to be around this place anymore. The comlink in his headpiece crackled . . . some other guard's voice trying to reach him, and he could hardly convey what was happening. He wanted to run.

Inside the vat, the screaming noises shrilled on, up and down. The gray liquid was pumping faster now, siphoned off to the black tanks. Armitage realized that each one of the voice boxes had been wired with some kind of amplifier, making it even louder, and he wondered who was studying the scream-capacity of these lungs and why. Behind him a set of monitors showed the waveform of the scream, mapping it out as a series of mathematical functions.

He turned to the door.

And realized he wasn't alone.

9/Descent

"I DON'T GET IT, CAP," VESEK SAID. "WHERE'D THEY go?"

Sartoris's party had just crossed the gleaming steel prairie of the main hangar and arrived back at the docking shaft, but Armitage and his team were nowhere to be seen.

Behind him, the captain heard Austin coughing again—the snotty, bronchial hacking noise was really starting to get on his nerves—and decided enough was enough. He cocked one thumb at the shaft.

"Must have gone back down without us," Sartoris said. "Let's go."

Vesek and Austin climbed back inside, onto the waiting lift, and Sartoris went in after them, followed by Greeley and Blandings with the box of scavenged components. The shaft sealed behind them and the platform began its slow descent. Austin kept coughing. Sartoris tried to ignore him. He was going to have to report back to the warden about the Star Destroyer and wasn't looking forward to it. No doubt Kloth would have all kinds of irrelevant questions about the ship and what they saw up there, every minute of it an endurance test for Sartoris's patience. Asking unnecessary questions was one of the warden's nervous tics when he felt pressed to make a decision, and—

"Oh no," Greeley said.

Sartoris glanced up. "What's wrong?"

The engineer started to say something, then dropped the box of parts, clutched his stomach, and bent over with a hoarse croak. Sartoris realized the man was throwing up, shoulders clenching in great involuntary spasms. Blandings and the other guards all backed away from him, muttering with surprise and disgust, but there wasn't much room in the shaft and within seconds the smell had filled it entirely.

"I'm sorry," Greeley said, wiping his mouth. "Lousy mess hall food, you can't . . ."

"Just stay there." Sartoris held up his hands. "You can get cleaned up when we get back to the barge."

"I feel fine, I just—" The engineer swallowed and took in a deep breath. His eyes and nose were streaming tears, and Sartoris could hear a faint chest-rattle as he sucked in a shallow breath. Over his shoulder he heard Austin starting to cough again.

"Captain." Blandings's voice was small as he glanced back up in the direction they'd come. "You don't think there was something up there . . . ?"

"Contamination diagnostics checked out negative," Sartoris shot back—too quickly, he realized. "That's what you said, isn't it, Greeley?"

Greeley gave a weak nod, tried to answer, and thought better of it. His skin had taken on a decidedly green shade, and it shone with a thin, oily layer of sweat. A moment later he sank down to his knees next to the box of electronics and lowered his head until it was almost touching the floor.

By the time they arrived back on the barge, Vesek and Blandings had started coughing as well.

10/Triage

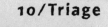

"HANG ON, I'M COMING." ZAHARA FOLLOWED THE 2-1B through the medbay to the bed where a guard named Austin crouched with his head between his knees. He'd come in along with another guard and a pair of maintenance engineers. Waste had triaged his new patients expertly, assigned them beds, and started working up Austin, who appeared to be the worst off.

"Thanks," Zahara told the 2-1B. "Go check on the others." Sitting down on the bed next to Austin's, she didn't wait for the guard to acknowledge her. "How are you feeling?"

He looked up at her stonily. "I want to talk to the droid."

"My surgical droid is otherwise engaged with your co-workers," Zahara said. "What happened to you up there?"

"What do you care?"

"It's my job. How many people were up there with you?"

Austin didn't respond. Twin rivulets of thick yellow snot were leaking out of his nose, down either side of his upper lip, and he smeared them away with his sleeve and started coughing again into his fist, a loose, rib-racking hack.

"Look," Zahara said, "I've got other sick inmates to look after. So how about dropping the attitude so we can focus on getting you better?"

"You're a piece of work," Austin said, "you know that?"

"I've been called worse."

"You and your *sick inmates*. I bet you . . ." He broke off into another coughing fit, Zahara leaning back as the guard sprayed the air around him with microscopic droplets, then pivoted his head to glare at her again. ". . . I bet . . . you probably . . ." More coughing, thicker now. "You're nothing but a . . ."

"Tell you what," she said, "you'll have plenty of time to call me names later. How about lying back and letting me have a look at you."

Austin shook his head. "Send the droid. I don't want you touching me."

"Don't be an idiot. You're—"

"Send the droid."

Enough was enough; Zahara stood up. "Suit yourself."

"Captain Sartoris was right about you, you know," he said as she walked away.

"Excuse me?"

"You're sweet on cons. I'll bet that if I were some low-life Rebel scum you'd treat me like your only patient. Every sob story that comes along, you're ready with a sympathetic ear."

"Wow." She almost felt obliged to respond with

some representational show of anger. "Your captain really knows me well, doesn't he?"

"He's a good man."

"Sure," she said easily. "Killing inmates is a real feather in his cap."

Austin gave a quick series of explosive coughs, then cleared his throat and whooped out a ragged breath. "That wasn't your call to make."

Zahara turned around to face him again. "Let me tell you something about your heroic captain. He was in trouble long before what happened with Von Longo—even the warden knew it. Regardless of what he might have once been, he's now a burned-out wreck of a human being, a claustrophobic sociopath with . . ." She broke off when she realized Austin was grinning at her, a narrow, vulpine grin—she was only confirming everything he'd suspected about her. "What Captain Sartoris did to Longo here in my medbay was just the end product of a long and messy downward slide."

"And that's when you really started to like him, right?" Austin asked, that hard smile still wrapped across his otherwise sickly face. "You like 'em hurt and needy. That really flicks your switch, doesn't it?"

She felt her neck beginning to turn red and was suddenly sure that Austin could see it, too. "If you say so."

"I'm not the only one."

"Dr. Cody?" a synthesized voice called out. "Are you available?"

She turned and saw the 2-1B gesturing to her from the other side of the infirmary. On the bed beside it, one of the new patients—she thought it was the other guard, Vesek—appeared to be having a seizure. The two engineers and the trooper who had accompanied him were all sitting up watching with a mixture of dismay and revulsion.

"On my way."

By the time she arrived at his bedside, Vesek had started to slide off his mattress despite the surgical droid's efforts to restrain him. The guard's face had gone a nearly translucent shade of pale and his eyes were rolled back in his head while the rest of his body flopped and twitched erratically as if responding to some high-voltage electrical current. Then without any warning he fell on his back, his mouth bursting open to emit an uncertain *urk* sound, followed by an almost solid spray of bright arterial blood that shot straight up into the air like a geyser.

"Watch out." Zahara raised her hands to shield herself and the engineers sitting next to her. On the other side of the bed, the 2-1B continued to hold Vesek in place. When it looked up, she saw that its cowling and visual sensors were covered with blood. Vesek collapsed backward on the stained sheets, as if the act of vomiting had drained all the fight from him.

"Get him in the bubble," Zahara said. "All of them, the guards, engineers, whoever came off that Destroyer, get them sealed off from the other patients—now."

The 2-1B's sensors had already cleared themselves and reflected back at her attentively. "Yes, Dr. Cody."

"Run labs on them, a full tox screen, find out what they were exposed to up there."

"Anything else?"

She forced herself to stop and think, taking inventory in her mind. "We better let the warden know what's going on. He'll want updates."

"Right away."

"Wait," Zahara said, "I'll take care of that myself." She didn't wait around as the surgical droid started giving instructions to the engineers. Their faces were freckled with Vesek's blood, and they looked frightened now, more scared than sick.

"You," she said, looking at the name on his badge, "Greeley, how many men went aboard the Star Destroyer?"

"Two teams of five," Greeley said, "but—"

"Where are the other six men?"

"They came back before us."

On the bed, Vesek made a throaty groaning sound and shifted his weight, rolling onto his side so that his back was to them. The other two men stared at him with matching expressions of encroaching panic as the droid led them away.

"Hey, Doc, what's the good word?"

She turned and saw that Gat, the Devish, had left his bed and made his way over to see her. He was gazing at the guard on the bloodstained bunk, fingering his broken horn with the unconscious compulsion of someone prodding a loose tooth with his tongue.

"Nothing you need to worry about."

"I heard you say something about the bubble."

"I'm just playing it safe," Zahara said, "until we get a better handle on things."

The Devish cocked his head and then nodded. "If there's anything I can do, let me know, okay?"

"Thanks, Gat. I'll keep that in mind." Without thinking, she put one hand on his shoulder and felt another pair of eyes on her from across the room.

Austin was glaring at her.

And smiling.

She walked back to her workstation, thumbed the console, and watched as Kloth's face materialized on the screen in front of her. Some kind of contrast malfunction had rendered the image too bright, making it appear bleached and monochromatic. He was sitting at his desk, the viewport behind him partly eclipsed by the massive bulk of the Star Destroyer's underside directly above. It blocked out more stars than she had expected and gave the odd appearance of having arrived at their destination.

"Dr. Cody? What is it?"

"I'm down here with four of the men from the boarding party," she said.

"How are they?"

"Not good. I'm placing them in the quarantine bubble. Where's Captain Sartoris?"

"In his quarters, I assume. But Dr. Cody—"

"I'll need him up here, too," she said. "What about the other five?"

"That's just it." Kloth shook his head and she realized for the first time that the pallor on his face had nothing to do with the contrast of the monitor screen. "The second team never came back."

11/Red Map

▄▬▬▄▬▄▬▄▬▄▬▬▄▬▄▬▄:

SARTORIS WAS DREAMING WHEN THE KNOCK ON THE door awakened him.

In the dream he was still wandering around the Destroyer, alone. The rest of his party—Austin, Vesek, Armitage, the engineers and troopers—was dead and gone. Something aboard the Destroyer had picked them off, one by one. Each man's departure had been marked by a scream, followed by a sickening crack that Sartoris seemed to feel as much as hear.

Sartoris kept moving, trying to ignore a nagging itch that had spread across the skin of his stomach like a rash. He knew it was only a matter of time before the beast, whatever it was, came after him. It wouldn't be long before he glimpsed its true face, if it had one. Maybe it didn't; perhaps it was simply sickness personified, a brainless and ravenous void that sucked in life.

A maze of hallways stood ahead of him, and Sartoris's pace faltered. He was lost and he knew it. He wasn't even sure if he was heading toward the thing or away from it. The skin around his abdomen itched worse and he stopped to scratch it and felt something impressed on the flesh itself, like a tattoo or a mesh of wrinkles. His dream-self tugged up his shirttail from his pants and he looked down at the skin of his side and saw that there was in fact something printed on his side, some kind of map—a map of the Star Destroyer. The diagrams disappeared into his flesh, and he realized he'd have to open himself up to read it. Steeling himself, he hooked the first two fingers of his right hand and raked them as hard as he could into the muscle above his hip, ignoring the dry-ice spike of pain and thrusting in deeper to peel back the outer tissue layer. The fat came loose from his flank with a sickening ease. Blood gushed out of his side, hot and steaming, running down his legs and filling up his boots.

When he woke up, a scream at his lips, the knocking had turned into pounding.

He sat up, shivered with a kind of all-over wetness, and for a queasy instant thought he was still bleeding. But the hot sticky moisture clinging to his skin was only perspiration—it pasted his hair to his brow and stuck his uniform to his back. The only part of his body that wasn't wet was the inside of his mouth; it was bone-dry.

Opening the door of his quarters he saw two guards in orange biohazard suits and masks standing there, looking like refugees from his interrupted dream.

"Captain Sartoris?"

He blinked. "What's this?"

"Sir, we've been instructed to bring you down to the infirmary."

"Why?"

A pause, then: "Orders, sir."

"Whose?" Sartoris asked, and made it easy for them. "The warden's or Dr. Cody's?"

The guards exchanged a glance. The glare off their face-shields made it hard to say which one responded. "I'm not sure, sir. But—"

"Who gave the order to gear up?" Sartoris asked, but he was already thinking about Austin's cough and Greeley's vomiting, and the others, all of them. Too late he wished he'd conferred with Warden Kloth about the other party before going back to his quarters. It had been a small act of defiance that had blown up in his face, another poor decision in a long and self-destructive chain of questionable choices. He ought to have reported back first: swallowed his agitation and just done it.

"Better come with us, sir."

Sartoris took a step forward to try to identify the men inside the masks. "I feel fine," he said, and although this was the truth, it felt like a lie, maybe because of the guards' reaction—when he came forward, they both took one big step back.

"How are Austin and the engineer, Greeley?"

"Austin's dead, sir. He died about an hour ago."

"What?" Sartoris gaped at them, feeling gut-punched. "That's impossible. I was just talking to him." How long had he been up here sleeping? A new thought occurred to him then—a desperate realization of an eventuality that he might have to face, sooner rather than later. "What about Vesek?"

"I really couldn't say, sir. They're all in quarantine. I think . . ." The guard, whom he'd finally identified as a short-timer named Saltern, was taking another step backward. "Maybe you better just come up and talk to her yourself."

"Dr. Cody, you mean."

"Yes, sir."

Sartoris didn't ask any more questions. He came out, and felt the guards falling in a step behind him.

"I can find my way up to the infirmary, Saltern."

"We were ordered to go with you, sir."

In case I bolt, Sartoris thought, and then: *Maybe I should.*

But he had told them the truth—he did feel fine. Whatever had happened to the others up on the Destroyer hadn't touched him. It was a localized phenomenon, and he wasn't going to let it get to him.

You won't have a choice.

"Take me upstairs," he said. "I need to talk to Vesek."

12/Big Midnight

THE RODIANS WERE SICK.

Trig looked at them in the cell across from his, sprawled on their bunks, shifting positions only sporadically. As unnerving as it had been when they'd stood there staring at him, Trig found this new development even more disturbing. Their respiration sounded terrible, a clogged rattle. The coughing was worse. Every so often one of them would groan or make a low, desperate whine.

"See anything?" Kale asked.

"Uh-uh."

A guard hustled by in an orange biohazard suit, followed by two more. "Hey!" Trig pounded on the bars. "What's happening out there?"

The guards just kept moving. Trig turned and looked back at his brother. "What is all this, anyway?"

Kale shrugged. "Who knows?" He rolled over on his bunk and closed his eyes, and a moment later was fast asleep. Trig listened to him snore.

"Hey there," a voice whispered.

Trig leaned forward. It was coming from the cell next to theirs.

"Hey," he said back, craning his neck, but he couldn't see around the corner. "What's happening?"

"Your name's Trig Longo, isn't it?" the voice from the next cell said.

"Yeah."

"And your brother . . . he's Kale, right?"

"That's right," Trig said. "What do they call you?"

The voice ignored his question. "Big price on your head," it whispered. "Ten thousand credits."

Trig didn't answer. Stepping back from the bars, he'd already begun to experience a cold slithery feeling moving into the pit of his stomach. The voice just kept talking.

"Ten thousand credits, that's big money. Thing is, nobody's going to collect."

"Why not?" Trig asked.

"Because I'm the one that offered it," the voice said, "and I'm going to kill you both myself."

Trig's entire body went numb. He suddenly realized that he knew that slushy pronunciation, made all the more inarticulate by the way the mouth had been injured when Kale yanked the piercings out.

"I requested a transfer just so I could be close to you," Aur Myss's voice said. "Greased the right wheels, you might say. The second they open these doors, I'm going to rip you and your brother apart with my bare hands. And that's just for starters."

"Why don't you shut up," Kale said from his bunk, startling Trig. He hadn't known that his brother was listening, or even awake.

Myss giggled. Trig realized the gang leader was probably the one he'd heard giggling earlier, when Wembly had come through, bellowing for quiet. "How do you want it?" he asked. "Quick and dirty, I'm guessing. We can do it somewhere private. The guards will find your bodies later, but it might be a while. Not that anybody's gonna care—not any more than they cared about your old man when Sartoris—"

"Shut *up*," Kale hissed, springing off his bunk now and joining Trig at the bars, shoving one hand out and groping blindly in the direction of the voice as if there were some way he could swing out and hit Myss.

"Kale, don't," Trig said, and by the time Kale seemed to realize what he was doing and tried to jerk his arm back, it was too late. Myss latched on to him now from the adjacent cell, yanking his face up against the bars. Trig could hear him giggling and grunting at the same time, holding on to Kale. In the cell opposite them, one of the torpid Rodians had actually sat up to watch with a vague expression of dazed interest.

"Just can't wait for it?" the voice asked. "You want it now? Is that it? You want me to—"

There was a sharp *whack* and the voice broke off with a surprised grunt.

"Get your meat hooks back inside," Wembly said outside the cell. He was wearing an orange suit and mask, the BLX standing behind him, and when he turned to the brothers' cell, Trig could see his own expression reflected back at him in Wembly's face-shield. "You still got all five?"

"Yeah," Kale said, holding his fingers and flexing them. "I think so. He was just messing with me."

"What's with the suit?" Trig asked.

For the first time, the guard appeared uncomfortable. The BLX droid standing behind him said, "There's been a—"

"Just a precaution," Wembly cut in. "Nothing to worry about."

"Is it bad?"

"Nobody knows anything. Dr. Cody's trying to figure it out." Wembly glanced at the Rodians, who were now back on their bunks again, coughing and making the quiet whining noise that Trig had heard before. "Looks like your neighbors aren't faring too well, either. Two less that you'll have to worry about, I guess."

"Wembly—"

Up the hall, somebody shrieked. Wembly spun around with remarkable agility for a man of his size and saw something he didn't like. Without another word, he burst into a shambling run in the opposite direction from whatever he'd seen.

Trig didn't have to wait long to learn what it was. The other guard charging down the hall wore a torn orange suit and no mask. He was still screaming when he slammed face-first into the bars of their cell, spraying a glut of blood through. It hit Trig's face, shockingly warm and wet on his cheeks and nose.

The sick guard stopped screaming and stood there, eyes wide and totally disoriented. His hands gripped the bars as if forcibly keeping himself upright. Fever blazed from his skin in palpable waves. His breathing was hoarse and raspy and when Trig saw the man's chest and shoulders rising to force out a cough, he had the presence of mind to stand back. Only after the guard coughed for what seemed like forever, making

no effort to cover his mouth, did he finally seem to realize where he'd landed.

"You can't stop it," the guard said, in a queer, flat
voice—the voice of a man talking in his sleep. "You
just can't."

"What?" Trig asked.

"There's no way." The guard shook his head, his
lower lip trembling a bit. Then he turned and started
walking crookedly up the hallway in the direction
where Wembly had gone.

Trig felt his throat go tight. He was suddenly miserably sure he was going to cry. He was scared, that was
part of it, but he was also thinking about his father.
Somehow the fact that he didn't know what time it
was—it could be midnight down here for all he
knew—made it all the worse. A few months earlier
they had been safe at home, the three of them eating
breakfast together. How had things gotten so horrible
so fast?

"Hey," Kale said, placing one hand on Trig's
shoulder. "Come here." He lifted the hem of his
shirt and wiped his brother's face off, the first tears
mixing with the guard's blood. "It's all right."

"This is bad," Trig said.

"We've been through worse."

Trig couldn't answer. He put his face against his
brother's chest, and hugged him fiercely. Kale hugged
him back. "Shh," he said. " 'S okay."

In the next cell, Myss was making noises of his own.
He was imitating Trig's sobs and giggling. In the Rodians' cell, one of them had started coughing a steady,
listless cough that didn't stop; it just paused long
enough for the thing to suck in a breath and keep going.

"Kale?" Trig asked.

"Yeah?"

"Do *you* feel sick?"

"Me? No, I feel fine." His brother shook his head right away. "You?"

"No." Trig drew back and looked Kale in the eye. "If you do, though, you have to tell me, right away, all right?"

"Sure."

"I mean it."

"I will," Kale said. "But that ain't gonna happen."

"You don't know that."

"Trust me, okay?"

Trig nodded. But he knew he was right. He sat back down on his bunk with his chin in his hands and stared out into the hall at the coughing Rodians.

In the next cell, there was the noise of something taking a breath, rearranging itself into position, and letting out a quiet, patient sigh.

"I'm gonna get you, kid," Aur Myss whispered. "When the time comes, I'll be waiting."

13/Molecules

ZAHARA WAS ADJUSTING THE AIR INFLOW ON HER ISO-lation mask when she sensed the 2-1B approaching behind her. "Dr. Cody?"

"Not now."

"It's important."

She hardly heard him. The afternoon had been a dark and bloody blur. All around her, the normally sedate infirmary was packed with sick inmates and guards, every bed occupied and more lying on the floor. The room was filled with the sounds of their coughing, rasping breaths, beeping monitors, and constant cries for help.

Whatever the boarding party had brought back with them from the Destroyer had spread so quickly throughout the *Purge* that she and Waste had already lost track of the new admits. Captain Sartoris had arrived in the custody of his own guards, and the surgical droid had ushered him directly into the quarantine bubble. Knowing that Sartoris was sitting in there waiting for her to examine him was the extra dose of stress she didn't need right now.

The warden had been calling her constantly from

his office for updates. He didn't understand why she couldn't at least diagnose what was wrong, if not cure it. Up till now she'd been too busy just trying to take care of the inmates, triaging them and treating their symptoms, which, depending on the species, varied from upper respiratory complaints to fever and GI symptoms to seizures, hallucinations, hemorrhage, and coma. And now the 2-1B was still standing next to her, awaiting her full attention.

"Look," Zahara said, "whatever it is, it's just going to have to—"

"It's Gat," the droid said. "He's dead."

Zahara turned around and frowned. *What?*

"He just had a seizure and went into respiratory arrest. I'm sorry for interrupting. I just thought you'd want to know."

Zahara took in a slow breath, held it for a beat, and nodded before letting it out. She followed the droid across the infirmary to Gat's bed. The Devish was lying on his side, pale-skinned, eyes open, already glazed. She looked at the vacant face, the broken horn and slackened jaw. Whatever had been good inside him— the rare element of decency and humor that had made him unique among her patients—was totally gone. She bent down and closed his eyes.

"And the warden is waiting to talk to you again," Waste said, actually managing to sound regretful.

Zahara knew what Kloth was going to ask. "How bad is it?" she asked the droid.

"Twelve fatalities so far."

"Including the entire boarding party?"

"With the exception of Captain Sartoris and ICO Vesek," the surgical droid answered, "yes."

"And they're both still in the bubble?"

"That's correct. Otherwise, the pathogen has already spread throughout the *Purge*. I'm following several reports of symptoms from all over General Population—inmates, guards, support staff. Rate of infection is nearly one hundred percent. Our medication and supplies will hold out for another week if nothing changes. However . . ." The droid paused, its voice modulating into a more confiding tone. "I have been unable to isolate the molecular makeup of this particular strain. Dr. Cody?"

"Yes?"

"As you know, my programming regarding infectious disease is quite wide in scope, and yet this current contagion is like nothing I've ever seen." The droid's voice lowered further, the synthesized equivalent of a whisper. "It seems as though the individual organisms are using quorum sensing to communicate with one another inside the host."

"Meaning what?"

"Individual cells don't activate to full virulence until they've reproduced to such numbers that the host can't combat them."

"In other words," Zahara said, "when it's too late?"

"That's correct. At this point I'm not even convinced that our isolation gear is an effective barrier."

Zahara looked down self-consciously at the orange suit that she'd put on immediately after placing the boarding party into quarantine. She didn't like wearing it, didn't like the message that it sent to the inmates who had already been exposed, but there wasn't any choice. She couldn't help anyone if she was sick or dead. And the droid was right, of course. As of now, it was impossible to say whether the suits and masks were helping—guards who had suited up immediately were already coming in sick, but she herself showed no sign of infection.

Not yet, anyway, a grim voice inside her amended.

From across the infirmary, an alarm went off, a steady high-pitched whine indicating that one of her patients had gone into full arrest. Zahara started to respond to it, and another alarm went off, and then a third. *There's got to be some kind of equipment malfunction,* she thought dazedly, but she could see from here that wasn't the case. Her patients were dying faster now, dying all around her, and the only thing she could do was sign the appropriate paperwork afterward.

"I'll take care of this," Waste said. "You need to talk to the warden."

"The warden can wait."

By the time she got to the bedside, though, it was already too late. The inmate had collapsed, the monitors feeding back a steady helpless whine. It seemed to be coming from everywhere at once. The patient to her right was having a seizure, and his alarm went off, too. For the hundredth time that day, Zahara wondered what Captain Sartoris's party had run across up inside the Destroyer.

She knew only one person she could ask.

14/Bubble

▬▬▬■▬■▬▬■▬■▬

THE ALARM WAS GOING OFF IN THE NEGATIVE AIRSPACE of the quarantine bubble just before she slipped inside. Looking in, she saw Sartoris standing over Vesek's bed while Vesek gaped up at him. The younger guard's face had gone so white that Zahara could see the fine blue veins tracing beneath his jaw and chin, rising up his cheeks. She ran the rest of the way, letting the flap seal shut behind her with a barely audible *thwap*.

"What happened?"

"You're the doctor," Sartoris snapped. "You tell me."

"He was stable just a few minutes ago." She checked the monitors. Vesek's pulse was gone, his oxygen saturation plunging and blood pressure crashing hard. "Did you do something to him?"

Sartoris glared at her. "Me?"

"Hand me that foil blister pack—the other one." She tore it open, withdrew the breathing tube, and smeared it with lubricant. "Tilt his head back."

Sartoris moved stiffly, watching as she eased the tube down Vesek's throat, going in blind. It hit an obstruction somewhere and when she tried to advance it, his chest heaved, and he made a gagging sound in the pit of his chest. It was a sound she'd come to know well over the last few hours.

"Watch yourself," she said, as dense red fluid started to spout up the tube, pouring out of his mouth. She reached for suction but couldn't see far enough to run the tube where it needed to go. All the while she could feel Sartoris hovering over her shoulder, literally breathing down her neck, and had to make a deliberate effort to ignore him. Working almost entirely by feel, she repositioned the tube and heard the first rasping noises of Vesek hungrily slurping up oxygen, then swabbed his face and taped the tube into place to keep it from slipping. She took a step back and made herself take a series of deep breaths, holding each one for a five-count until she began to feel steady again.

"Is he going to make it?" Sartoris asked.

"Not for much longer. Not like this." She turned to face him. "I need to speak to you."

"I was just leaving."

Zahara gave him an incredulous look. "Excuse me?"

"I came to talk with Vesek." Sartoris shot a glance at the tube taped into place around the guard's mouth. "Not much chance of that now."

"You can't leave."

"Who's going to stop me?" His eyebrow hiked up. "You?"

"You're in quarantine because you're one of the primary carriers of this infection," Zahara said. "You need to stay here."

Sartoris eyed her levelly, taking her measure. The cold indifference in his face was unlike anything she'd ever encountered before, as if it were permanently etched beneath the features, across the very bones of his face.

"I'm going to make this very clear," he said. "You have no authority over me. And there's nothing you can do for me or my men or any of these inmates. You're useless, Dr. Cody, and you know it. If you were one of my guards, you'd be gone by now . . . if you were lucky. Otherwise you'd be dead."

"Look—" she started.

"Save it for your precious inmates," he said, standing up and starting to walk toward the sealed hatch. "I've already heard enough."

"Jareth, wait."

At the sound of his first name, he stopped in his tracks, and when he turned around and saw her expression, a grin twisted like barbed wire across his face. "You're scared stiff, aren't you?"

"That's got nothing to do with this."

"You ought to be. They're going to remember you for this."

"What?"

"You might think you're through with the Empire, but they're not through with you." He glanced outside the bubble, where the 2-1B was hurrying from bed to bed as the alarms switched on, each one signaling cardiac and respiratory arrest. "Every exposed inmate and guard on this barge is going to die in the next few hours, while you stand there in your isolation suit with your tools and your droids. I hope you enjoy answering questions, because there's going to be plenty of them waiting for you." He reached out with one finger and very gently placed it against her sternum. "You'll spend the rest of your life living this down."

"What did you and your men see up in that Star Destroyer?" she asked.

"What did I *see*?" Sartoris shook his head. "Nothing—not a thing."

Sighing, she glanced at the monitor screens alongside the bubble's inner membrane. "Your blood work is coming back clean. The infection doesn't seem to be affecting you whatsoever."

"Benefits of clean living," he said, and shoved past her. "If you think you can detain me, you're welcome to try. Otherwise I'll be up in the warden's office. I'm sure he'll be interested in hearing about how you and your staff are bearing up in this crisis."

Before she could move to stop him, he'd already walked out of the bubble and through the medbay. Something about his motives bothered her. There was no way he was going waste time talking to Kloth just to report on her inefficacy here. How much more trouble could she really get in now, anyway?

Zahara started to follow him and paused, feeling momentarily light-headed. She stopped short, scrutinizing herself for any of the symptoms she'd seen in her patients. Her breathing was fine, she felt no pain or lethargy—was she just feeling the accumulated tension of the whole situation?

"Waste?"

"Yes, Dr. Cody." The droid didn't look up from the inmate whose bunk it was squatting over, administering some sort of IV injection.

"I need you to run some blood and cultures."

"On what patient?"

"Me," she said, and held out her arm.

The 2-1B looked at her. "But that would require me to violate the isolation barrier of your suit."

"The suits don't work, anyway," she said. "You said so yourself."

"I was speculating—"

"Enough." She peeled off the mask and tossed it aside, yanking off the gloves and pulling her sleeve up to expose her bare arm. From the nearby beds, the inmates gazed at her blankly.

"Dr. Cody, please—" Waste's synthesized voice was edging perilously close to panic. "—my theories regarding the efficacy of the barge's isolation gear are hardly conclusive, and in any case, the prime directive of my programming plainly states that I am to protect life and promote wellness whenever possible."

"Just do it," she said, and locked her eyes on the droid's visual sensors, waiting for the needle.

15/VHB

SARTORIS WALKED BACK UP THE CORRIDOR TOWARD the warden's office with a pair of E-11 blaster rifles, their stocks collapsed so he could hold one in each hand. He'd taken them off two of the stormtroopers in the hallway—one of them, right outside the infirmary, had attempted to shoot him with it. The guard in question, a man that Sartoris had known for years, had staggered toward him with his helmet in his hand and blood in his eyes, coughing and ranting at the top of his lungs. He didn't seem to have any idea where he was but kept insisting he get medical care. He said his lungs were filling up with fluid and he couldn't breathe, he was drowning from the inside but they wouldn't let him into the medbay. Sartoris tried to shove past the man, and the guard pulled the blaster and pointed it at him. When he finally realized who he was about to shoot, the trooper stopped and swayed sideways against the wall.

"Cap, I'm sorry, I didn't realize—"

Sartoris grabbed the E-11 from him, switched it to stun, and shot him point-blank. Twenty meters later, another stormtrooper came at him, and Sartoris had been faster this time, dropping him on sight. It had been like that the rest of the way up. Guards and troopers in ineffective infection-control gear stumbled up and down the hallway, coughing and puking blood into their masks, reaching out to him for help and begging him for answers to what was going on. Many of them had already collapsed and lay facedown on the floor. The farther he went, the more bodies lay in his path. Sartoris stepped over them when he could; other times he stepped on top of them. With every passing meter, the musty fug of bile and stale sweat hanging in the air grew more oppressive. He had never smelled anything like it. If things were this bad up here in the administration level, he couldn't imagine how bad it was down in Gen Pop—it would be a nightmare down there. He wondered if the warden had already pulled all the remaining guards up from the detainment levels entirely, sealed the whole thing off, and was waiting for the inmates to die.

Reaching Kloth's office, he pressed the call-switch and waited for an acknowledgment, but the warden's voice didn't answer back.

"Sir, it's Captain Sartoris. Open up."

No reply, but Sartoris knew he was in there. Historically the warden had faced all crises big and small from the sanctity of his office—today would be no different.

And the warden had something that Sartoris needed.

The access codes to the escape pods.

Maintaining the pods had been one of the duties of ICO Vesek, and Sartoris knew that Vesek had the launch codes to activate the pods. And so he had sat next to Vesek's bunk in the quarantine bubble, staring down into Vesek's hallucinating expression, those disoriented rolling eyes, asking him over and over for the launch codes. But Vesek had been less than forthcoming. Eventually Sartoris had lost patience with the guard—he could be forgiven for that, couldn't he? Wouldn't it make sense that eventually he'd need to apply a bit more pressure, to help Vesek focus on what he was asking?

He hadn't meant to pinch Vesek's nose shut for as long as he had. If Vesek had cooperated, simply snapped out of it for a moment and given him the codes, none of that would have been necessary. All Sartoris had needed was information, the same way he'd wanted information from that old inmate Longo, but the old man hadn't been very forthcoming, either, and this was a prison barge, after all, wasn't it?

Accidents happened.

But Vesek wasn't an inmate, a voice inside Sartoris's head whispered. *Vesek was one of your own men, and you—*

"He was on his way out, anyway," Sartoris muttered, and turned his attention back to the task at hand. Warden Kloth was in there, and he needed to talk to him more urgently than ever. Sartoris was going to convince Kloth that they needed to get off the barge now if there was any chance of staying alive. There was plenty of room in the escape pod for both of them—or just himself, if Kloth didn't see things his way.

"Warden?" Sartoris shouted.

Still nothing from the other side of the door. Sartoris glanced down at the blasters in his hands, and back at the door. It was probably blastproof, and shooting his way in would only start a volley of ricocheting bolts that might end up killing him. But he needed to get the access codes, sooner rather than later, if—

Then the door slid open, all by itself.

At this point, Sartoris hadn't been expecting it, and he actually hesitated for a moment, peering inside the chamber. Kloth's office appeared empty—the holo-mural desert scene, an abandoned console, the view outside unobstructed.

Sartoris stepped inside, and the smell hit him hard. It was the same ammoniac odor that had accumulated in the corridors outside, only a more concentrated version, and he cupped his hand over his nose and mouth, laboring to suppress his gag reflex.

"Captain," something gargled from the other side of the console. "How nice to see you."

Sartoris took another step and looked forward, then down. Warden Kloth was lying on the floor below his console, curled on his side in the fetal position, in a pool of something grayish red. When he saw Sartoris standing over him, he lifted himself up on both elbows and took a raspy, shaking breath. Webs of sticky fluid dribbled from his nose and chin. The sickness had stripped away any remaining affectation of toughness and cruelty, leaving only the trembling, skinned thing that Sartoris had known was inside him all along.

"I've been watching the monitors," he said. "This infection from the Star Destroyer—" He coughed again. "It's spreading too quickly to stop. Would you agree?"

"Yes, sir."

"Then we're left with only one choice . . ." Kloth sucked in another labored, snorkeling breath. "We have to abandon ship."

"My thoughts exactly."

"You'll help me to the escape pod," he said between hacking coughs. "That's SOP. I'll make . . . my full report from there. Imperial . . . Corrections won't question my decision—they can access all the data from the infirmary afterward—they'll see I had no choice—"

Sartoris had to smile. Even in extremis, the man was still thinking about how to cover himself in front of his superiors.

"You have the access codes for launch?" he asked.

Kloth coughed and nodded, and coughed harder, the force of it making veins bulge like twisted blue worms in his temples.

"I think," Sartoris said, "that you should tell me now."

The warden stopped coughing. His eyes narrowed, then widened. Sartoris was pointing both of the E-11s at Kloth's face, close enough that he knew Kloth would be able to smell the tinge of ozone that still clung to their barrels, and see that Sartoris had switched them back to kill.

"You're an animal," Kloth said. "I should have relieved you from duty when I had the chance."

"It's not too late," Sartoris said, holding the blasters steady. "You could make it your last official act as warden."

"Put those down. You'll need both hands to help me to the pod."

"I think I can manage," Sartoris said. "After you give me the codes."

"I don't have much choice, do I?"

Sartoris regarded him blandly. "I suppose you could try lying to me. But I deal with liars and con artists every day, so under the circumstances I wouldn't recommend it."

"The codes are already imprinted here. I couldn't alter them if I tried." Kloth handed him a datacard, his hand trembling only slightly, and held Sartoris's gaze steadily as he did so. "Captain?"

"Yes?"

"There's a subsection of the Imperial Corrections Psychological Profile Exam known as the Veq-Headley Battery. It's specifically skewed to indicate any underlying psychopathological attitudes in the applicant . . . with the understanding that such things might come in handy in service to the Empire." His tongue came out and moistened his upper lip. "Would you like to know how you scored on your VHB, Captain Sartoris?"

"I think we both already know the answer to that, sir," Sartoris said, and squeezed both triggers.

The effect at close range was nothing short of spectacular. Warden Kloth's entire cranial vault sheared away in a dense cloud of scarlet, gristle, and bone. His neck and shoulders flopped sideways, torqued on some invisible axis with the leftover momentum of the energy blast, and then landed with a wet splat, skidding backward in the spattered reservoir of blood.

Sartoris pocketed the datacard and turned to face the still-open door. That was when he saw the young guard in the isolation suit standing out in the corridor, staring at him slack-jawed, his fever-blotched face gone abruptly pale so the blisters stood out like stars. When the guard realized that Sartoris was looking at him, he jerked both hands up and backed into the hallway behind him, his chin going up and down trying to yammer out words.

"Captain? You j-just shot Warden Kloth."

"Did him a favor," Sartoris said, taking note of the guard's runny nose and the fever sores clustering around his lips. "You want one?"

The guard looked as if he'd just lost control of his bladder and bowels simultaneously.

"Get out of here." Pointing with one of the blasters: "Go that way."

The guard nodded, turned, and fled, boots clattering, rasping audibly for breath. Sartoris wished him well. He went the other direction, and started making his way to the escape pod.

16/In the Cage

▬▬▬:▬▬▬:▬▬▬

ALTHOUGH THERE WAS NO LONGER ANYONE ALIVE TO monitor it, the surveillance system of Imperial Prison Barge *Purge* did an excellent job relaying the conversation between Trig and Kale Longo in their cell in Detention Level Five. The screens, now playing to a retinue of Imperial guard corpses in the barge's main surveillance suite, showed the brothers' faces peering from between the bars. And although the audio systems were perfectly calibrated to capture the slightest conspiratorial whisper, there was very little sound coming through the speakers. In fact, all throughout the detention level, it was quiet. The last of the screaming and coughing noises had already stopped, leaving only a vacant, sucked-out silence that went on and on.

Then, softly, the audio sensors picked up Trig's voice:

"They're all dead. Aren't they?"

And Kale, falteringly: "I don't know."

"Whoever's left alive, they're already gone, they just left us here. We're going to die in here, too."

"You need to stop talking like that," Kale said. "Right now. You understand?"

Trig didn't reply. Not long ago, he had watched the Rodians die in the cell across from them. In the end, they'd coughed themselves to death, hacking and choking up pieces of their strange gray organs until they'd finally just writhed silently on the floor of their cell, twitching and whining and—after what felt like an eternity—falling still. Now the bodies had started to smell. Of course there was no way the surveillance system could capture *that*, just as there was no way for anyone who was actually in the area to avoid it.

Trig told himself the decay process shouldn't be happening so quickly, but the smell was there just the same. Maybe it was how the sickness interacted with the individual alien chemistry. It was everywhere, creeping up and down the corridors, trickling through the bars. He imagined rows of cells filled with corpses, dead inmates slumped on their bunks and sprawled on the floor, limp arms hanging through the bars, hundreds of them, gray and seeping, up and down the corridors of the different sublevels. The barge had turned into an immense floating crypt.

So why weren't he and Kale dead . . . or even sick? Trig wondered if they were destined to survive through some rare quirk of genetic immunity, only to die of starvation or dehydration like neglected animals, here in the cage. He thought of something his father had always said: *The universe has a sense of humor, just not a nice one.*

"What happens next?" he asked.

Kale went to the bars, cupped both hands around his mouth. "Hey!" he shouted. "Is there anybody out there?" His voice was surprisingly loud, ringing through the emptiness. "Hello! We're alive in here!

Hey!" He took in a deep breath. "We're alive in here! We're—"

There was a loud clank, and the cell doors up and down the corridor all began to rattle open at once. Kale turned and glanced back at his brother.

"Somebody heard us."

"Who?"

"Doesn't matter," Kale said. "Right now we have to—" He stopped.

Trig watched him. "What is it?"

Kale held up one hand, inclining his head to listen. Whether or not Trig actually heard a noise from the cell next to theirs, he couldn't be sure—his imagination, always active, was now working overtime to pluck something of substance from the void. "Stay there," Kale whispered, leaning out of the cell and looking around. Then he gestured Trig forward.

They went out together, Trig just half a pace behind Kale, and then he remembered—

"Wait!"

It was too late. The figure in the next cell burst out at him, scrambling forward with a snarling howl of rage. Trig saw Aur Myss fall on top of his older brother and drive him into the opposite wall, limbs flailing, hands slashing, already going for Kale's eyes.

Kale collapsed, caught completely off-guard, and for an instant Myss's body covered his entirely, his entire torso struggling spastically for air. The Delphanian seemed to be laboring equally hard to rip Kale's face apart and draw in another breath.

He's sick. The thought flashed through Trig's mind almost faster than he could recognize it. *Now's your chance. Maybe your only one.*

Hardly thinking, he swung down and grabbed Myss's throat from the back, laced his fingers over the doughy wads of flesh surrounding his neck, and squeezed. *Please, please, let me do this.*

But the attack brought a surge of strength through the Delphanian's body. Twisting around, Myss slashed free, the ragged up-and-down fissure of his mouth constricting into a grin. "Boy, you've overstepped your boundaries for the last time."

He grabbed Trig's face, clamping it between scaly hands, the pressure excruciating. Trig could feel blackness swarming in, eclipsing all reason. He wanted to scream but he couldn't open his mouth.

Suddenly the hands fell slack.

Trig's vision cleared, and he saw Myss still staring at him. But shock had taken the place of rage. Through the thing's open mouth, a glint of steel shone like a sharp metallic tongue. Then Myss toppled forward, and Trig saw the handle of the blade that his brother had shoved through the back of the Delphanian's skull.

"He came at me with it," Kale said shakily.

Trig found he couldn't speak.

"Come on, let's go."

They walked quickly down the long hallway toward the main exit, passing cell after cell of dead bodies. Kale said nothing. As much as Trig wanted to talk about what his brother had done—to thank him, to say *something* about it, to at least acknowledge the fact that it had happened—he didn't know where to start. So he, too, remained silent.

Up at the end of the corridor, Trig saw another figure hunched in the control booth, this one wearing an orange isolation suit.

"Wembly," Kale said.

The guard was hunched forward next to the release switch for the cells, the control he'd engaged to open up the wing. Kale reached into the booth and touched his shoulder.

"Hey, Wembly, thanks for . . ."

Wembly's corpse slouched forward and sideways out of the booth, his forehead striking the floor with a hollow thud. His sagging lips hung open, encrusted with dried blood and mucus, and his upturned eyes were vacant. Staring at him, Trig thought he saw a tremor, one last spasm passing through the shoulders and gut, but that, too, was probably just his imagination.

"He let us out. Probably the last thing he did."

"It was," a voice said.

They looked around to see Wembly's BLX unit standing in the corner of the booth. The droid stood awkwardly with its arms at its sides, looking utterly lost without its master.

"Come on," Trig said. "You can come with us."

The BLX seemed to consider the offer, but only for a moment. "No, thank you. I belong here. When we're rescued . . ." He allowed the thought to trail off, perhaps unable to convince itself of that eventuality.

"You're sure?"

"Forget it," Kale said. "Let's get out of here."

Trig cleared his throat. "Where are we going?"

"There's got to be an escape pod somewhere up above—maybe on the administrative level."

"You don't think somebody already took it? The warden, or the guards?"

Kale faced him, gripped Trig's shoulders in his hands, and held on firmly, even a little painfully. "We need a plan, and right now that's as good as any. So unless you've got a better idea, you can help me find a way up there."

Trig bit his lip. Nodded. Made himself say, "Okay."

It took a long time to find the turbolifts up from Main Detention. Most of the bodies they ran across were like the inmates on his level, corpses in bunks, corpses on floors, corpses curled up in corners, arms already stiffening around their folded knees as if somehow balling themselves up could stave off the eventuality of death. There were suicides—one inmate had hung himself from the bars, another had wrapped a bag around his head. Dead guards and stormtroopers lay on the floor, while puzzled-looking maintenance droids hovered over them, trying to make sense of the mass carnage, picking them up and putting them down again. Kale collected blasters from two of the bodies, but Trig could tell just by the way he carried them that he wasn't entirely comfortable with the weapons, although he tried to act casual about it.

They saw other things as well.

Outside one cell, a dead guard lay with his back against the bars. Trig saw that he'd been tied by the wrists and around the neck by the two dead inmates inside the cell. The inmates had since died of the disease, but that hadn't been what killed the guard. The cons had somehow lured him close enough to bind him there and then tortured him to death, stabbing, slashing, and mutilating him with the crude, sharpened instruments that were still clutched in their dead hands.

They saw an inmate, an alien species that Trig didn't recognize, comprising two conjoined bodies, one twice the size of the other. The smaller body had already died and fallen limp, while the larger one cradled it weakly like its own child, weeping and trying to breathe. It didn't even look up at them as they walked by.

They saw a maintenance droid carrying on a cheerful, one-sided conversation with a dead stormtrooper.

They saw two Imperial guards slumped dead over a dejarik holo-chess table while the figures on the table lumbered aimlessly around the board awaiting instruction.

Finally they found a turbolift and waited for the hatchway to slide open. There was a pair of dead guards inside, both of them armed, slouched in opposite corners, their torsos torn apart and scorched by blaster bolts, as if, in the final throes of delirium, they'd turned against each other. Kale hoisted them by their biohazard suits and dragged them out of the lift, and Trig was glad his brother didn't ask him to help. Looking at the bodies was one thing but touching them, lifting them up . . . hoisting their deadweight . . . that wasn't something he felt prepared for.

What if one of their cold dead hands was to reach up and grab hold of him?

Would he even be able to scream?

There was a clicking sound behind them, and Trig glanced back over his shoulder. He thought about Myss in the cell next to theirs, the cell that had been empty when he'd looked. Myss must have run out immediately after Wembly had sprung open the doors for them. Did that mean Myss was immune, too? Trig wondered if he was following them. Just because he didn't see anything didn't mean it wasn't there.

On the uppermost level of detention they heard a faint mewling sound like something crying. It was plaintive and child-like, with a despondency all the more resonant to Trig because he recognized it in his own heart. He stopped and looked in the direction of the noise.

"You hear that?"

Kale shook his head. "It's not our business."

"What if they need help?"

Kale flashed him a tired look but didn't argue. They filed up the hallway, passing more cells of dead inmates, reminding Trig once more of neglected domesticated species that had been forgotten and left to rot by their masters. Kale kept the blasters half raised at his sides. The mewling noise grew louder until Trig stopped and stared into the final cell in the line.

A young Wookiee was crouched inside the cell. He was much smaller than Trig, probably not much more than a toddler. He was crouched down over the bodies of what had to be his family, two adults and an older sibling, clutching their hands to his face and holding their arms around himself as if to simulate a hug.

"Look at this," Kale murmured.

Trig saw what his brother was pointing at. The sickness had affected the dead Wookiees differently. Their tongues had swollen until they dangled like grotesque, overripe fruit from their mouths, and their throats had ruptured completely, splitting open to expose deep red musculature within. When the young one looked up and saw Trig and Kale standing outside the cell, his blue eyes shone with fear and dread.

"It's okay," Trig said softly. "We're not going to hurt you." He glanced at Kale. "He must be immune, like us."

"So what are we going to do about it?"

"Wait here." Trig ran back down the hallway to the abandoned guard station, the door left wide open by whoever had left their post to creep off and die in private. Stepping inside the booth, he found the switch to open the cells—the one that Wembly had died activating for them down on their own level. The bars rattled open, and he went back to where his brother still stood, looking in at the young Wookiee.

"Come on out," Trig told him. "You're free now."

The Wookiee just stared at them. It wasn't even making the crying sound anymore, but somehow its silence was worse. That was a lesson Trig was already learning—the silence was *always* worse.

"You can't stay here." Trig extended his hand toward the Wookiee. "Come with us."

"Careful," Kale said, "he'll take your hand off if—"

"It's okay," Trig said, keeping his hand where it was. "We won't hurt you."

Kale sighed. "Hey, man, look—"

"He's all alone."

"And he obviously wants to stay that way, all right?"

For a moment the Wookiee peered at him cautiously, as if—like Wembly's BLX—it was actually considering the offer. Trig waited to see if anything was going to happen. In the end, though, the youngster just bent forward and picked up the slack arms of its parents and pressed them to either side of its small frame. It wouldn't look up at Kale and Trig again, not even when they turned and finally walked away.

They were at the far end of the corridor when they heard it start to scream.

Trig froze, the fine hairs prickling all down his back. Just the sound made him feel as if his entire body had been coated with a layer of slick, half-melted ice. His breath lodged inside his lungs, caught just below his throat. The Wookiee's screams kept going—strangled, agonized screams, mixed with a horrifying, slobbering sound of something eating.

The screams stopped, but the grunting eating sounds continued, greedy and breathless, slurping and crunching. His mind flashed to Aur Myss in the cell next to theirs, the whispering and giggling and the sensation that it had been following them.

But that's impossible. Myss is dead. You saw it yourself.

"What is it?" he whispered.

"Not our business." Kale grabbed his hand. "Keep going."

17/Tisa

THE LAST OF ZAHARA'S PATIENTS DIED THAT NIGHT. IN the end it happened very quickly. About half of them had been human, the others different alien species, but it didn't make a difference. In the last moments some of the nonhumans had reverted to their native languages, some had clutched her hand and talked to her passionately—if brokenly, through uncontrollable coughing—as if she were some family member or loved one, and she'd listened and nodded even if she didn't understand a word of it.

At Rhinnal they taught her death was something you got used to. Zahara had met plenty of physicians who claimed to have adjusted to it and they always seemed eerie to her somehow, more detached and mechanical than the droids that served alongside them. She tended to avoid such doctors and their cold, clinical eyes.

Waste brought the news of the final deaths with a neutral tone that she'd never heard before, a lack of affect so peculiar that she wondered if it had been programmed for the worst eventualities. Perhaps it was what passed for sympathy in the droid world.

Then, in an almost apologetic voice, the 2-1B added: "I've finished the analysis of your own blood as well."

"And?"

"You're obviously immune to the pathogen. What I meant was that I believe I've had some success in analyzing the immunity gene within your own chemical makeup and synthesizing it."

She stared at him.

"You found a cure?"

"Not a cure, necessarily, but a kind of anti-virus, if what we're dealing with is indeed viral in nature, something that can be administered intravenously." The droid held up a syringe filled with clear fluid and looked around at the infirmary, the bodies in their beds. "If there are any survivors aboard the barge, they ought to get this as soon as possible."

Zahara looked at the needle, belated salvation dripping from its spike. She should have felt some kind of relief. And later, perhaps, she might. But her first reaction to the news—*if there are any survivors aboard the barge*—was a profound sense of personal failure, manifesting itself as a sandbagged heaviness in the legs and belly. The health of the barge and its inmates and staff had been her responsibility. What had happened here over the last few hours was unthinkable, a collapse of such glaring magnitude that she couldn't look at it except through the filter of her own personal culpability. Sartoris might have been taunting her, but he was right. She would never live this down.

There's no time for self-pity, a voice inside her head said. *You need to find out who's left, sooner rather than later.*

As usual the voice was right. She did herself the favor of recognizing that fact, and pushed down on the black feeling inside her belly. To her mild surprise, it collapsed, or rather burst like a bubble.

"I'll be back."

"Dr. Cody?" Waste sounded alarmed. "Where are you going?"

"Up to the pilot station. I need to run a bioscan on the barge and locate any survivors."

"I'll go with you."

"No," she said. "You need to stay here in case anyone else comes for treatment." And then, sensing the droid's reluctance, "That's an order, Waste, get me?"

"Yes, of course, but given the circumstances I would feel much more comfortable if you would simply allow me—"

"I'll be fine."

"Yes, Doctor."

"Watch for survivors," she said, and walked out the door.

She didn't have to go far before the notion of survivors struck her as an increasingly unlikely prospect.

She stepped over and around the bodies, breathing through her mouth when the odor became too much. Almost immediately she wished she'd allowed Waste to come with her. The droid's prattling would've made everything else easier to take.

She arrived at the pilot station and slipped through the doors, braced for what she found there. The *Purge*'s flight crew had not abandoned their posts, even in death. The corpses of the pilot and co-pilot, a couple of rough-hewn Imperial lifers she'd never really gotten to know, slouched backward in their seats, mouths gaping, algae-gray flesh already beginning to sag from their bones. As Zahara approached them, the barge's instrumentation suite recognized her immediately, panels blinking, and a computerized voice cut in from some hidden speaker.

"Identification, please." The voice had been synthesized to sound female, business-like but pleasant, and Zahara tried to remember what the pilots called her and then remembered—Tisa. Word was that on the longer flights, various guards had been caught up here after hours, chatting her up.

"This is Chief Medical Officer Zahara Cody."

"Thank you," Tisa said. "Confirming retinal match." There was a pause, perhaps five seconds, and a single satisfied beep. "Identification confirmed, Dr. Cody. Awaiting orders."

"Run a bioscan of the barge," she said.

"Acknowledge. Running bioscan." Lights pulsed. "Bioscan complete. Imperial Prison Barge *Purge,* previous inmate and administrative census five hundred twenty-two according to the—"

"Just tell me who's left."

"Currently active life-form census is six."

"*Six?*"

"Correct."

"That's impossible."

"Would you like me to recalibrate the bioscan variables?"

Zahara stopped and considered the options. "What *are* the variables?"

"Positive life-form reading is based on algorithmic interpretation of brainwaves, body temperature, motion, and heart rate."

"What about alien species whose normal body temp or pulse don't fit within those parameters?" Zahara asked. "They wouldn't show up on the scan, would they?"

"Negative. Scan parameters are continuously recalibrated to incorporate the physiological traits of every member of the inmate population. In fact, current calibration standards reflect accurate life-form census with a point-zero-zero-one percent margin of—"

"Where are they?" Zahara asked. "The six?"

Tisa's holoscreen brightened to extend a transparent, three-dimensional diagram of the barge. It looked much cleaner in miniature, etched out with fine, straight lines, a drafter's dream of perfect geometry. The pilot station occupied the uppermost level. On one end of it, rising like a periscope, stood the retractable docking shaft that still connected them to the Destroyer. On the other end of the pilot station, a wide descending gangway led downward to the conjoining administration level, flanked on port and starboard sides by the barge's escape pods. The mess hall, infirmary, and guards' quarters occupied the far end of that same level, and below that, the six individual strata that constituted Gen Pop. Any farther down, Zahara knew, and you'd find yourself amid a series of beveled hatches giving way to numberless sublevels, including the bottommost holding cells.

In all she counted the six tiny blips of red light distributed throughout it.

"Current life-form census," Tisa was saying, "indicates one active reading in the pilot station, one on the administration level, two in General Population, Detention Level One, and two in solitary confinement."

Solitary. She hadn't even thought about that until now. Reserved for the worst and most dangerous inmates on the barge, a haven for maniacs and extreme flight risks, it was the one place where the sickness might not have had an opportunity to spread. The question was whether she should risk going down there alone. Of course there were plenty of weapons lying around, but she didn't relish the idea of letting two of Warden Kloth's worst inmates free only to blast them into oblivion when they attacked her.

Still, what choice did she have?

"Can you patch me through to the infirmary?"

"Acknowledged," Tisa said, and the monitor above the hologram brightened to show the medbay. At one corner of the screen Zahara saw Waste walking from bed to bed, removing monitors from the last of the dead, gathering up old IV lines and ventilator tubing. He was talking to himself in a voice too low to hear, perhaps only reviewing the diagnostic data, but seeing him like this made her feel suddenly, inexplicably sad.

"Waste."

The 2-1B stopped and looked up from the screen. "Oh, hello, Dr. Cody. Was the bioscan a success?"

She wasn't sure how to answer that one. "I'm going down to solitary. Can you meet me down there?"

"Yes, of course." He paused. "Dr. Cody?"

"Yes?"

"How many remaining life-forms are there?"

"Six."

"Six," the droid repeated tonelessly. "Oh. I see."

For a moment he glanced back at the infirmary full of bodies, all the patients who had died on their watch, despite all their efforts, and then up to the screen again. "Well. I suppose I'll meet you down there, then."

"See you there," she said, and signed off.

18/Solitary

ZAHARA LEFT THE PILOT STATION AND TOOK THE TUR-
bolift straight down to the barge's lowest inhabited
level. She almost never descended this deep into the
barge, had maybe been down twice since she'd started
here, to treat inmates who were too sick or dangerous
to come up to the infirmary. The only thing that lay beneath it was the mechanical and maintenance sublevel,
the cramped domain of eyeless maintenance droids that
never saw the light of day.

The lift doors opened to release her into a bare hallway with exposed wires dangling from the overhead
girders. Zahara squinted, trying to make out the details. Apparently the main power circuitry didn't work
so well down here. Somewhere above her a steam vent
hissed out a steady current of moist, rancid-smelling
air like the stale breath of a terminal patient. She
didn't see any sign of the 2-1B anywhere and wondered whether she should go any farther without it. It
didn't really matter, if there were no other survivors
except—

"Oh!" she said aloud, startled out of her thoughts,
falling forward and catching herself on the damp cor-

ridor wall, where her palm slipped, almost landing her flat on her face.

She'd tripped on the bodies of the guards in front of her. She counted five of them, sprawled out in a harrowing tableau. They were all wearing isolation suits and masks except for one, a younger guard whom Zahara recognized from a month or so earlier, when he'd come to the infirmary complaining of some minor skin irritation. She'd liked him well enough, and had fallen easily into conversation. She remembered him talking about his wife and children back on his homeworld of Chandrila.

Looking down at his body, Zahara saw a sheet of flimsiplast curled in his hand. She knelt down to pick it up and started reading.

> Kai:
> I know I told you and the kids I would be home after this run. But that is not going to happen. I am sorry to say that something has gone wrong on the barge. Everybody is getting sick and nobody knows why. Almost everybody has died so far. At first I thought I was going to be okay but now it looks like I have it, too.
>
> I am sorry, Kai. I know this is going to be hard on the boys. Will you please tell them their daddy loves them? I am so sorry this is how things turned out, but tell them I served to the best of my abilities and I was not a coward and never scared.
>
> And I love you with all my heart.

At the bottom the guard had attempted to write his name but the letters had come out so crooked and helpless, probably from his trembling hand, that the signature was little more than a scribble.

Zahara folded the note and slipped it into the breast pocket of her uniform next to the vial of anti-virus. She slipped the keycard from the guard's uniform and turned toward the sign marked SOLITARY. Then she stopped. Where was Waste? She'd given the 2-1B ample time to get down here, and usually he was so prompt—

Something happened to him.

It was that voice again, the one inside her head, the one that was never wrong. She wondered if she should go, if she even should have come down here to begin with.

You came this far.

With real reluctance she bent down and picked up one of the blasters from a dead guard's hands. It was cold and felt heavier than she remembered. Zahara had received the requisite weapons training before signing on and was able to locate the safety mechanism and switch the blaster over to stun.

There were three separate cells.

Each had a solid metal door, dull gray and coffin-sized, with a control pad and a slot for the keycard mounted up and to the right.

Zahara stepped up to the first door. She realized she'd stopped breathing. Her body felt weightless, as if her legs had simply vanished beneath her. Faintly she could smell the hot coppery scent of her own fear coming off her body, an unpleasant, unnecessary reminder of how little she really wanted to be doing any of this.

You don't have to.

Yes, I do, she thought, and brought the keycard to the slot. Her hand was shaking, and it took a moment to line it up properly and push it in.

The door began to slide open.

She jerked the blaster up, pointing it into the semi-darkness. Light from the outside cast her silhouette into the cell like an outline cut crisply from black fabric with very sharp scissors. Squinting in, she could make out an empty bench, a table—but the silent two-by-two cube was otherwise absolutely empty.

There was no one here.

She stepped back and turned to the second cell, slotted the card, and—

The noise from inside the cell sounded like a snarl of surprise and rage. Zahara lurched backward, the blaster suddenly loose and clumsy in her hand, somehow unable to find the trigger as the cell's occupant charged toward her. The thing was huge, big enough that it had to duck and twist its shoulders to fit through the cell doorway, with sharp white teeth and eyes that shot back splintered gleams of intelligence.

Stumbling backward, Zahara tried to say *Hold it,* but the words got clogged up in her throat. It was like trying to cry out in a dream, struggling to push words through strengthless, suffocated lungs.

The thing stopped directly in front of her and lifted its shaggy head, perhaps seeing the blaster. It was a Wookiee, she realized, and at the same time she was aware of a pounding noise from the last remaining cell, a muffled shouting on the other side of the wall.

"Hold it," she said again, more clearly this time. She aimed the blaster upward. "Don't move."

The Wookiee moaned. Zahara raised the keycard and wondered how she was supposed to hold both convicts at bay with one blaster. But it was too late now.

The last cell door rattled open to reveal the figure standing immediately inside. Zahara flicked her eyes back at the Wookiee, but he hadn't moved from his spot. Glancing back at the other convict, she realized she was looking at a dark-haired man probably in his late twenties, dressed in an ill-fitting prison uniform. He was staring at her with dark and questioning eyes.

"What's going on down here?"

"I'm Dr. Cody," she said, "chief medical officer. There's been—"

"So you didn't bring us dinner?"

"What? No." She'd expected hostility, confusion, or disdain, but the inmate's cavalier attitude already had her flustered. "I'm afraid there's been an incident." She raised the blaster, and the Wookiee threw back its head and let out a restless, deep-chested bray that seemed to shake the air around her.

"Okay, okay," the man said, "put the blaster down, huh? You're making Chewie nervous."

"Chewie?"

"Chewbacca, my co-pilot," the dark-haired man said, coming forward so she could see his face more clearly, the half smile quirked across his face. "I'm Han Solo."

19/Pod

By the time they found the escape pod, Trig was sure they were being followed.

He could hear breathing noises behind them, the occasional thumping footstep of something tracking them gracelessly through the central hallway of the admin wing, no longer bothering with stealth. Sometimes it made little scratching noises. Other times he could only hear it breathing.

He didn't even need to say anything about it to Kale. Kale knew it, too. Rather than bringing him comfort, the unspoken awareness between them had the paradoxical effect of accelerating the near panic building up in Trig's nervous system; it was as if he were dealing not only with his own apprehension, but Kale's as well.

Finally they saw the escape pod, just up ahead on the outer wall.

"There it is." Kale didn't bother hiding the relief in his voice as he lifted the hatch of the pod. "Go ahead, get in there."

Trig climbed in. "Not much room."

"Enough for us." Kale got in behind him and looked

at the array of controls. "Now we just have to figure out how to get out of here."

"Can you work it?"

"Sure."

"You don't know what you're doing, do you?"

"Will you give me a second to think?" Kale made a fist and bit his knuckle, gazing at the instrumentation array. "I thought these things were automated, but—"

A voice behind them said: "What have we here?"

It was Sartoris.

He was standing there with blasters in both hands, looking just as unhappy to see them as Trig felt staring back at him. Intuitively, just from his posture, Trig understood that there was something between them and the man, something Sartoris knew about them or their father, although Trig didn't know what it was. But he felt it nonetheless, some deeply personal schism of unease, emerging across the guard's face and then vanishing again almost as quickly, like an exhaled breath across a pane of glass.

"Get out," Sartoris said flatly.

Kale frowned, shook his head. "What?"

"You heard me. Get moving." Sartoris twitched the barrel of one blaster rifle at Trig. "You, too."

"There's plenty of room for all three of us."

"Sure." Sartoris grinned without a trace of humor; it did nothing to improve the surliness of his expression. "And I'm sure we'd be very cozy together. But that's not the plan. Now get out of here." He was still aiming the blasters at them. "What are you waiting for?"

"You're just going to let us die here?" Kale asked.

"Boy, you can go running naked through the mess

hall for all I care. The only reason I haven't already shot you is I'd have to drag your carcasses out of the escape pod. So why don't you save me the trouble?"

"You don't understand," Trig said. "There's something aboard the barge and it's still alive. It's been following us. If you leave us here—"

"Sonny, I am sick unto death of hearing you talk." Sartoris pointed the blaster at Trig's face, the hole in its barrel looming huge, black, and endless, and Trig felt his whole body just disappear. Faintly, from what felt like light-years away, he could feel his big brother's hand on his shoulder, tugging him back.

"Come on," Kale's voice said.

Still weightless, Trig allowed himself to be pulled backward, the rest of the way out of the pod. As he stumbled he saw Sartoris taking a flat black object from his pocket and slotting it into the pod's navigation system, the two of them already forgotten, a problem that no longer concerned him.

The hatch sealed shut with a barely audible *whoosh*. It was almost anticlimactic. There was a muffled *thunk* as the bolts blew and the pod was gone, ejected, leaving Trig and Kale standing there looking at the empty place where it used to be.

Kale cleared his throat. After a long pause, he seemed to remember that Trig was standing next to him.

"Hey," he said. "It's going to be okay."

Trig looked up at him. He felt not only weightless now but transparent, barely there. It was as if somebody had hooked a vacuum to his soul and sucked all the hope out of it.

"Come on," Kale said. "I've got an idea."

20/Lifeday

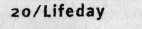

IT TOOK ZAHARA LESS THAN A MINUTE TO REALIZE that Han Solo, whoever he was, was one of the most unusual inmates she'd ever encountered. The realization struck her most forcefully when she tried to explain to him what had happened aboard the barge, and how critically he and the Wookiee needed her assistance if they were going to stay alive.

"Whoa, whoa, whoa," Han said, waving an impatient hand in her face. "You're saying everybody on this flying trash can is dead except for us?" He looked at the Wookiee standing next to him as if to confirm what his ears were telling him. "Are you buying any of this?"

The Wookiee gave a plaintive, honking growl. Zahara didn't know much Shyriiwook, but most of what she'd picked up had to do with vocal inflection, and Chewbacca's was incredulity, pure and simple.

"Yeah," Han said, "me, either." He looked back at Zahara. "That the best you can do, Doc? Or you got another tale you want to try out?"

"You'll see for yourself soon enough. The

infection—it's some kind of virus—has an estimated mortality rate of ninety-nine-point-seven percent."

"Sounds like somebody's been getting their statistics from a droid." Han took a step back, taking his first real look at her and breaking into an appreciative smile. "Although I must say, Doctor, all things considered, *you* seem to be in pretty good shape."

Zahara felt her cheeks redden. "I'm . . . immune."

"Well, I guess we must be, too, huh?"

"It's possible, but I doubt it."

"So how come we're still alive?"

"You've been sealed away in solitary. Now that you're out here and exposed, though, I need to inject you with the anti-virus." She took the syringe from her pocket along with the basic medical kit that she carried with her everywhere. "This will only take a second. I just need to see your arm, and—"

At the appearance of the needle, the Wookiee snarled at her, a noise that went right through Zahara's thoracic cavity, and for the second time she saw the glint of his teeth, the bright white incisors, and caught a whiff of something feral, from either his fur or his breath. She took a step back.

"You need this," she said, and turned to Han. "Both of you do."

Han shook his head. "Wookiees aren't too big on needles. Neither am I."

"I'm a physician."

"Yeah, well, you might want to work on that bedside manner." He glanced at the weapon still in her hand. "Or has blasterpoint medicine become standard operating procedure for the Empire?"

"This was just a precaution. We can't afford to

stand around and discuss this. Too many people have already died."

"Listen, Doc, I...," Han said, and stopped. Glancing back, following his line of sight, Zahara saw that he was staring at the outstretched leg protruding from around the corner, one of the guards whose bodies she'd stepped over to get here. Han craned his neck farther, and she knew that he could see some of the other corpses as well.

When he looked back at her, the defiance in his expression had faded, replaced with something else— not fear necessarily, but a kind of acute awareness of his surroundings. He looked over at Chewbacca, and the Wookiee sniffed the air and let out a low, restless *thragghh* sound from somewhere deep inside his throat.

"Yeah," Han muttered. "Me, too." And then, begrudgingly, to Zahara, "I'm not crazy about my options here, Doc."

"Please," she said, holding his gaze. "You need this."

He reached down and pushed up his sleeve. Zahara realized that she wasn't going to be able to hold on to the blaster rifle and treat him at the same time. She set the blaster aside, kicking it out of the cell behind her, into the hallway, then took Han's arm, swabbed it, then slipped the needle in. Han winced as she pushed down the plunger.

"You tested this, right?"

"You're actually the first."

Han's eyes went huge. *"What?"*

"Relax," Zahara said. "How's your breathing?"

"I'll let you know in a minute," he said, "if I'm not already dead."

Zahara tried not to let the worry show on her face. She'd trusted Waste's analysis of the anti-virus implicitly, but that didn't mean there couldn't have been some margin of error along the way, and who knew exactly how it would interact with any individual's unique chemical makeup? And what would it do to a completely different species, a nonhuman?

But the alternative was to allow Chewbacca to become infected. And she wasn't at all sure that the anti-virus could make a difference at that point.

She turned to the Wookiee. "Your turn."

Chewbacca put out his arm. Finding a vein on a Wookiee was always a challenge, but she felt one beneath the thickly matted fur, sliding the needle in. He growled but didn't move.

"There," she said, "now we can—"

The Wookiee screamed.

The first thing Chewbacca felt was the pain of the young ones. It came at him from everywhere at once, a threnody of wounded voices, assailing him from all sides. He didn't know what it meant except that something bad had happened here aboard the barge, and now it was happening to him, too. In a horrible way he felt as if he were part of it, complicit in these unspeakable crimes, because of the injection that the woman had given him. The sickness she'd implanted under his fur, under his skin, was alive and crawling through him, a living gray thing going up his arm to his shoulder to his throat, and the sickness clucked its tongue and whispered, *Yes, you did those things, yes, you are those things.*

Had he done it? *Had* he somehow hurt them?

But that couldn't be right. The doctor hadn't poisoned him; she'd injected him with a cure. Then why did it hurt so much, and why did he still hear the young ones screaming?

His skull felt like it was filling with fluid, blocking out his sense of smell. But his hearing was keener than ever. Voices were shrieking at him, no longer pleading but accusing him of unspeakable atrocities, and when he looked down at his hands he saw that they were dripping with blood, while the rank, salty flavor of their blood was in his mouth.

And then the sickness was in him.

And the sickness wanted to eat.

He snarled louder, lashed out, wanting to make it go away, but it was too deep already, burrowing through his memory, bringing back details he hadn't remembered in nearly two hundred years. He heard old lifeday songs from Kashyyyk, saw faces—old Attichitcuk, Kallabow, his beloved Malla—except their faces were changing now, melting and stretching, mouths hooking into strange, contemptuous grins. His father's eyes lit upon him, saw all the shame he tried to hide. They knew what he was now that the sickness was inside of him and what the sickness would make him do to the little ones. They knew how he would slaughter them in their cells and feast upon their steaming entrails, shoving them into his mouth without bothering to chew, enslaved by the sickness and its appetite. They saw how the sickness could not be sated, how it wanted to keep on killing and eating until there was nothing left but blood that might be lapped up from the cold durasteel floors. They said, *These are the true songs of lifeday, these songs are eat and kill, eat and kill.*

No, it's not true. It's not.

Screaming louder, a deafening roar, at least in his own mind, he felt the oblivion of the sickness coming and was grateful for it, an opportunity to hide, to get away from the things he was experiencing. He did not try to escape; he ran toward it eagerly.

Zahara jumped back, instinctively ducking and flinging both hands up to protect herself. Chewbacca's arm swung out blindly, the syringe still protruding from it, and the needle sailed across the cell like a poorly thrown dart, hitting the wall and disappearing somewhere in the half-light. If she hadn't dropped down when she did, the Wookiee's arm would have crushed her throat.

"Hey, pal, take it easy," Han said, reaching over to him. "Chewie, it's just—"

Chewbacca rounded on him with a full-throated howl, and Han jerked backward, frowned, and stared at Zahara.

"What did you do to him?"

"Nothing. He got the same thing you got."

"Maybe it works differently for his species, did you ever think about that?" He looked back at Chewbacca but the Wookiee's expression was completely alien now, unfriendly, no trace of recognition in his eyes. He seemed confused, frightened, and ready to attack whatever threat he perceived was nearby. The ripe, feral stink that Zahara had caught a whiff of earlier was back, stronger now, almost overwhelming, as if some aggression gland inside his metabolism had started spurting violent hormones through his brain. He was growling steadily now.

Then Zahara noticed the swelling. It was already affecting his throat, causing it to balloon up, and what she'd thought were growls had actually become a series of suffocated breaths.

"What is *that*?" Han asked. "What's happening to his neck?"

Zahara didn't answer. She couldn't make coherent sense of her own thoughts, except that somehow she'd managed to find some of the last survivors aboard the barge, only to help the disease do its job even more efficiently.

She pulled herself together, flashing through options: somehow the anti-virus had either weakened the Wookiee's immunity to the pathogen, or the sickness itself had become more aggressive in the past few hours, shortening its incubation time from hours to minutes. Either way—

Chewbacca fell to his knees with a crash, clasping his arms over his head, and rocked back and forth with a diminishing series of horrible, gargling groans. When he lifted his head again, it was with monumental effort, and Zahara saw that the rage was draining away from his face. But this was only a side effect of oxygen debt, his gaze fogging over even as his enormous shoulders sagged forward, giving way to gravity until the entirety of his body slumped facedown to the floor.

Zahara squatted down. "Help me roll him over."

"What? Why?"

"Just do it."

Han grabbed Chewbacca's shoulder and Zahara lifted his hips, tilting the massive bulk of the Wookiee's body and tumbling him onto his back. She put her hand behind his furry head, down beneath his neck, and lifted upward.

"Find the syringe."

"Uh-uh, no way." Han shook his head. "You're not giving him another drop of that stuff."

"You want your friend to live? Find the karking syringe."

Han took a second to digest this and then went back into the far corner of the cell, muttering under his breath. Zahara understood that, right now, a huge part of saving the Wookiee's life was just a matter of making Han believe her. If he didn't, if he tried to interfere, there was nothing she could do except to make Chewbacca comfortable until he died.

Han came back a moment later with the syringe in his hand. "I hope you—"

Zahara grabbed it from him, squirted out the last of the anti-virus, and tilted Chewbacca's head back, palpating the clogged airway. Carefully avoiding the arterial passageways, she slid the empty needle in, felt the *pop* as it found the pocket of fluid, and pulled the plunger back. *Droids still can't do this,* she thought. *There's not a droid in the world that would try this.*

And probably for good reason.

Pinkish gray liquid began to fill the barrel of the syringe. Han didn't say anything, but she could hear the dry click as he swallowed hard. She emptied the syringe, put it back in, and tapped the fluid again.

After three full syringes, the swelling began to go down.

The screaming in Chewie's head got louder.

What are the true songs of lifeday?

I am inside you, the sickness whispered, *and you will sing the songs as I teach them and those songs are to kill and to eat. And you will sing them while I am still inside you. While I am still hungry and I am always hungry and you will sing my songs.*

Yes, Chewbacca told it, his thoughts moving in the oddly formal way they sometimes did when he was thinking of things very seriously, yes, you are inside of me. I breathed you in when the prison door was opened just like Han breathed you in and you made him cough and start choking. But then the doctor gave us the medicine.

The sickness screamed at him and raged. But he didn't hear it anymore.

He felt the pressure loosening from his chest. He was breathing again, the stricture in his throat abating, allowing for the first tentative passage of air. Vision was clearing, too, becoming stable, allowing him to see Han and the doctor standing over him, their faces worried.

—those are the true songs of lifeday—

The strength coming back through him now was the strength of his family and homeworld. He sat up but did not try his voice. He didn't trust it yet. He looked down at his hands. They were clean. Relief sagged through him and it was like coming home to faces that recognized him and welcomed him in. There was no more screaming now. Inside the house where he had been born, someone was playing music.

"Easy." Zahara broke open a packet of bandages and adhesive and tried as best she could to dress the tiny pinhole incision she'd left on his throat. She couldn't see through all the fur, but her fingers knew instinctively where it was. "We'll have to clean that up as soon as we can. How do you feel?"

He gave a hoarse cry, then a louder one.

"You okay, pal?" Han asked, and when Chewie gave a quick bark of acknowledgment, he turned to Zahara. "Lady, you just got really lucky."

"Hopefully we all did," she said. "If that anti-virus works, you should both be protected."

They helped Chewbacca to his feet, a process that fully required both of their strengths. Han watched him closely, preparing for a relapse, but the Wookiee seemed steady enough once he was standing up.

"Think you can travel, buddy?" Han asked.

Chewie barked out another growl.

"Okay, all right," Han said. "Forget I asked."

"The turbolift's back this way," Zahara said, pointing around the corner. "We can go back through, just be careful you don't trip over the . . ."

They all stopped.

"What happened to the bodies?" Han asked. "The dead guards?"

Zahara blinked down at the floor where the corpses of the prison guards had been sprawled out. They'd all seen them.

But now they were gone.

"Maybe they weren't dead," Han said doubtfully.

"I examined them."

"So somebody came and moved them. I dunno, maintenance droids or something." He looked at her. "Is there a reason we're still standing here discussing this?"

Zahara thought about it. She wondered if maybe the 2-1B had come down to meet her and moved the corpses. But that just didn't make sense. The blasters were gone, too, she realized—including the one she'd just kicked out of the room.

Somewhere in the semidarkness she thought she heard something creak, some random self-activating servo coming to life inside the walls, and she jumped, startled. Suddenly she realized that Han was right. They had to get out of here, not soon but now.

"The turbolift's over this way," she said.

Han and Chewie followed her in, the doors closing as they glided upward. "Where are we going?"

"Medbay. I've got to talk to Waste."

"Who's Waste?"

"My surgical droid."

"And you call him Waste? Like waste of space?"

"Waste of space, waste of programming . . ." She shrugged, relaxing a little now that they were out of that damp, shadow-crawling lower corridor. "I started it as a joke and it just kind of stuck."

"He doesn't mind?"

"He thinks it's a term of endearment," she said, and upon saying so, realized it was true.

Han grunted as the lift reached the infirmary level and stopped. Zahara remembered the corridor vividly, how it had been littered with bloated corpses of guards and stormtroopers who had died waiting to get into medbay—dozens of them, sometimes stuck to one another with the fluid they'd been heaving up when they finally collapsed. The smell would have intensified, too, she knew. She expected Han would say something, maybe cover his mouth and stand there a moment taking it all in, the way that she had when she'd first laid eyes on it.

The turbolift stopped and the doors slid open on the hallway. Zahara braced herself for the shock—and looking out, felt a different kind of shock go through her, quick and jolting, making her legs feel heavy and weak at the same time.

All the bodies were gone.

21/They Woke Up

Han and Chewie followed Zahara down the corridor without talking. Han in particular didn't like it, nor was he crazy about the way the doctor kept glancing back over her shoulder. She was easy on the eyes, he had to admit, but fear didn't do much for her face. And she was keeping something from him. In his experience women and secrets mixed together to form something only slightly less volatile than an unstable fusion reactor.

"How much farther is it?" he asked.

She didn't answer or even look at him, just held up her hand, meaning either shut up, stop walking, or both. Han turned to glance at Chewie, wondering aloud how much longer they were supposed to put up with this.

It had been a while since they'd been free—weeks, he guessed, since the Imperials had boarded the *Millennium Falcon* and impounded the ship and her cargo. The shuttle had ferried them here to this barge, just another pair of anonymous smugglers whom the galaxy couldn't care less about.

And that would've been the end of it, if Han hadn't

gotten impatient and tried to escape a number of days earlier during a well-choreographed mess hall riot. He'd clocked a prison guard, Chewie had thrown a stormtrooper across the table, and the next thing they knew everything went dark.

Very dark.

Down in the hole, he'd spent most of his time speculating about what was going to happen next—who, if anyone, he and Chewie could rely on for a rescue. A smuggler's friends were few, and those who would actually stick their necks out for the likes of Han were effectively nonexistent. For the first time he had begun to wonder if he and Chewie were destined to spend whatever remained of their lives in some cramped and poorly lit Corrections dungeon.

In front of him, the doctor stopped walking again, turned, and looked through an open hatchway. Though he'd never been up here before, Han figured it was the medbay. He came up alongside her and peered inside, then back at the doctor. From the expression on Zahara's face, Han guessed this wasn't how it had looked when she'd left it.

Every bed was empty.

All the medical equipment, monitors, and medication pumps were active, blinking and twittering to themselves, but the IV lines, tubes, and cords dangled loose, some of them dripping liquid medication in puddles the size of small lakes. Bedsheets and blankets hung in twisted disarray, stained with sweat and blood, dragged across the floor and left there. Han realized the silence was making his shoulders tighten up and his right hand feel particularly lonely where his blaster ought to have been. He made a quick but conscious decision to calm down.

"Busy place," he remarked.

She shook her head. "It was full when I left."

"No offense, Doc, but maybe this sickness is affecting you, too."

"You don't understand," she said, "they were all dead—twenty or thirty of them, guards, inmates, plus the ones lying on the floor, I wouldn't have left them here if there was something I could still do to help."

"Where's your droid?"

"I don't know." She raised her voice. "Waste?"

The 2-1B didn't answer. Han and Chewie walked around her on either side, looking at the rows of empty beds. Chewie growled, and Han murmured, "Yeah, me, either." He stepped over a bloody hospital gown that looked as though it had been ripped in half, then looked back up at Zahara. "Say you're right and there's nobody else left alive. How are we going to get out of here?"

"There's the Star Destroyer."

Han was sure that he'd misheard her. "Excuse me?"

"Up above us. Apparently it's a derelict. The barge docked on it to scavenge for parts for the thrusters—that's when everything really started going wrong. I have no idea whether the engines were repaired before the maintenance team died. Otherwise . . ."

"So this contagious disease came from the Destroyer?"

She nodded.

"Sounds like a good place to keep clear of."

Zahara didn't answer him. She had bent down to

study a patchy streak of bloodstains from under one of the beds. Reaching under, she touched something—Han couldn't tell what it was—and dragged it slowly into view.

"What is that?" Han asked, and then he saw.

The hand was human, and had been ripped free by sheer force, the bones of the forearm cracked and severed by some blunt object. Two of the fingers were missing, plucked from the knuckle. Zahara looked at it with no particular emotion evident on her face.

"It belonged to a guard," Zahara said.

"How do you know?"

She pointed out the signet ring. "ICO ACADEMY." She dropped it, and it landed with a soft thud.

Behind her, on the other side of that row, Han heard Chewbacca growl.

"Uh, Doc?" Han said. "I think we found your droid."

Zahara looked, and as soon as she did, she realized that some small, dismal part of her had been expecting exactly this outcome, from the moment she'd arrived in solitary and Waste had not been there.

The 2-1B lay in pieces across the floor behind the last of the beds. Its arms, legs, and head had all been systematically dismantled and crushed, its torso beaten so the instrumentation panel flickered listlessly, erratically, beneath the cowl. It was still trying to talk, making garbled noises through its vocabulator.

"Dr. Cody?" it said.

"Waste, what happened?"

"I'm sorry. That test pattern wrote on the owl wall. It was marvelous. Would you like to taste it again?"

"Waste, listen to me," she said, crouching down next to it. "The patients, the bodies, where did they go?"

"Look, Doc," Han said behind her. "Let's get out of here, huh? This whole place—"

"Shh," Zahara said, not looking back, keeping her attention on the droid. "The corpses, Waste," she prompted. "Did someone take them?"

"I'm sorry. There isn't any left. It doesn't walk without three and the two places. I'm sorry. Every reasonable attempt was made." The 2-1B clicked and something sparked and clanked deep inside its lower processors. "We must uphold the sacred oath of . . ." It stopped, hiccuped, and seemed to regain some sense of what she'd asked it. "An amazing thing. They're miracles, really. Marvelous." And then, with terrible brightness: "They woke up!" There was one last small internal click, although this one sounded more jarring, broken, and when it spoke again its voice sounded thick and sluggish. "They just . . . eat."

"What?"

The components in the droid's torso flickered again, but it didn't say anything else. "Hey," Zahara said, turning around to Han and Chewbacca, "do either one of you know anything about droids?"

But Han and Chewie were gone.

22/Bulkhead

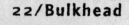

THE GRAFFITI SCRAWLED ON THE INNER BULKHEAD WAS written in Delphanian, but Trig could guess what it meant. *Face Gang. Keep out. Blood toll.*

"Will you relax?" Kale said. "Myss is dead. They all are."

It didn't make Trig feel any better. At first all the corpses had frightened him, but there was something worse about *not* seeing them. They hadn't seen any more dead people since Sartoris had chased them away from the escape pod. Now they were traveling crosswise through the admin level, in accordance with Kale's plan. Trig had initially thought that it was because of the hidden route they were using, down these tight passageways, alongside conduits within the walls, but now he wondered why they hadn't seen a single body.

"Hold this for me." Kale handed him the blaster rifles he'd been carrying. "Here we go." He removed a loose panel from the wall, reached inside, and slid out a pair of power packs. "Right where Dad left them." Sticking his hand deeper, he groped around for a moment and came up with another blaster, a pistol. "Here, you take this one."

"I don't want it."

"Did I ask if you wanted it?"

Trig realized his brother was right. Whether or not there still was something following them, he was going to need a weapon. He inserted the power pack into the blaster, clicked it home, and tried to find a way to carry it that didn't feel awkward or self-conscious before realizing that there was no way of doing that. His father's voice spoke to him: *When you're carrying a blaster, whatever else you're doing comes second.*

Kale gestured forward, up the walkway. "Let's go find that other escape pod."

"How do you know there *is* a second escape pod?"

"It's here because we need it to be here."

Trig just shook his head. Circular logic: their father would be proud. "Seriously, though."

"Seriously?" Kale said. "The Imperials build everything symmetrically. They're not creative enough to do anything else. So where there's one, there's got to be another, same location, opposite side." He shrugged. "I don't know, what do you want me to say?"

Trig just nodded. He'd liked the first explanation better.

Fifteen minutes later, Kale let out a small but energetic whoop. They had reached the opposite side of the barge's admin level. "What did I tell you?"

The pod looked exactly like the one that Sartoris had taken. Trig wondered how they were going to activate it without the launch codes, but he didn't want to puncture Kale's enthusiasm. It was nice to see his brother smiling again. He walked over to the pod's hatch and put his face against the viewport, peering into a darkly luminous chamber of softly glowing lights.

He felt a wave of coldness slip over him and turned around fast.

There was someone coming up the hall.

It wasn't his imagination this time, no chance; Kale heard it, too, Trig saw it in his brother's face, both of them registering the deep-chested growling noise getting louder as whoever it was rounded the corner.

"Stay behind me," Kale murmured, raising both his blasters up to chest level. "If anything happens, shoot first and then run, got it?"

"Wait," Trig said, fumbling with the pistol, "where's the stun switch?"

Kale said something in an even lower voice, but Trig could hardly hear him over the beating of his own heart. He realized he was about to fire a blaster for the first time and his life would depend on how well he used it. If it was another guard they might have to kill him. This was why he hadn't wanted to carry a blaster in the first place, but that didn't seem to make a difference now, because—

A man in an orange inmate's uniform came around the corner with a Wookiee next to him.

"Hold it!" Kale shouted.

When the man and the Wookiee saw them they stopped walking, but neither of them appeared particularly surprised. The man raised his hands, but the Wookiee growled louder, shoulders hunching up, looking like it still hadn't ruled out attack as a possible response.

"Easy, kid, put the blasters down."

"No way." Kale shook his head. "What are you doing here?"

Han's eyes flicked over to the escape pod. "Looks like we both came looking for the same thing."

"There's not enough room," Kale said. "So why don't you and your friend turn around and go back where you came from."

"What are you guys, brothers?" Han didn't move, but he shifted his attention to Trig, the corners of his mouth twisting upward in an odd grin, crooked but genuine. "You ever use one of those things before?"

Trig didn't know if he was talking about the blaster or the pod, so he just nodded. "Sure."

"Yeah, I bet. Come on, kid, give up the heat, huh?" Stretching out both hands, that casual, crooked smile on his face, he started sauntering toward them again, as if he'd already decided how all of this would transpire and it was only a matter of going through the motions until everybody else realized it, too.

"You take another step and I'll shoot!" Kale cried out in a voice that broke high at the end, but by then it was too late. Both he and Trig had been watching the man when they should have been watching his partner.

The Wookiee made it look easy, closing the gap in what felt like no time at all, plowing straight into Kale and knocking him flat, both blaster rifles clattering to the floor, rolling and pinioning one huge furry leg out so that it caught Trig in the side. Trig heard himself make a noise like *uff!* and felt all the air leave him like it had been sucked out of a vacuum. He went down, too, hand at his side, and realized he'd dropped his blaster. It had somehow already materialized in the man's hand.

The Wookiee kept the blaster rifles pointed at them, and Trig felt the last vestige of hope draining out of him like dirty water from a bathtub. What had ever convinced them that they could hold off a pair of career criminals with nothing to lose?

The man, meanwhile, walked over to the escape pod. "Well, we'd love to take you boys along, but as you pointed out, space is at a premium, so—"

"You'll never make it," a voice said.

Trig looked around and saw the woman standing there. It took him a moment to realize it was Dr. Cody, the *Purge*'s medical officer. He hadn't seen her since the day their father died, but now her pretty face— normally smiling, usually amused about something or other—looked gray and strangely lifeless, aged twenty years since the last time they'd met. Even her voice had changed. It lacked that easy, pleasant twinge of irony that he'd heard before, that tone of *I'm working on an Imperial prison barge, how much worse can it get?* Now she only sounded tired and resigned.

"What do you mean?" Han said.

"Go ahead," Dr. Cody said, in that same oddly inert and shrugging voice, "try to get inside."

The man pulled on the escape pod hatch, but it didn't open. "What, it's locked? How do you know?"

Zahara pointed at the steady red light next to the SECURITY SYSTEM ACTIVATED sign by the pod's hatch. Trig hadn't noticed it until now, either. "It's locked down."

"So how do we get in?"

"There's a manual override up in the pilot station." Dr. Cody turned to the Wookiee. "And enough with the blasters, all right? I hardly think either of you has anything to fear from a couple of teenage grifters."

"Hey, they pulled 'em on *us*," Han protested, and the Wookiee barked out a contentious whinnying rejoinder, but both lowered their weapons.

"The pilot station's directly above us," Dr. Cody said. "I'll go up and see about unlocking the pod."

"Chewie and I'll go up with you, take a look at the thrusters." Han glanced at Kale and Trig. "You kids tagging along?"

"We'll stay here," Kale said, "you know, stand watch."

Han shrugged. "Suit yourself."

"What . . . ?" Trig glanced at his older brother, uncertain, but felt Kale reaching down to squeeze his arm gently yet firmly.

"Here." Dr. Cody handed Trig a comlink. "I'll call when I get it open so you can check it before we come back. We'll come back as soon as we can."

"Leave us the blasters," Kale said.

Han snorted. "Yeah, right."

"Go ahead," Zahara said, "you can spare one."

Han looked expectantly at Chewie. "What? He's not taking *mine*," but the Wookiee just continued to stare back at him. "Great," Han muttered, thrusting the weapon back at Kale. "Here you go, boy. Try not to shoot off your own foot."

Kale took it and nodded, and Han, Chewbacca, and Dr. Cody started to walk away.

"Dr. Cody?" Trig asked.

She stopped and looked back.

"Is there anyone else left besides us?"

"I don't think so," she said, and Trig could tell from her expression that she'd been anticipating a different question. It wasn't until they were gone that he realized what he should have asked her.

What happened to all the dead bodies?

23/Inside

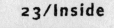

THEY'D BEEN WAITING FOR FIVE MINUTES WHEN THE first alarm went off.

Kale had been explaining the plan for why he'd volunteered both of them to wait here. "When Dr. Cody gets up to the flight deck and unlocks the pod, we climb in and comm her back to tell her it's asking for launch codes like the ones that Sartoris had. She puts them through and we're out of here."

"She's not stupid," Trig said. "Besides, we can't just leave her here."

"The Imperials will send a rescue ship."

"How do you know?"

"She's high up," Kale said, gesturing vaguely in the air. "You know, connected."

"That still doesn't mean they'll come back for her."

"You're really creased about this, aren't you?"

"She helped out Dad in the end," Trig said. "That means something."

"Look." Kale regarded him with a maddening smile. "I know you're sweet on her, but—"

"What?" Trig felt his face and the tips of his ears growing hot. "Yeah, right."

Kale shrugged, the very picture of fraternal indifference. "Whatever you say. It's pretty obvious, though, just the way you stare at her. Not that I blame you—she's not bad looking." His expression darkened. "Just don't forget who she works for."

"What's that supposed to mean?"

Kale started to say something and that was when a high, shrill squeal cut through the hallway from the other side of a sealed doorway, some kind of localized alarm system. They both jumped and Kale swung the blaster rifle around a bit too brazenly, Trig thought—he was getting used to carrying a weapon.

"What is that?" he asked.

"Wait here," Kale said. "I'll be right back."

Before Trig could argue, his brother started down the corridor, the blaster held up by his chest. The sealed doorway in front of him opened with a soft hydraulic gasp and Kale stepped through it, paused there, and threw one last look over his shoulder at Trig. "Stay where you are," he said, and the doors sealed behind him.

A moment later the alarm fell silent. It was like something at the end of the hall had woken up crying, eaten Kale, and fallen back to sleep again. Trig shuddered at the image, trying to shake it out of his head and having no luck. He stood with his ears ringing, wondering what he was supposed to do, how he was even supposed to mark the time that everyone was away.

Restless, trying to keep his mind occupied, he turned back to the escape pod. The little red light was still on, but he tried the hatch anyway, tugging on it just in case Dr. Cody had already sprung it by remote. It didn't open. What had he expected? He put his nose to the viewport again, cupped his eyes, and squinted, trying to see if anything had changed in the arrangements of the glowing instrument panel, but he couldn't make anything out clearly.

Then, inside the pod, something moved.

Trig jerked his head back, his entire body stiff with shock, and he stumbled backward on unstable legs. His nerve endings seemed to have been replaced with thin hot copper wires, pulse racing so he could hear it clicking in his gullet. *I didn't* really *see that,* his brain whirred, *the lights inside are just making it look like I did, but—*

He held his breath, listening.

There was a faint scratching sound coming from inside the pod.

Trig took another step back, until he felt his shoulders make contact with the opposite wall. His eyes rolled over to the doorway that Kale had gone through a few minutes earlier, but Kale wasn't back—there was no sign of him. And the scratching sound inside the pod was only getting louder, an irregular but insistent scrape of fingers—or claws—against the inside of the hatch. As Trig listened he realized it was becoming faster as well as louder, more eager, as if it knew he was out here and wanted to get out with him.

Trig realized he was squeezing the comlink hard enough to make his hand cramp. He lifted it up and thumbed the power switch. "Dr. Cody?"

There was a long pause, and then her voice came back, clear and strong. "Trig?"

"Yeah."

"We're up on the bridge now. We're still looking for

the override to open the pod. It shouldn't be much longer."

"Wait," Trig said. "Hold on. There's something inside the pod already."

"What's that?"

"There's something in it. I can hear it scratching."

"Hold on, Trig." Another long silence, this one stretching out until Trig thought he'd lost the signal. Then at last, Dr. Cody's voice said, "Trig? You there?"

"Still here."

"I've got the bioscan running up here for the entire barge."

"Yeah?"

"We're not picking up any life-form reading inside that pod."

Trig stared at the hatch, where the scraping had become maniacal clawing, and he could hear something else along with it, a wet, slobbering, toothsome sound, as if whatever was inside was almost trying to gnaw its way out.

Should have asked her about the dead bodies, he thought again, a little hysterically. *Yeah, that probably would have been a good idea.*

The words drifted out of him like smoke: "There's something in there."

"Missed that, Trig."

"I said—"

"Okay," Dr. Cody's voice said, "here we go, I found the lock override."

"No, hold on, *wait*—"

There was a click and the hatch swung open.

24/Futureproof

▄▄▄■▄▄▄■▄▄▄■▄▄▄▪

When Kale came back, Trig was gone.

The hatch to the escape pod stood open, and he crouched down and crawled inside, the green display lights glowing across his face.

"Trig?"

His brother wasn't in there, either, but the gassy, festering smell was bad enough that Kale didn't linger for a closer look. It reminded him of some kind of predator's den, the kind you might find littered with the picked-clean bones of its last meal. He supposed he'd have to put up with it if the pod was their only means of getting out of here, but for now he had to find his brother.

Stepping back out, he bumped his foot against a small flat object. It let out a little electronic gurgle. He looked down and saw that it was the comlink Zahara had given Trig. Kale frowned. It wasn't like Trig to leave something like that, any more than it was like him to wander off for no reason.

He picked up the comlink and switched it on. "Dr. Cody? This is Kale."

"I hear you, Kale," she said.

"Listen, something happened to my brother."

"Say again?"

"An alarm went off and I went to go check it. When I came back, he was gone. The pod hatch is open, but he's nowhere in sight."

"Just a second, Kale. Let me check something."

Kale waited, and looked back down at the inner wall of the escape pod door. It was scored with dozens of scratches, some of them deep enough to gouge into the metal itself. He reached down to touch it and discovered it was wet. When he drew back his fingers, they were dripping with blood and something sticky and warm. He wiped it off on his pant leg with a shudder of revulsion.

"Kale, the scanner's showing a life-form about fifteen meters up the corridor to your immediate right. Do you see it?"

He turned around but there was nothing but the same dirty familiar walls, dim lights, and low cramped ceiling, yellowing and dingy, as if stained by the doomed and hopeless breaths exhaled by thousands of inmates over the years. "No," he said, "there's nothing here."

"You're positive? The signal's strong."

"No, it's just an empty hallway, I—hold it."

He put the comlink down and raised the blaster, walking over to the wall for a closer look. In front of him, at shoulder level, he saw a separate wall panel and the words:

MAINTENANCE ACCESS SHAFT 223

Kale placed the barrel of the blaster rifle against the spring-loaded panel and pushed it open to reveal the widemouthed shaft within. A gust of foul-smelling air rushed up into his nose and he groaned, almost gagging, covered his nose and mouth with his free hand, and leaned back into the ripe blackness, looking down.

"Trig?"

The sound of his voice reverberated down the metallic emptiness, ringing shapeless in the void. Kale thought back to what he'd seen when he'd gone through the doorway to investigate the alarm. It had been nothing special, nothing at all really, probably just a malfunction somewhere, although one particular aspect of it had stuck with him—a single bloody handprint on the wall, half smeared and still so fresh it was dripping. When he'd seen that, he'd realized it wasn't a good idea to leave Trig alone, even for a few seconds, and that was when he'd come back to find this.

He decided to try once more, leaning back into the shaft. "Trig, are you there?"

His brother came vaulting up and out of the shaft with a scream. He smashed face-first into Kale, knocking him to his knees with a speed and momentum that probably saved his life. If it had happened any slower— if Kale had been given any time to get his blaster back up again—he probably would have shot his brother on pure reflex. As it was, Trig was already on top of him, still screaming, fists flying, clawing, kicking, and sucking in great drafts of air. He was crying, too, Kale could see, sobbing in a high, choking, desperately frightened voice that made him sound much younger than his actual age.

"Easy," Kale said, holding on to him, noticing now how badly torn Trig's uniform was, like an animal had been at it—the collar ripped to expose Trig's slight, hairless chest, one sleeve torn completely away to show his skinny arm. Parts of the cheap fabric were damp and clammy, like the inside of the escape pod hatch. Kale held on to him. He hugged Trig tightly to his chest until he started to feel, if not the fight going out of him, at least a kind of exhausted fatigue slowing the panicked thrashing, and kept holding on to him after that until Trig was quiet except for the occasional hitching breath.

"It's okay," Kale said, and then drew back enough to get his first real look at Trig's face. "What happened?"

Trig just stared back at him with bloodshot eyes. If he'd been any paler his skin would have been translucent. Nothing moved in his face except for the slight tremble in his chin.

"Did someone attack you?" Kale asked. "Inside the pod, was there . . . ?"

He waited, letting the question drift out to where Trig might pick it up and respond to it, but Trig didn't. The longer he stared at Kale, the more Kale wondered if his brother was seeing him at all. He put his arms around his brother again and held him.

"Listen," he said, "it's going to be okay. I won't let anything bad happen to us, okay? I promise."

But the thought of the bloody handprint came back to him again, and he realized that for the first time in his life he'd made a promise to his brother that he knew he couldn't keep.

25/Deadlights

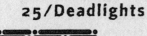

"THESE THRUSTERS ARE COMPLETELY SCRAGGED," Han said as he crawled up from a dislodged floor panel in the center of the barge's pilot station, wiping the grit and reactor grease from his hands. "Whatever the engineers were trying to do down here, they didn't get very far. We're not going anywhere in this floating scrap pile."

"I got the escape pod open," Zahara said. "Launch codes are—"

"Dr. Cody?" Tisa's voice broke in. "I'm picking up new life-form readings on the bioscan."

"New readings?" Han glanced at Zahara, frowning. "I thought you said everybody was dead."

"They are." She looked at the bank of electronics. "Tisa, display all positive bioscan readings."

"Yes, Doctor." In front of them an array of glowing pencil-thin lines began to shimmer into view, their intersecting geometry deliquescing once again to create the barge in miniature.

Han said, "What the . . . ?"

The three-dimensional multilevel outline of the

vessel—previously an empty, almost elegant intersection of clean, digitized spaces and lines—was now crawling with blood-red pinpricks of flashing lights. They were moving together, bunched and swarming up from the lower detention blocks en masse, advancing level by level toward the admin area. In the hologram, at least, they appeared to be seething forward at a disproportionate, insectile speed.

"Wait a second," Han said. "What are those things?"

She shook her head. "Life-forms."

"Thanks, Doc," he said. "Got anything more specific, or are we supposed to just fill in the blanks?"

Zahara stared at the clusters of tiny lights, each one an independent organism. They were moving faster than she could believe, coming up stairwells, ventilation ducts, and utility shafts. "That's impossible. They weren't there before. Tisa, how come you didn't pick up on them earlier?"

"There *were* no positive life-forms earlier, Dr. Cody."

"Where did they come from?" As she watched, more red lights began to appear in the lower levels, seeming to spontaneously generate out of nowhere. Her thoughts flashed back to what Waste had told her about the molecular behavior of the virus, how it masked its lethality until it had reproduced to a level that the host could no longer successfully fight it— *quorum sensing,* he'd called it. Abruptly she felt as if two tight iron bands had closed around her, one blocking her throat, the other clamping down over her chest, freezing her breath.

"How many ways are there out of here?" Han asked,

and she realized he was shaking her. "Hey, Doc, I'm talking to you."

"Just—" She pointed to the hatchway and the stairwell they'd taken up from admin. "—just the way we came in."

"Any other escape pods?"

"Only the one we left behind." Zahara stretched out one hand and pointed one level down, to the west admin wing. It was already totally overrun by colonies of red lights. That was the last place she'd seen Trig and Kale. She didn't want to think about where they were now.

The diagram of the barge showed a wide stairway leading up from the admin level to the bridge. And now the red lights—*deadlights,* Zahara's mind gibbered frantically—were moving in that direction.

"Great," Han muttered, raising his blaster and turning to face the door. "Looks like we're gonna be shooting our way out. Again."

Chewbacca growled, shook his massive head, and brandished the rifle, looking profoundly unhappy about the odds.

"Wait," Zahara said, pointing to the tower protruding from the top of the hologram, and then turned behind her, across the bridge itself. "About twenty meters behind us, on the opposite end of the flight deck, there's a docking shaft that goes straight up."

Han gaped at her in disbelief. "What, *into* the Star Destroyer?"

"It's our only chance."

"Yeah, well, where I come from, they've got a saying—out of the nexu's den and into its mouth."

"Whatever those things are, there have to be hundreds of them. How long do you think your power packs will hold out?"

Then she heard them coming.

It was a thunderous, bullying shriek, charged with rage and hunger and condensed down into a solid wall of inhuman noise. It stiffened the blood in her veins. They were rising up from the admin level, pounding up the steps. Zahara looked forward to where she knew the docking shaft stood. As she whirled back to look in the direction of Han and Chewbacca, yelling that they needed to get out of here, *now,* she saw Kale Longo burst through the half-open hatch leading up from the admin level, hauling his younger brother's body in his arms.

"Run!" Kale shouted, and he himself was running so hard, so frantically, that his feet barely seemed to touch the ground. His head was on some kind of loose pivot, spinning to look everywhere at once, and his eyes were almost perfectly round with dread. Trig flopped and jostled in his arms. Zahara thought she'd never seen someone look so terrified in her life.

"Where's the other blaster, kid?" Han shouted.

"I had to drop it to carry my brother—"

"Well, shut the door behind you!" Han's voice rang out, but Kale was already bolting away from the door, across the bridge. Han braced himself to yank on the sliding hatchway. "Chewie, give me a hand with this, will you?"

The Wookiee fell to work alongside Han, both of them forcing the panel closed again.

"This way," Zahara shouted, and broke left, she and Kale sprinting almost shoulder-to-shoulder across the bridge in the direction of the docking shaft. Up ahead she didn't see anything between the banks of instrumentation panels except for a single open hatchway.

It better be in there, she thought. *Please, let it be where Tisa says it is.*

Looking back, she saw Han and Chewbacca charging to catch up. Ducking through the hatch, Zahara could see the docking tower doorway in front of them now, the turbolift open and ready.

We're going to make it, she thought.

That was when the sliding door that Han and Chewbacca had just pulled closed exploded wide open.

26/Army of Last Things

KALE JUMPED INSIDE THE DOCKING TOWER WITH TRIG still in his arms, followed by Dr. Cody. He looked back and saw Han Solo and Chewbacca still halfway across the pilot station, the Wookiee firing back at whatever was coming their way. Kale couldn't see what that was, nor did he particularly want to. He could *hear* it, though, and hearing it was enough.

"Hurry!" Dr. Cody shouted back at Han and Chewie. "I have to close off the shaft!"

From where Kale was crouched with his little brother in his arms, all he could see was the medical officer reaching up to seal off the lift doors, and then Solo and the Wookiee diving inside, Chewbacca still shooting, the volley of blasterfire ringing in his ears.

Suddenly Trig sat up, eyes wide. "Dad?"

Kale stared at him. "Trig, what—"

"*It's him.*" The younger boy had already pulled free from his arms, twisting sideways past Han and Chewbacca, crawling back out of the docking shaft turbolift to the pilot station. "Dad's out there!" he shouted. "I saw him! He's—"

Kale sprang out after him. He flung out one arm as far as it would go and grabbed Trig's pant leg, hooking his fingers around the cuff. He felt a low, dull thud as Trig fell to the floor, then got his other hand up around Trig's waist and began dragging him back into the docking shaft.

Then he looked up.

And saw his father.

Von Longo was staggering toward them in a shambling half run like something that been wrenched three different ways at once—wrenched and broken at the hips and shoulders. He was surrounded by a group of prisoners and guards.

Except, Kale saw with dawning horror, they weren't prisoners and guards anymore, not exactly, and neither was the old man. His dead yellow skin was mottled with two weeks' morgue rot, his skull grotesquely swollen and partially collapsed on one side so that Kale could see, very clearly, the grinning hinge of the old man's jaw clicking in its socket.

Kale couldn't move. For what felt like an eternity he watched his father stagger-swaying toward him with that horrible, clutching gait, his face lit up with a kind of drooling familiar eagerness.

At last Kale broke out of his paralysis and screamed. Scrambling to his feet, propelling himself back in the direction of the shaft, he saw Solo and the Wookiee pulling Trig inside, but they were looking over and beyond him, into the corridor from which the noise was coming. As if in a dream he saw that Dr. Cody's face had gone completely white with fright.

Kale saw the doctor reach up and cover Trig's eyes with her hands.

Then he felt something grab his leg.

He didn't even hear himself scream.

27/Say It Three Times

▬▬▬:▬▬:▬▬▬:▬▬

WHEN KALE CAME TO, HE WAS SPRAWLED ON HIS back, Dr. Cody kneeling beside him. There seemed to be a great deal going on around him that he couldn't see. Zahara's hands moved with easy efficiency, wrapping a blood-soaked strip of fabric around his lower leg, once, twice, pulling it snug, tying it off. Kale hissed through his teeth, cold strange air that tasted like iron shavings, and felt his guts recoiling.

Where are we?

"It's all right," her voice was saying from across a great distance. "We made it. We're up inside the Destroyer's landing bay."

Kale rolled over and tried to look around. The pain in his calf was incendiary, intense enough that for a moment he didn't trust himself to speak. He sipped in a shallow, tentative breath and held it until he thought he probably wasn't going to be sick, then glanced up at Dr. Cody again, the scope of his vision broadening a little. Behind her, Han and Chewie stood outside the sealed docking hatchway.

"Where's my brother?" Kale asked hoarsely.

"He's right over there," Dr. Cody said, "he's fine. Just try not to move."

Kale craned his neck and saw Trig sitting on the floor against the docking shaft's outer wall, curled up with his chin resting on his knees, rocking back and forth, staring at nothing. He didn't look fine. Kale thought of Trig's stunned voice saying: *Dad's out there,* seeing the eager thing that had come after him, and wondered if his little brother would ever be fine again.

Say it, he told himself, and thought back to an old superstition he'd heard as a very young child. *Say it three times and make it real.*

"It bit me," Kale said, "didn't it?"

She tightened the makeshift dressing. "Is that too tight? I have to stop the bleeding."

"It bit me."

"They're crawling up the shaft," Han Solo muttered, taking an uneasy step back, and glanced back at Dr. Cody and Kale. "How soon can we get going?"

Kale could hear it—the scraping. It was coming from inside the docking tower. Hands pounded and scratched on the other side of the shaft. Gnawing sounds. Those things down in the barge had climbed right up after them, he realized, up the tower. Right now they were breaking their brittle fingernails and teeth inside that metal tube, trying to get out. He thought about what he'd seen when he'd looked back into the barge's pilot station. It wasn't possible but it was true. The sound of their hunger and anger, along with the stinging pain in his leg, made the memory real.

The corpses of the prison barge had come back to life and his father was among them.

His father had bitten him.

Kale felt his mouth flood with coppery spit and leaned forward, opening his lips to vomit, but nothing came out. His stomach wouldn't quit trying, though, wouldn't say die, as his dear old dad might have said. *Dead* old dad, his brain blathered, and his diaphragm kept jerking and heaving spasmodically with the awful insistence of an involuntary muscle twitch.

"Look, kid," he heard Solo's voice saying, its impatience penetrating the thick cloud of horror that had accumulated around his thoughts. "We gotta go."

"Which way do you suggest?" Dr. Cody asked.

"If we can find our way back to the Destroyer's command bridge, maybe we can actually get this big beast moving."

Chewie gave a dubious growl.

"It's a ship, isn't it?" Han said. "You've flown one, you've flown 'em all. We just gotta get past . . ." He gestured vaguely. ". . . all this."

Kale wiped his eyes and took his first real look around at where Han was indicating. The main landing bay and hangar that surrounded them was an endless durasteel desert whose perimeters stretched out so far that they seemed to elude the eye. Even now, the notion of crossing it was more than he could fathom. And yet . . .

"Help me up," he said.

Dr. Cody reached down. He took her hands and lifted himself, straightening his back as she guided him. At first he thought it was going to work—he actually might be able to put weight on the other leg as well.

"Take it easy," she said. "We don't have to rush."

The pain hit hard, and Kale fell back to the floor with a silent cry that came out as little more than a groan. He looked down. Blood was spurting recklessly from the wound in his leg, soaking the tourniquet and turning it dark red. He saw Trig staring at him but didn't know if his brother was worried about him, or about what he'd seen down below. Did it matter? It was all one thing now, their situation spelled out around them in spilled blood.

"You can't travel like that," Dr. Cody said.

"Just give me a second."

"You'll bleed out before we make it across the landing bay."

"I'll be fine."

She stared at him, then leaned down, close enough to whisper. "Listen to me. I want you to understand this. If we try to move you now, you're going to die." Without moving her head, she indicated Trig, hunched over. "And he'll have to watch that happen. Is that what you want?"

Kale shook his head.

"I'll stay here with you," she said, loud enough for the others to hear. "Han, you and Chewie can take Trig and head for the command bridge."

At the mention of his name, the younger boy jerked as if shocked and sat up straight, shaking his head. "No." He stared at his brother. "I want to stay with Kale."

"Come here," Kale said.

The younger boy stood up and walked over.

"I told you I wouldn't let anything happen to you,"

Kale said, "and I won't. But to keep that promise I need you to go with the others, right now."

Trig shook his head again, violently, tears filling his eyes. He spoke in a fierce whisper. "I'm scared," he said. "Dad's face—"

"Listen to me," Kale said. *That wasn't Dad.*

Trig stared at him.

"That was something else. We know what Dad was like. We remember him from before, and that wasn't him." He waited. "Right?"

"But . . ."

"Was it?"

Trig shook his head.

"You have to go. I'll catch up later."

"What's going to happen to you?" Trig asked.

"Dr. Cody and I will catch up to you guys as soon as we can."

"You promise?"

"I promise," Kale said, and was glad when Dr. Cody put her hands on Trig's shoulders to turn him toward Solo and the Wookiee. Looking at his brother's heart-broken, terrified expression was becoming close to unbearable now, but Kale made himself do it for one more second. "Trig?"

The boy's eyes shone on him.

"I love you," Kale said.

"Then don't make me go."

"Doc, you want the blaster?" Solo asked.

Zahara looked up at him, surprised. "You'd really give me your last blaster?"

"Well," Han said, looking away, "you know, if those things start coming through the shaft—"

"That's all right."

"You sure?"

She nodded. "We won't be here that long." Glancing at Trig: "We'll see you soon, okay?"

Kale watched his brother's expression, but Trig didn't say anything, didn't even nod, as Han Solo and Chewbacca led him away.

28/Things You Don't Forget

THEY STARTED ACROSS THE HANGAR WITHOUT talking.

Han went first, carrying their sole blaster at his side. He and Chewbacca seemed to know where they were headed, and Trig followed, a dragging, somnolent half step behind. Every so often the Wookiee tossed his head, gave a snort or a grunt like he was sampling the air and didn't like the way it smelled, and Han would say, "Yeah, I know," but they just kept moving forward.

The silence was a black cloud that hung over them. The only noise was the tapping, echoing sound of their shoes against the vast steel floor, and outside, the creaking of the Star Destroyer in the black vacuum of space. Otherwise, there was no sound at all. It only accentuated the size of the ship and the limitlessness of the surrounding void.

Trig hated it.

In such silence his mind wandered—except *wandered* was far too tame a word. His mind ran wild, capered shrieking up and down his skull like some lunatic who'd murdered his entire family, jerking to a halt here or there to ruminate upon some grisly trophy or another.

Why am I thinking like this?

But he knew exactly why.

He thought back to the thing that had lunged out of the escape pod at him, the thing he hadn't gotten a chance to tell anyone about, even his brother. The pod-thing had once been an inmate, a human—it had worn an inmate's uniform—but circumstances had turned it into something else entirely. Its puffy dead face and caved-in black eyes had been still vaguely human, but it had jumped out of the pod with a snarl that was decidedly *not* human. It had gone for his throat, and Trig's reflexes were the only reason it hadn't succeeded.

Spinning around, he had gone blundering down the corridor and plunged through the maintenance shaft, clinging to the inner wall while the thing went plummeting down past him with a frantic yodeling scream. And then, holding on inside the shaft, his fingers slowly going numb, Trig had listened to it hit the bottom of the shaft with a crunch, its shallow breathing broken, still hungry, still trying to drag itself back up to get him.

He thought about that inmate, as horrible as it was, over and over, and told himself it was better than thinking about the other thing.

The thing weaving its way across the pilot station toward the docking shaft.

The thing with his father's face.

That face, also bloated and sagging, had hung off the thing's skull like a poorly fitted mask, stretching at the eyes. Trig's mind refused to leave it alone. He kept thinking about the way it had grinned at him, as if it recognized him. And all the rest of them, the guards and prisoners.

Not Dad, he told himself. *Kale said it wasn't and you could see it, too. Dad's dead, you said good-bye to him, whatever that thing up there was, it wasn't Dad.*

And he could almost believe it.

Almost.

Except around the eyes.

His father's eyes had always been his strongest feature, those faded blue irises streaked with flecks of gold, the dark inquisitive pupils, their quickness and clarity, how they sought you out, making you feel like you were the only person in the room. Trig had always liked talking to his father, and his dad could always make him laugh just by looking at him.

The thing upstairs had had his father's eyes.

Behind him now, Trig thought he heard something scuffling across the Destroyer's main hangar and jerked around fast to look back. He could feel the blood tingling in his fingertips. There was nothing there, nothing but the long flat durasteel floor they'd been walking across, and far away, on the other side, almost out of sight, the tiny huddled shapes of his brother and Dr. Cody.

I'm going crazy, he thought, and the idea brought no sense of dread—in fact, it was almost a relief. He'd been losing his grip on things over the last several days, and what he'd just seen only solidified it. Crazy, of course, and why not? What else were you supposed to do when the dead came back to life and tried to rip out the soft part of your neck?

And if the dead man was your father?

But Kale said—

"Kale's wrong," he muttered, "he's just *wrong*," and he nodded along with his own words because being crazy meant you could tell the truth. You didn't have to pretend it was okay anymore, and that was good.

He heard that furtive scuttling noise behind him again and spun back around, but there was still nothing there. He couldn't even see his brother and Dr. Cody across the hangar, their outlines absorbed by distance and the lack of light. Or maybe the thing that was following them had already eaten them, and they were dead, too, which meant Trig would be seeing them again soon, wouldn't he?

In the end, the sickness would bring them back. In the end maybe the sickness brought everyone back.

Trig began to feel as if he were sinking into a warm deep bath. His hearing was becoming muffled, his vision softening around the edges, blurring into deeper shadows across the bay. No wonder the Empire had abandoned this Star Destroyer out here in some remote corner of the galaxy—the sickness here was worse than anything he'd ever heard of; it made Darth Vader and his endless armies seem almost innocent by comparison. Thinking about it now made him want to puke and laugh at the same time because that was what you did, that was just what crazy people did, when their fathers came back from the dead and tried to attack them.

Kid?

Hey kid, are . . . ?

He realized he'd stopped walking. Han Solo was

standing in front of him, staring at him through what felt like a thick and motionless cushion of air. Trig could see his mouth moving, saw him frowning, asking a question—

. . . you gonna . . .

But for the life of him he couldn't figure out what Han was saying. It was like he was speaking a different language. Now the man was shaking him by the shoulders, and the soft wax that had plugged Trig's ears was starting to melt away, opening up his hearing.

". . . all right?" Han asked.

At the sound of his voice, Trig felt the still air around him stirring, become less stifling, as if he'd just snapped out of some invisible chrysalis and drawn his first clean breath. It stung his nose and made his throat ache like he'd tried to swallow too big of a bite of something, and he realized he was going to cry again. Even if he didn't have any more tears.

Han stood there looking at him awkwardly.

"My dad . . ." Trig managed, and that was all.

Han opened his mouth to say something but didn't. To his left, Chewbacca leaned forward and put his arms around Trig. It was like being wrapped up in a warm, slightly musty-smelling blanket. Trig could feel the Wookiee's heartbeat, and a soft, comforting growl from deep inside that cavernous chest. Slowly he made himself release and draw away.

"Okay," Han said, and cleared his throat. "You all right?"

Trig nodded. It was a lie, he wasn't all right, not at all, but he was better—a little.

He looked around and saw that they were standing among several smaller ships, the ones he'd first seen from the other side of the bay, old rusted vessels, jetti-soned escape pods, captured Rebel ships and shuttles, a small Corellian freighter. They lay in piles around them, a modest assortment of ruined aeronautics.

The Wookiee barked out a question.

"Nah," Han said, "I seriously doubt it." He pointed. "We can get up to the main concourse, follow it up."

"Yeah," Trig said, because he knew some kind of answer was expected of him.

"It's going to take us a while to get to the command bridge. These things are a kilometer long. But if it's got an engine, we can fly it."

Trig nodded. They kept walking.

Behind him, far off in the distance he heard a new sound.

Screaming.

29/Sine

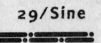

ZAHARA JERKED SIDEWAYS AND STARED BACK AT THE docking shaft. The screaming coming from inside of the shaft was inhuman. It was shrill and sharp and hateful, comprising maybe hundreds of voices pitched up together—*EEEEEEEEEE*. It oscillated in a waveform that the mathematical part of her mind insisted on graphing, rising up to squeeze her eardrums, sloping toward silence, then coming up again to the same frequency of precision dynamics.

Kale groaned. He was muttering something. She leaned down to listen.

". . . ut it off . . ."

She looked at him, startled by what she understood him to be saying. And in case she *didn't* understand, he was fully awake now, staring at her, pointing at his bandaged leg.

"Doc, please. You have to."

Another scream Dopplered by, *eeeEEEEeeee*, and she waited until it ended.

"What?"

eeeEEEEeee—

"Cut it off."

eeeEEEEeee—

"That's not necessary," she said. "Not right now."

eeeEEEEeee—

"I can feel it coming up through me. You have to." His eyes were bright and scared and absolutely lucid. "Please, I don't care how much it hurts, just do it, cut it off."

eeeEEEEeee—

"I can't do that."

"Then kill me."

The screaming spiraled up again, louder than before, surging up and edging off in that same pattern. It continued throughout their conversation, and Zahara started shouting so she could be heard over it.

"Your brother went with Han and Chewbacca, they're on the way now to find communications and medical supplies. You're going to get through this, trust me. How bad is your pain?"

"There is no pain."

"What?"

"It's not like that. It doesn't hurt. I can just feel it, where my d—where it bit me." His eyes were very wide now, glittering like broken glass, and she could hear the whistle of air through his nose as he lost the battle to panic. "Unwrap it at least, so I can see it. I'll show you."

"I need to keep pressure on the—"

"It's coming through me!"

"Kale, don't!"

He sat up and grabbed the bloody tourniquets from his calf, ripping them off in layers. Zahara tried to stop him and he shoved her back without so much as a backward glance, intent on peeling away the canvas strips that she'd torn from her own jacket. The last of them fell away in a sodden red heap.

"See?" Kale's face was flushed with horrified triumph. "I told you."

Zahara stared at it. There was a fist-sized chunk of flesh missing from the meaty part of his lower leg, the exposed shinbone gleaming visibly through a web of the torn muscle and viscera. The puckered flesh around the wound had gone a bruised, gangrenous gray. She found herself watching in fascinated horror as that same gray hue began to reach up his leg, past his knee to his thigh, causing it to pulsate visibly with gelatinous vitality. It was like a hand sliding up underneath his skin, reaching eagerly upward toward his torso.

"Get rid of it!" Kale shrieked, his own voice high and reedy, slapping at himself as his voice joined those of the screamers inside the shaft. *"Cut it out, get rid of it, get it out of me!"*

Zahara felt the wheels of time grinding to a halt. Her mind flashed back to one of her teachers at Rhinnal, something he'd said once in the classroom: *The day will come when you'll be faced with a situation you're completely unprepared for, both physically and emotionally. On that day you'll find out what kind of doctor you really are, by how much you give up to fear, and how much you remember your training.*

She tore open the pocket of her cargo pants and pulled out her medical kit, breaking it open. Inside were scalpels, gauze, tape—the most rudimentary tools of her trade. Down in front of her, Kale kept screaming. The gray swollen pulsation she'd seen earlier had already crept up past his waistline, rippling inside his abdomen, turning pink skin into dull, mottled pewter. Seeing it made her sick—it was like watching meat rot from the inside.

He's dying. Or worse. So do something.

She took a scalpel from the kit and lowered its sharpened tip into the exposed flesh just below his belly button. For an instant Kale's screams of fear became screeches of pain and he gaped at her in total confusion as she widened the incision, fingers probing through a slick jacket of fat to the constricted abdominal muscle beneath. A cold sweat had broken out over her forehead and upper lip. She put it out of her mind, extinguished every detail except what was right in front of her.

The strands of muscle slithered between her fingers like taut damp cords of yarn. She could see them in her mind, feeling the abnormal heat beneath them, that intrusive presence, that thing, cutting its slickly twisting path upward. A whisper of motion brushed against her fingertips, and she seized it and squeezed. There was a sudden rupturing spurt and something beneath the muscle layer burst over her, a thick slimy pustule of nacreous liquid, coating her hands to the wrists.

The screaming coming from inside the shaft was beyond deafening now.

Zahara yanked her hands out and looked at them, staring at the way the clotted fluid first seemed to coagulate, then wiggled, and now actually appeared to *crawl* over her flesh like living gloves, looking for an opening, a wound it could use to get inside her. It stung worse with every passing second of exposure to the open air, and she wiped it off on her pants, forcing her gorge back down, telling herself if she lost her nerve now she'd never get it back.

Below her on the floor, Kale's face had gone pale, ashen. He was staring at her in a state of shock. She kept hoping that he'd pass out but so far he hadn't, though he'd at least stopped screaming.

"I have to go in again," she said, "I have to make sure I got it."

Before he could say anything she shoved her hand back through the incision, sliding in, feeling around, waiting for that little wiggling clot of activity against her fingers and not feeling it. When she looked down she saw that the grayish black rot color was still there, just above his waistline, but it hadn't come any farther up.

"I think we got it."

She took a deep breath and looked at Kale. He'd finally blacked out, eyes mostly shut, rolled to the side. She gathered up the shirt she'd ripped off him and started to fold it up, pressing it down over the wound to stanch the new bleeding she'd created. Sitting back, holding pressure, taking in breaths and letting them out, she willed her own heart rate to slow down to something approaching normal. Whether she'd done more harm than good, she wasn't sure, except now Kale was still alive and breathing and if she hadn't done anything, that might not have been the case.

It wasn't until later, when she'd finally calmed down a little, that she realized the docking shaft next to them had fallen totally silent.

The screaming in the shaft had stopped.

And then, from a great distance away, she heard another noise, some faint respondent roar.

Something on the other side of the Star Destroyer was screaming back.

30/Black Tank Blues

▬▬▬:▬▬▬:▬▬:

CHEWBACCA WAS WORRIED ABOUT THE BOY. TRIG wasn't talking. Han wasn't, either, but Chewie was used to that, depending on the circumstances. The boy, though—that was something else. Young ones needed to express themselves. In the short time that the Wookiee had known him, he'd seen the boy dealing with things far beyond his age, and if he kept them bottled up inside, it could be very bad for all of them.

It had started when they'd heard Kale screaming on the other side of the hangar. Trig had wanted to go back and Han had to physically hold on to him to prevent him from running away.

"He'll be all right," Han had said, and although Chewie could tell he wouldn't, he knew what Han was doing—getting the boy as far away from the docking shaft as possible before those things broke through. Trig fought him, anyway, fought hard, kicking and punching, trying to squirm away, until Chewie had to intervene and physically pick the boy up and hold him back, not a hug this time, not even close. The boy was stronger than he looked. Chewie ended up carrying him for the next twenty minutes until Trig, in a low voice, had muttered, "You can put me down now."

It was the last thing he'd said.

As much as he understood the mission, putting distance between themselves and the shaft, Chewbacca didn't like venturing any deeper into the Destroyer. The long corridors, the vacant spaces they kept coming upon, turning corners and seeing nothing but random droids, the emptiness that didn't really feel like emptiness—who had designed all of this, and who had left it here? Had they all died, and if they had, what had happened to the bodies? Some of the avionics were still functioning, and they occasionally came across whole empty suites of blinking lights, navigation and atmospheric systems operating on and on endlessly without the influence of any living thing.

At the end of one hall they came across a stormtrooper helmet lying on its side like a broken skull. A second one dangled from a chain above it, its faceplate stained with dried blood. Han kicked the first helmet over and Chewie could smell something horribly rotten and sweet inside it: the plasteel mouthpiece had been carefully ripped out to expose the wearer's lower jaw. It looked like an artifact from an ancient civilization, a cannibal cult. Why would anybody have a thing like that?

It felt like they had been walking for a very long time, without even putting a dent in the distance that they still needed to travel. And what would happen when they did reach the command bridge? Despite his partner's bravado, Chewie wondered if they really would be able to fly the Star Destroyer.

They had found a second blaster—it was the one

worthwhile discovery so far, and Chewie was glad to have one of his own, if only to better protect the boy.

"What's this?" Han said from ahead of them. "Chewie, gimme a hand with these, huh?"

Chewbacca looked back to make sure the boy was coming—he was, not looking up from his feet—and went to meet Han, who was pointing to a stack of shipping crates blocking the corridor. They appeared to have been shoved here by someone in a hurry to get on to other things. Chewie studied the writing on the side of one of the boxes.

IMPERIAL BIOLOGICAL WEAPONS DIVISION

When he glanced back up, Han was already hauling the boxes aside, trying to clear their path. A big crate on top fell over, and Chewbacca saw a red steel canister go rolling off to the side. It slammed into the wall with an empty clang, rebounded, and stopped under Han's boot.

"What were these creeps messing around with out here?" Han said, more to himself than Chewie, but the Wookiee gave his opinion anyway, which was that none of this made him feel any safer about their prospects.

"This one busted its pressure valve," Han said, inspecting the tank. "There's no markings on it at all, like the whole thing's just been painted red. You see any more of these lying around?"

"Up here," Trig called out. While Han had been talking, Trig had climbed on top of the next pile of crates, twenty or thirty at least, stacked two or three deep. The boy was nimble. It took Chewbacca almost twice as long to clamber up the stack next to him and yank off the top to look in.

The crates were full of cylinders, dozens of them, stacked in neatly ordered rows. There were a few loose red tanks up here, but all the rest—the ones that had been repacked with military precision—had been painted jet black. Chewbacca lifted one of the black ones and heard something sloshing around inside.

He held it up so Han could see it and spoke in Shyriiwook: *It's still full.*

"Different formula, maybe," Han said. "Different combustibility or something—who knows?" There was a whack as the bottom of the tank slipped from Chewbacca's grip and hit the others inside the crate. "Hey, be careful with that thing, will ya?"

Chewie put the black canister back in its place, noticing that the gauge readout already stood at maximum pressure. He wondered how long it would be before these tanks started leaking like the red ones and what would happen when their contents filtered into the Destroyer's atmosphere.

He didn't tell Han what he'd felt inside the tank that had made him almost drop it. The sloshing motion inside had kept moving back and forth, and in fact it felt like it was moving by itself. Like there was something slopping around inside the black tanks, dripping off its internal walls and trying to get out. Something alive.

"Whose idea was it to come aboard this thing anyhow?" Han asked with disgust, not awaiting an answer. He'd already climbed up the makeshift barricade of crates, following Chewbacca and Trig down the other side. Chewbacca had the best hearing of the three of them, and he could have sworn as he walked away that he heard something start hissing.

Han froze in his tracks.

"What's that?"

Chewie stopped and cocked his head, and then looked up with a growing feeling of apprehension. He could hear something overhead, he realized—a rising scream. It was accompanied by a rumbling sound, some gargantuan, many-legged thing plodding heavily directly above the durasteel-paneled ceiling.

Han pointed in the direction they were headed. "It's coming from that way."

Chewbacca saw the boy's mouth fall open in shock. The lights started shaking and the Wookiee heard the creak and pop of metal overtaxed with the weight of whatever was approaching.

"Get back, kid," Han said, pushing Trig aside as he aimed the blaster up. "I think it's gonna—"

The ceiling buckled, twisted, and split open. Through the hole Chewbacca glimpsed a solid mass of dark-eyed faces, arms and legs already trying to push through. Some wore Imperial uniforms; others were dressed in stormtrooper armor, a leg piece here, a shoulder piece there, or wearing broken helmets. Only then did he get a true sense of how many there were up there, perhaps hundreds, maybe more—an entire army of the dead. They were reaching down for him.

Reaching down for the boy.

Chewie wasn't sure who fired first. One of them, he or Han, or maybe both of them at the same time, squeezed off a round of blasterfire into the tangled mass of squirming bodies. After that it didn't matter:

some vital piece of infrastructure inside the ceiling gave a sharp *pop*.

It was as if a hole had been torn open between the worlds of the living and the dead. Bodies came spilling down in front of them, an avalanche of stinking yellow flesh and broken armor, grasping hands and shrieking mouths. Some of them landed on their feet; others hit the ground with all fours and stayed that way like animals, grinning up at them, baring their teeth. Their eyes were flat and lifeless and hideously hungry.

"Get behind me!" Han shouted.

Trig didn't move—paralyzed, Chewbacca thought, grabbing Trig by the arm and yanking him around behind him as he and Han turned and opened fire.

The dead things recoiled as if they hadn't expected blasters. Chewie sprayed them point-blank, watching stormtrooper helmets explode and burst to reveal swollen, half-decayed faces whose only expression was a kind of cheated rage. Next to him, Han was shouting something, but Chewbacca couldn't hear it over the blasters. The corridor in front of them was filling with smoke. Distantly, from what felt like the other side of space, he could feel Trig gripping him tightly, the boy's fingers digging into his arm, clinging for dear life.

In front of them and up above, more of the things were tumbling down, half falling, half jumping, fresh corpses piling on top of the ones already there. Chewie realized that it didn't matter how long or hard they pounded the bodies with blasterfire; they were just going to keep coming. He growled loudly.

"I know, I know!" Han's fingers gripped his arm. "Go on, I'll cover you!"

He saw Han pointing to another hatchway at the end of the corridor. Scooping up the boy, Chewie pivoted and broke for it, diving through the hatch without a look back. An instant later Han leapt through behind him, slammed the console on the other side, shutting the door, and fired a round into it. Chewbacca realized he could already hear them on the other side, attacking the door, screaming.

He and Han exchanged a glance, and Chewbacca saw something on his friend's face that he hadn't seen in a very long time—true fear. For a moment Han was so pale that the scar on his chin stood out in bold relief. It was like watching him age prematurely, twenty years in an instant.

Han opened his mouth to speak, and then something hit the other side of the hatch with unthinkable weight and force. It was as if everything that was inevitable about their future, however brief it might be, had just arrived outside that hatchway with a gullet full of gleaming yellow teeth.

They ran.

31/Coffin Jockeys

WHEN JARETH SARTORIS OPENED HIS EYES, HE WAS still strapped inside the escape pod. His skull felt like it had been split down the middle with a gaffi stick, and his right leg was twisted around sideways, pinned down by the partially collapsed front panel.

Cautiously, with great effort, he managed to extract it, sliding his knee up and rotating the ankle slowly, steeling himself for the sharp slash of pain and not feeling it.

Nothing broken.

He breathed in, exhaled a sigh of relief, his senses still coming back to him a little at a time. Was he in space? How long had he been blacked out?

He glanced down at the pod's navigational display and checked the counter, still ticking off minutes and seconds since his departure from the barge. According to the readout, he'd ejected almost four hours earlier, which meant he'd been unconscious since—

He turned his head and looked out the shattered viewport.

Then he remembered.

* * *

The pod had ejected from the *Purge* as planned, leaving the Longo brothers standing there with matching looks of anguish stamped across their faces. The slight twinge that Sartoris had felt at that moment had actually caught him by surprise. Had they really expected that he'd take them with him?

No, of course not. Imperial Corrections had a saying: *There are no children here.* They were inmates, convicts, nothing less than enemies of the Empire, and whatever had happened between him and their father—Sartoris had already started thinking about Longo's death in the vaguest of generalities—had nothing to do with anything now.

Still, that voice spoke up within him, faint but implacable:

You killed their dad and now you're leaving them to die.

Okay. So what? The galaxy was a hard place to grow up. Sartoris's own father, a petty thief and death stick addict, had beaten him savagely throughout his childhood, sometimes stopping only when he was afraid he'd killed the boy. One night when Jareth was sixteen his dad had come after him with a rusty torque-bludgeon; for the first time the boy had stood his ground, ripped the weapon away from him, and bashed in his father's skull. He'd never forget the old man's face as he died, his expression of abject bewilderment, as if he couldn't understand why his son had turned on him. Afterward Jareth dragged the body out of the hovel they shared and abandoned it in an alleyway. The local law enforcement would simply assume the old man fell victim to the latest of his countless bad decisions. The next day Jareth had lied about his age, joined up with the Empire, and never looked back.

To this day, Sartoris had never fathered any children of his own—none that he knew of, anyway, and that was a mercy. Throughout his adult life he'd rarely wasted a thought on the roaring, chaotic creature that had once called himself his father, let alone the prospect of his own fatherhood. But as the pod blasted off from the prison barge leaving Trig and Kale Longo behind, Sartoris realized he'd been remembering the old man more vividly than he had in years. In fact, *remembering* was too sentimental a term for it. It was almost as if Gilles Sartoris were sitting next to him, beaming in approval at the way his son—after a lifetime of misdeeds—had finally lived up to his own full destiny. Just because Jareth Sartoris never spawned offspring, it hadn't stopped him from relegating another man's sons to permanent darkness.

He'd been thinking all of these things, four hours ago, when he'd realized something was wrong before the klaxons started blaring inside the escape pod—something inside the guidance system had gone seriously wrong. Rather than spiraling off into space, he had felt its trajectory curving back upward, pitching around on its side, rising up alongside of the barge. He'd stared up through the viewport—

And then he'd seen it overhead, the open maw of the Star Destroyer's docking bay descending from above, as the pod rose up into it.

A tractor beam, he'd thought, as the shadows of the hangar engulfed him. *That's why we couldn't keep going, even with the thrusters repaired: there was a tractor beam turned on.* He remembered thinking that at a little over two hundred meters, the prison barge was too big to be pulled inside the hangar, but the Destroyer could have locked on after they had docked, holding it there with the tower connecting them. By the time the engineers figured out what was going on, it had probably been too late.

As the pod swung up inside the bay, he'd felt himself swiveling sidelong, then a lurch and an abrupt bone-jarring smash. The pod sank a little, metal squealing against metal as if pinned between two larger objects, and then the sides began to crumple inward. Sartoris's leg gave a loud bray of pain as the navigation panel caved in around it. Everything jolted forward again. His head snapped face-first and hit something on impact.

The last thing he'd glimpsed before blacking out was the vision of his father, smiling beside him.

Now that he'd regained his bearings, Sartoris released the shoulder restraints and took in a deep breath, shoving all doubt aside. He was alive and that was all that mattered. Switching the internal locking system to manual, he bent his leg and shot it forward to kick out the door. It fell off its hinges, waffled through the air, then disappeared. A moment later, he heard it clatter distantly to the floor.

He stuck his head out and looked around. The pod had lodged between two other ships, an old X-wing fighter and an upended TIE fighter lying on one solar array wing. Lucky for him the pod had landed hatch-up; otherwise he would have been trapped in here permanently, imprisoned between two icons of the galactic power struggle. The notion of starving to death inside the pod, beating his shoulder against the hatch until he was too weak to move, didn't allow him to appreciate the irony of such a death.

Lowering himself, he stepped over onto the X-wing and paused a moment before dropping to the floor, looking around the hangar.

It was exactly the way he remembered it, mostly desolate with a handful of abducted ships strewn out across this end. Sartoris moved forward, mindful of his sore ankle, taking his time so he wouldn't slip and make things worse. The last time he'd passed through here, he'd ordered the rest of the boarding party onward without pausing for close inspection, but now he wandered among the vessels with the sharp eyes of a man evaluating his resources. Back in his early days they'd joked about the pilots who flew these smaller TIEs because of the high mortality rate on such missions—they called them coffin jockeys. Gazing up, Sartoris could see how the hatches and canopies had been ripped open, sometimes with such force that they dangled on their hinges. He wondered if these particular coffin jockeys had been fighting their way out, or if some unknown predator from the outside had been trying to get in.

What sort of predator? It's deserted in here, remember?

As if in answer, a high, frantic chorus of screams rang out across the hangar, ripping a hole through the silence. It was so unexpected that Sartoris actually jumped and felt the skin on his back bristling upward over his shoulders and down his arms. His scalp abruptly felt too tight on his skull. For an instant he stood perfectly straight and still, feeling a leaden sense of profound and unreasonable terror bulking down in the pit of his stomach, and looked across the hangar but couldn't see anything.

Another mutated blast of screams, this one louder.

Straight out of childhood, another vision of his father flashed through his mind, for no good reason at all: the old man smacking his lips—the death sticks had always given him dry mouth. Sartoris never forgot the moist, soft smacking sound his father made as he slipped into his room to deliver the nightly beating.

"Get a hold of yourself," he muttered, heart thudding against his sore ribs, unaware that he was even speaking aloud. "Right now. I have to—"

Then the scream came yet again, this time seeming to emanate from everywhere at once. It was cycling up and down, bouncing off the walls of the hangar like a living thing hunting for food.

Sartoris whirled around, now close to screaming himself. He couldn't see anything. The screams—there were more of them now, a cyclonic outcry of rage—kept rising up, filling the hollow docking bay with ear-shattering din. He wished he could have convinced himself that it was some kind of alarm, a leaky air lock, anything but what it was, a cacophony of human voices.

His eyes widened farther, starved for input and seeing nothing. The gray crepuscular reaches of the main hangar just went on and on, an equation for which there was no final quotient. It occurred to him that they'd never found out what happened to the other boarding party, the ones that had disappeared up here. The screams he heard now didn't sound like anything he'd ever heard, except perhaps in his worst childhood nightmares. They were the screams of the dead, his mind babbled, corpses who didn't want to stay buried.

And they sounded hungry.

Suddenly he wanted to run.

Where?

That was when the shooting started.

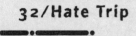

THE FIRST TIME SHE HEARD THE BLASTERS, ZAHARA jumped back away from the shaft on animal reflex. Then conscious thought took over, and she went back and grabbed Kale under the arms, dragging him away from the shaft. As she pulled him across the hangar floor, the weight of his damaged body sagged sideways in her hands, head lolling, but she saw that his eyes were partially open, a pinpoint of lucidity still buried deep inside there somewhere.

"Shooting . . . ," Kale managed. "Why are they . . ."

His eyelids lifted a little, awareness dawning over his features, and he frowned. His mouth went up and down, trying to shape more words, a question she couldn't hear over the noise.

She pulled him along faster, running backward so she could keep an eye on the shaft. At that moment the first bolt of blasterfire pierced the docking shaft's outer shell. She simultaneously heard and felt it recoiling through the durasteel floors, a sizzling *crack* that left a black gash in the wall of the tower like a crooked, idiot grin, admitting a tiny puff of smoke. Then another explosion burst through it, and another, the smell of cooked metal already wafting through, the ozone smell and acrid smoke that she associated with broken machinery. There was another series of blasts, even bigger, some heavier-gauge artillery, followed by a swarm of shrapnel spitting through the air in front of her face.

She kept moving backward, not looking away.

The hole in the shaft was big enough now that she could see them inside the shaft, leering out at her as their hands gripped the hot, twisted durasteel and tried to peel it back. They had packed the shaft with their bodies—prison inmates still in their uniforms, human and nonhuman alike, guards, administrators, no longer segregated but jammed together with a pressing, eager confederacy they'd lacked in life. She could already see their faces. Sagging lips. Wrinkled noses. Dead yellow eyes lit up with a kind of stupid animal cunning. A scaly green arm came out clutching a blaster rifle and fired a shot blindly across the hangar, the red streak fading off in the distance, slamming into something too far off to register. More blasters fired inside the tube, widening the hole they'd created, making it longer and bigger on all sides.

Be careful, you can't see where you're going, if you go too fast—

Even as she thought it, her feet tangled over each other and she went down hard, Kale's body landing on top of her.

Go, go, get up, now!

She jumped back up, groping for Kale, struggling to haul him off the floor, and made the mistake of looking up one more time.

They had started crawling out.

The blaster-twisted hole they'd created in the shaft was jagged and they cut themselves along the way, twisted spikes of durasteel slashing their uniforms and gouging deep into the pouched sacks of rotten innards that were their bodies. One of them—a guard whose face she vaguely recognized from his visits to the infirmary—was instantly impaled and hung there flailing while the others scrambled over him.

In her arms, Kale groaned, tried to straighten his body, writhing around to look at her, and then fell slack again. He was trying to talk to her, she realized; despite his injuries, he'd actually found the strength to shout, but she still couldn't hear him over the blasters.

She pulled him faster, moving blindly, taking shorter, quicker steps. His weight was slowing her down, and now the first few of the things were already making their way toward her. One of them was Gat, his once familiar face contorted into a hideously hungry grin. *I am going to eat you,* that grin said, *and you are going to taste good to me.*

There was a brief moment of silence, an incidental lull, and although Zahara's ears were ringing, she realized what Kale was shouting.

"Let me go!"

"No," she said, not concerned with whether he heard her or not. The important thing was that she'd said it to herself—she wasn't leaving him here. In front of her, perhaps six meters away, three dead guards and maybe a dozen inmates paused as if acclimating to their new environment. Then they broke into a loose, shambling, openmouthed run straight at her, arms swinging, legs clanging, firing all the way. They were already getting better at it. The shots were actually getting close to hitting her now.

"Drop me!" Kale screamed. *"Just go! Go! Run!"*

Shut up, she thought—her adrenaline hit hard, erupting through her skull base, and her backward run became a backward sprint, her legs not even feeling like part of her now, paddling the floor beneath her with a crazy, blurring speed. The things were receding, trying to run but not as fast as she was, she could outrun them all, even dragging Kale behind her, she—

There was another metallic jolt, and Kale jerked violently in her arms and fell still.

She stopped running, aware of a damp warmness spreading through her lower torso and legs. Everything below her waist was soaked in blood.

She looked down.

The right half of Kale's face was gone, a pulped half-moon. The broken skull protruded from his scalp like shattered terra-cotta, the jawbone dangling crookedly on one hinge. He'd taken the shot that would have torn straight through her abdomen. His good eye rolled up, fogging over. Already she smelled the terrible sweet odor of cauterized hair and skin.

As his head swung down, Zahara saw that the left side of his face was almost completely untouched, except for a single freckle of scarlet under his eye.

There was a muffled snarl, and she looked up again.

In front of her, the things were moving faster now, motivated by fresh bloodshed.

Zahara dropped him and fled.

33/Catwalk

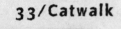

THEY WERE LOST—TRIG KNEW IT.

It had happened when they were running blindly from the other side of the hatchway that Han had blasted shut. Nobody had spoken up and said which way to go, they'd just *gone,* sprinting as fast as they could, away from the scratching, screaming things they'd left behind. They'd run for what felt like whole kilometers—impossible, he knew, but the subjectivity would not be argued with. Eventually, too exhausted even to breathe, they'd slowed down, gasping for air and still not speaking. That was the first time Trig thought Han had somehow gotten turned around and was now leading them in the wrong direction.

Maybe back toward those things in the ceiling, maybe—

Trig cut the thought off, refusing to give it any further credence. Better to concentrate on where they were headed. The long corridors and main transit shafts had long since become identical, air exchangers and manifolds all starting to look the same, and when they arrived at yet another bank of turbolifts that looked just like the last set, Trig couldn't keep it to himself anymore.

"We're going in circles," he said.

Han didn't say anything, didn't even glance back at him. He was looking back and forth down the upcoming nexus of concourses, running the options in his head.

Trig cleared his throat. "Did you hear me? I said—"

"You think you can get us to the command bridge, kid?" Han snapped. His eyes looked hollow and deepset. "Be my guest."

"I'm just saying—" He pointed the way that Han appeared to be favoring. "—this doesn't feel right."

"Yeah, well, we're on a Star Destroyer, being chased by the living dead. *None* of this feels right." Han rubbed his hand over his face, and when he lowered his palm and looked at Chewbacca, his expression showed a deeper gradation of doubt. "We came back from that way, right?"

The Wookiee gave a mournful, uncertain groan.

"Great. You're supposed to be the one with the keen sense of direction."

"I think if we just take this turbolift, you know, up—" Trig started.

"We're almost to the conning tower." Han squatted down and touched his fingertips to the deck below their feet. "You feel how the floor's vibrating?"

Trig nodded tentatively.

"We're probably standing right on top of the primary power generator." Han cocked a thumb off to the right. "It's this way and then straight back, I can feel it. We're almost there, right through this hatchway."

He palmed the switch on the wall. It hummed, the entire platform reverberating even harder under their feet, and a huge space gaped in front of them.

Almost simultaneously, they all took a step back, staring down into the void.

Sickish green and yellow lights illuminated it from above, and Trig leaned slightly forward, craning his neck as far down as he dared, but he couldn't see the full dimensions of it. As his eyes began to adjust, he saw they were standing at a precipice overlooking a deep cavernous chamber that for a moment appeared to be nothing less than the atmospheric null set of space itself. He realized that his lungs were aching for air, and allowed himself to inhale a shaky breath.

"See?" Han said, a little weakly. "Told you we were at the top."

Trig stared down at the massive cylindrical shape, only half visible, so far down, their voices sounding very small against the opening.

"What is that down there?" he asked.

"Main engine turbine, probably."

"It's big."

"It's a big ship, kid—the Empire likes 'em that way." Han pointed to the other side, voice solidifying with all kinds of manufactured confidence. "See that square service shaft on the other side? That's probably the main lift platform up to the bridge."

Trig squinted. He *couldn't* see across, and he doubted that Han could, either. His attention kept getting sucked downward in the direction of the silent turbine. What would it be like to fall that far down? You would have a long time to scream, that was for sure—one endless, diminishing shriek as the darkness swallowed you up. He wondered what might happen if the lower part of the Star Destroyer was open and you fell through it—if it was possible to drop straight down into the hostile, icy bath of the galaxy itself.

"How do we get across?"

Han pointed. "You're looking at it."

Trig frowned. The catwalk in front of them was so narrow that at first he thought it was just an extra contour of the wall. It ran along the edge, stretching out as far as he could see, presumably ending on the other side.

"There's no guardrail."

"Yeah, well, beggars can't be choosers."

"There's got to be a regular way of getting over there."

"I'm sure there is," Han said. "Me, I don't plan on standing around out here any longer than I have to."

Trig thought back to the turbolift he'd suggested they take, a few turns back. No doubt that had been the usual means of getting to the bridge. But did he want to go back there alone? Could he even find it at this point?

He glanced at Chewbacca, but the big Wookiee seemed unconcerned, and Han was already stepping out onto it. He put his back to the wall and crept forward, keeping his palms flattened on either side to maintain his balance. "Just keep your head up and don't look down and you'll be fine." He jerked his head at the Wookiee. "Well, what are you waiting for?"

With an unhappy yawp, Chewbacca stepped out after him, and Trig knew that it was his turn. He thought that Han was probably right about the conning tower—in his headstrong, cocksure way, he *did* seem uncannily well informed about the general layout of the Destroyer—but as Trig approached and put his foot onto the catwalk, he felt his guts go loose and turn to water. His legs felt so weightless that his knees trembled all the way up to his thighs, and when his palms started sweating he was abruptly sure that this was how he was going to die, falling down into the pit. Any remaining sense of balance and equilibrium fled.

"I can't," he mumbled.

Han turned and looked at him. He could feel the man's eyes on him, making his face blaze up hot all the way to his hairline.

"Come on, we don't have time for a pep talk here."

Trig tried to swallow but his throat was too gummy. He forced the words out. "There's got to be another way. Maybe I'll go back to the turbolift."

"Alone?" Han asked.

"Then I'll wait for you here. Once you get the engines going again—" He bobbed his head up and down, selling the idea to himself. "I'll just meet you back here, okay?"

Han looked at him one last time. The distance between them was already wide enough that Trig couldn't make out the expression on his face, but some small and shameful part of him guessed it was probably a mixture of exasperation and maybe a little contempt.

But if there was contempt, it wasn't evident in the man's voice. "All right," he said. "We'll come back for you." Then he and Chewbacca turned back in the opposite direction and continued to pick their way along the catwalk.

Trig stood staring at the two shadowy forms advancing deeper into the shadows until he wasn't sure he saw them anymore. Then they were gone, and he was standing there all alone.

He'd never hated himself more than he did at that moment. It struck him that Kale would have gone out there without question, that his own life had been full of these failures of nerve, large and small, and that this was probably the most recent of many to come.

He stood at the edge of the abyss, for what felt like a very long time, waiting to hear Han call out, *We're here,* or *We made it,* from somewhere far off in the distance, but no such sound came to him.

Maybe they fell, a craven voice inside him whispered. But if they had, wouldn't he have heard them scream?

He sat down by the open hatchway, a careful distance from the edge, and stared down into it, listening to the sounds of his own breathing, the steady thud of his pulse.

Eventually he began to hear sounds from down inside the chamber. Low rustling noises from far below where he couldn't see.

It's them. They're down there.

He bounced to his feet, more startled by the thought than the popping sound that his knees made, and tried to look deeper into the pit. He'd heard that Star Destroyers carried a crew of eight thousand or more—suppose they'd all been infected? They would nest somewhere, wouldn't they, a place together in the dark? Maybe this was where the ones in the overhead ventilation shaft had come from, where they'd been waiting. And they were headed forward in the direction of the main hangar, as if summoned there by—

He turned around, struck by the feeling that he was being watched.

It wasn't just a feeling.

At the far end of the shaft, ten meters away, a face was peering at him out of the half-light, in three-quarter profile. Even at this distance, Trig recognized it instantly, though it took a moment to get the name out from his shock-numbed lips.

"*Kale?*"

His brother regarded him from the side without turning his head, as if in a trance. Then he reached out and pushed a button on the wall, and a door opened in front of him.

"Kale, wait! Don't—"

Kale stepped through the door and disappeared.

Trig chased after him, running back up the concourse, staggering a little, feeling pins and needles creeping up through his lower legs from all the time that he'd sat motionless—had he really been waiting there that long? His knees had the trembling, wrung-out feeling that made him wonder if they might actually buckle underneath him.

He got to the hatchway that his brother had opened and pressed the switch. The door that hissed open wasn't as big as the one that Han had discovered above the turbine. It was just a normal hatchway, and that somehow made him feel better, too.

He stepped through it.

"Kale? It's—"

His voice broke off with a choke.

The chamber was even darker than the concourse

he'd left behind. At first glance it appeared as big as the abyss he'd refused to cross—but this was some type of main refuse depository. A mountain of trash rose up to the ceiling, and the fetid, brown, excremental stink simmering off its peaks was beyond nauseating.

Trig clamped his hand over his mouth and looked around through watering eyes, trying to keep from gagging. He couldn't see his brother in here, but Kale had just come inside, seconds earlier.

"Kale," he said again, strangely hesitant to shout out in here. "It's me. What are you doing in here?"

Behind him, the hatch sealed shut.

34/Skin Hill

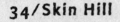

IT WASN'T TRASH.

Trig came to this realization as he took another step toward the mountain, hoping to find some trace of Kale around the other side. That was when his toe struck something soft and yielding, and when he glanced down he saw it was a human leg.

Very slowly, he looked up.

The leg was connected to a torso, covered up by another, and another, the pile growing in front of him comprising what he realized was hundreds of dismembered corpses—heads, arms, legs, and whole bodies, bare bones, many of them still dressed in rotten Imperial uniforms and incomplete stormtrooper armor. The pile rose up to the ceiling. Details leapt out at him from everywhere. The bodies had been mangled like parts at an abattoir, some of them in handcuffs and manacles, others hacked recklessly to pieces, still others looking partially devoured, whole gobbets of flesh gnawed off. Many of the parts were bloated to the point where the skin itself had begun to split open like sausages, and Trig realized he was standing in a tacky puddle of whatever had leaked out of them to coat the floor.

He felt the room start to spin. A scream ballooned in his throat and died there, snuffed out by his own inability to open his lips and release it. Instead, he stumbled backward, trying not to look at what was in front of him, all around him, wanting it not to be there but unable to get away from it. Somewhere behind him was the door he'd come through, the hatchway that would get him out of here, but he couldn't find the switch to activate it. He began slapping the walls blindly at random, pounding them, and nothing changed.

At last the seal broke in his throat and he let out a shriek, a combination of "help" and "Kale," and that was when he heard the sounds, a soft, moist rustling noise from inside the mountain. Bodies shifted, shoved aside and rearranged by something within.

And then he saw the thing come burrowing out.

First the white head, maggot-white, then the rest of it, slithering through to emerge outward on the floor.

It rose to its feet, a figure in dripping, ragged clothes and a bloodstained stormtrooper helmet, staring at him. The black polarized lenses of the helmet were streaked and filthy, clotted with slime and gore. The breath filter had been broken off on one side, and Trig caught a glimpse of the scaly infected throat of the thing underneath it. There was blood caked around the mouthpiece, and it occurred to him that the thing might possibly have eaten its way out.

It staggered toward him.

Trig backed away, immediately tripped, and fell. Jumping up, lunging sideways, he started running around the edge of the mountain. He imagined that he heard the thing coming after him, but it might have just been his own heart hammering in his ears. He didn't dare look back. But he could feel it there, growing closer, a steadily intensifying presence like pressure buildup behind his eyeballs and chest cavity, pushing him onward, faster.

The room spun around him. Trig jerked his head right and left. The door, wherever it had been, was utterly lost to him now. Fear had robbed him of all sense of direction. He didn't even remember where he'd come from.

As he bolted around the edge of the pile, lunging over three corpses that appeared to have been bundled together, wrists and ankles bound with cords, something caught his eye from up above—a glint of light.

Looking up, he saw the open ventilation shaft in the ceiling, at least ten or fifteen meters up, maybe more.

He finally stopped and looked back, saw the thing in the trooper helmet coming around behind him. It was moments away.

This time Trig didn't give himself time to think.

He started climbing.

It was even worse than he'd expected. The huge pile of dismembered parts and severed heads made up a loosely knit, constantly shifting terrain, moving and tumbling down as he clawed his way up and over it. The stench only seemed to thicken as he uncovered submerged levels of decay that hadn't yet been exposed to air. Struggling against his gag reflex was a nonstop battle, one he didn't always win, and the wobbling sensation of continuous near nausea only made climbing more difficult.

He tried to focus on the vent shaft, forcing himself to think only of getting out. Every few seconds, though, he did look back—he couldn't help it.

The thing in the helmet was climbing up after him.

It crawled with the steady relentlessness of something out of one his nightmares. And in fact, even in the depths of his own scrambling climb, Trig couldn't help but flash back to the voice of Aur Myss from the cell next to theirs, how he had promised to come for him and his brother. Was that an undead version of Myss behind him now? How had it gotten here to this part of the Destroyer before him, and what had it been doing inside this heap of human rubble? None of those questions even rose into his mind—only that it had followed him here to satisfy whatever undying urge drove it forward.

Rage.

Murder.

Hunger.

Something moved underneath him in the mountain.

It's just another body part, don't think about it, don't let it—

He felt a scabby, clay-cold hand reaching up out of the pile to seize his ankle.

Trig let out a painful squeal of fright and wrenched his leg free, almost losing his balance and falling. He was struck by the vision of his small, helpless frame bouncing back down the slope of corpses, as hands and arms and mouths lunged out, ripping off pieces of his flesh, until they'd finally added his own bleeding carcass to the mountain.

Instead he climbed faster, forced himself to dig in, yanking himself upward, dumping down bodies as he went. He was close enough to the top now that he could actually see inside the vent, the oversized duct that had been exposed there.

Go. Just go.

With what felt like enormous effort, he thrust his entire body upward. His brain had shut down completely at this point. He no longer smelled the room or even truly felt its awful, gelid presence sticking to him. He was aware only of what lay ahead, and how much he needed to get there, and the last few moments, as he got to the top of the pile, left no imprint in his memory whatsoever—they might as well have happened to someone else entirely, a stranger.

Consciousness snapped back through him as his fingers scraped cold metal, the blessed solidity of the ductwork's outer rim, and he levered his upper body through it with a gasp, jerked his legs up behind him and only then allowed himself to breathe. The vent was not much bigger than his shoulders, but it was large enough.

Trig looked around in a kind of mild hysteria. His heart was slamming, trying to smash a hole through his chest, the muscles in his throat working up and down wildly.

I'm going to start bawling again. Well, go ahead and cry. I suppose you've earned it.

But he realized his eyes were dry. At last, at the top of a pile of human bodies, he had arrived at a place beyond tears.

There was a whistling, breathing noise below him, and when he looked down he saw that the thing in the trooper's helmet was still climbing up the mountain of bodies.

Trig looked back and forth through the open duct. Then he picked a direction and began to crawl.

35/The Whole Sick Crew

ACROSS THE MAIN HANGAR, SARTORIS WATCHED DARK figures moving toward him.

He'd first seen them coming right after all the shooting had died down, only a handful at first, then more, now dozens—traveling en masse, a single organism made up of countless smaller components. They were close enough now that he could make out individual faces, men he'd worked with for years on the prison barge, guards he'd called by their first names, soldiers who had followed his command with the utmost unquestioning loyalty, prisoners who had once shuddered in fear at his passage. They traveled together now, their swollen, disease-ravaged bodies pressing against one another, death as the final brotherhood.

They were coming for him.

Behind him, there was a sharp clank of metal on metal. A low, collective groan escaped the shadows, deep and ravenous, and Sartoris spun around and looked through the captured ships to catch a flicker of movement beneath the X-wing. Somehow they had slunk around behind him, too. He could see them down there, huddled in the shadows, watching him.

Where did they come from?

That was Lesson One from Imperial Corrections playbook, one you never forgot—never turn your back on the cons. Now Sartoris realized it was too late. The certainty of his death filled his belly like a big gulp of contaminated ice water. Droplets of sweat began to trickle down his spine, creeping between his shoulder blades and down into the waistband of his pants.

The figures in front of him had jerked closer, seeming to advance in the interstitial space between moments, like footage from which the transitions had been removed. Their eyes never left his, and there was a slinking, primitive slyness to their movement; he wondered if they were still sizing him up, or if they just derived some atavistic pleasure watching him squirm. Within seconds it wouldn't matter—they'd be close enough to launch themselves at him and tear him apart. They could even shoot him now if they wanted. They were all carrying blasters.

The things behind him hooted out a scream.

The inmates and guards in front of him screamed back, a call-and-response. Sartoris saw ropy strands of drool swinging from their mouths, human and nonhuman alike. There was a group of Wookiee prisoners with what looked like whole waterfalls of saliva pouring down between their fangs and slopping over their chins, soaking their fur. They looked like they'd eat him alive instead of blasting him—maybe they preferred their meat uncooked.

"Come on, then," he said grimly. "What are you waiting for?"

As if awaiting the invitation, they broke ranks and charged, and Sartoris, who up till that moment had

had no idea what his next move would be, looked around at the abandoned X-wing and grabbed the fighter's wing, lifting himself up and onto it. He made his way with a jouncing, bandy-legged run up the wing toward the cockpit canopy, pivoted, and dropped down into the pilot's seat, reaching up to try to seal it shut, but the canopy was broken and wouldn't close.

Within seconds every flaw in his reckless plan became glaringly apparent. He could already feel both groups of the things moving below the X-wing, their thudding collective strength and hunger surging as they rocked the fighter back and forth underneath him, trying to flip it over, while others climbed up the nose cone in front of him. The three Wookiee prisoners he'd glimpsed earlier had already taken hold of the canopy and were trying to rip it loose, or maybe just haul themselves up high enough to attack him where he sat. He could picture their three woolly bodies hunched over the stump of his exposed torso, ripping and tearing whatever was left inside the kettle of blood that had once been the X-wing's cockpit.

For the first time his eyes flashed down at the avionics display. The instrument panel held the milky glow of sleeping electronics, but it was brightening slowly now as if activated by his arrival. Just above the throttle, the green targeting scope blinked steadily, and Sartoris saw switches for weapons activation, laser cannons, and proton torpedoes coming online.

From above, several hands reached down at once and sank their claws into his neck. He could smell them now, the infected Wookiees, the salivating, bronchial snorts of their hunger as their breath drew closer. Wet hot saliva dribbled down over his face and he felt the press of something sharp and hard.

Sartoris squeezed the trigger.

His whole world jolted backward. The laser bolt burst from both sets of cannons at once, a blinding muzzle flash that vaporized the mob of inmates in front of him even as it threw him into reverse. The Wookiees that had been reaching for his throat disappeared, jerked away with a howl of anger and shock, and Sartoris realized the X-wing was still skidding, propelled along the hangar floor by the recoil. It all ended abruptly with a jarring crash, the thrust engines of the ship hammering into something even bigger than itself, probably the hangar wall.

He lunged up and out of the seat and saw he'd collided with an Imperial landing craft, a *Sentinel*-class shuttle that looked like it had been sucked in by the tractor beam and dropped flat on the deck.

There's an emergency hatch here somewhere. Where is it?

He vaulted onto the shuttle's hull, ran up and felt the craft lurch underneath him—they were already down there, waves of them, and that screaming noise was cycling up again. When they hit the underside of the shuttle he lost his balance completely and fell forward, through the hatch.

What came next was blackness.

With a silent groan, Sartoris opened his eyes. He was lying on his back in the shuttle's darkened cabin, the corrugated steel pressing against his neck. Outside the reinforced durasteel hull he could hear them faintly, scratching, slapping, pounding. There was a brief pause. Something much heavier slammed into it, an explosion—blasters again, he thought wearily, and wanted nothing more than to just black out.

"Did you bring them with you?" a voice croaked in the darkness.

Sartoris jumped a little and stared up at several sets of eyes peering down at him. As his vision adapted he realized he was looking at a group of men in ill-fitting Imperial uniforms leaning over him from seats mounted to either side of the shuttle's cabin walls. Reacting without thinking, he jerked backward and tried unsuccessfully to scramble away.

"It's all right," the voice said. "We're not infected."

Sartoris examined them more closely, his heart still wedged up in the tight pocket of his throat. Even amid everything else that was happening outside, the appearance of the men remained a shock. Their starvation-ravaged faces were little more than skulls with parchment-yellow skin stretched over them, lips drawn back in permanent sneers, cheekbones bulging grotesquely outward. One of them attempted what Sartoris supposed was a smile.

"I'm Commander Gorrister," the man said, clearly waiting for Sartoris to introduce himself. When he didn't, Gorrister sank back with a sigh and continued, "From what's going out there, I can only surmise that you ended up here the same way we did."

Sartoris grimaced. "Something like that."

Gorrister started to say something and a sharp slamming noise cut off his words. Outside the ship, the blasterfire continued, smashing and pounding against the armored hull. The commander waved it away with scarcely a glance.

"They'll give up after a moment," he said. "It's really just a reflex on their part—"

Sartoris raised an eyebrow. "Reflex?"

"Mm. Certain learned behavior patterns are difficult to unlearn, even when grossly ineffective."

Another round of explosions slammed into them, the firing intensifying.

"Sounds pretty effective to me," Sartoris said.

The commander shook his head. "Our hull is specially reinforced. We're essentially impervious to handheld weapons. Until they're able to decipher the heavier artillery, we're relatively safe. Of course, that's only a matter of time, isn't it?" His upper lip disappeared in his mouth with a soft sucking sound. "They haven't pulled in many ships yet, but I suppose that's to be expected, hovering out here at the edge of the Unknown Regions. There's not much traffic this far out."

He made a weak effort to point up to the cockpit, where the shuttle's instrument panel shone faintly, a myopic eye afflicted with cataracts of energy-lack.

"We saw how it dragged your prison barge in," Gorrister said, and then, uttering a terrible, humorless chuckle that was more like a gasp: "Too bad they can't eat their own."

"Who?" Sartoris asked.

The man favored him with a wan expression that was less incredulity than outright disbelief. "What, did you actually think your inmate friends out there were the only ones aboard?"

"Who else is there?"

"Who . . . *else*?" This time the commander actually mustered a laugh. It sounded like a layer of dust being blown from a very old book, perhaps one that had been bound in human skin. "Oh, dear. You really don't have any idea what's going on, do you?"

Sartoris felt a stirring of irritation he didn't bother to suppress from his voice. "Suppose you bring me up to speed."

"It started ten weeks ago, when the first tanks began leaking."

"What tanks?"

Gorrister ignored him. "There were those conspiracy theorists among us who still insisted it wasn't an accident, that we were all part of some larger experiment, which I suppose is possible."

"Hold on," Sartoris said, sitting up to face the man straight on, "start at the beginning."

The commander paused, and Sartoris realized that the deputation of skeletons sitting on either side of him had leaned forward, listening intently, as if they'd never heard this story before, despite having ostensibly lived through it.

"What can it matter now?" Gorrister said. "We left Meglumine hauling top-secret freight. Experimental military-grade ordnance for the Empire, all the usual caveats, on Lord Vader's own directive. Our destination was a testing base on Khonji Seven, outside the Brunet system . . . but we never got through the Mid Rim." He took a breath and let it out with great effort. "At first the breach seemed minor, and it appeared that our engineers were able to confine it. Some of our scientists were even able to study the effects it had on human physiology, the lungs and larynx in particular. We assumed that they had it contained." He paused and cleared his throat. "But that turned out not to be the case for long. The infection spread quickly through the entire Star Destroyer—soon no one was safe."

"Wait a second," Sartoris said. "You're telling me there's ten thousand *more* of those nightmares staggering around out there?"

"Oh my goodness, no. Some of us did manage to escape, obviously—or tried to, and a few showed signs of natural immunity. Using their blood, our medical officers were able to synthesize an anti-virus, as I'm guessing yours probably did, too . . . based on the fact that you're still here."

Sartoris just grunted, not inclined to go into his own random immunity to the sickness. Gorrister didn't even seem to notice.

"We sealed off part of the ship," he said, "and injected ourselves with the anti-virus. At first it seemed like there would be enough to go around." Another thin and ghastly attempt at a smile: "It didn't last as long as we'd hoped. There was more in the bio-lab, but of course we couldn't get back to retrieve it. That was when the plan began to change somewhat. Of course many of the crew were eaten before they could change over—torn to pieces and . . . well, *consumed,* I suppose is the word."

Gorrister swallowed, seeming to find something particularly distasteful in this part of his narrative.

"At first we tried to gather up the remains—we put them in a waste facility, chopped them up, thought it might be a way to keep them from changing, you know, and even that isn't always successful. But in the end we were outnumbered and there really wasn't anything to do but run." He flashed a cold, flat glance up at Sartoris. "Until they found out how to activate the tractor beam."

"They can think?" Sartoris envisioned the screaming things staggering around outside the ship, pounding and firing at it almost randomly with blasters. "That's crazy."

"Oh, it's madness," Gorrister agreed, blinking at him with the mildest of curiosity. "All I know is that they were waiting for us inside the hangar when we came back in. The first man out of the hatch got his head ripped off at the shoulders." He licked his lips. "After that we sealed ourselves back in, sent a distress signal, and settled in to wait."

"How long have you been trapped here?"

"Ten weeks."

Sartoris felt his mouth drop open—he couldn't help it. "You mean you've been canned up here inside this ship for ten *weeks*?"

"There were thirty of us originally. Now we're down to seven, including myself." The commander sighed, eliminating what sounded like the last of the air from his lungs, and sagged against the bulkhead behind him again. His filthy uniform was so big on his now emaciated body that it bulked up almost comically around the shoulders, like a child playing dress-up. "We keep trying to make comm contact but all frequencies are jammed. I believe that also might be a deliberate countermeasure on their part." When his eyes found Sartoris's again, they were colorless and dispassionate, the eyes of a man delivering a lecture that he'd prepared years earlier. "You asked earlier how I thought they could activate the tractor beam. They *learn*, you see. That's part of it."

"Those things out there?" Sartoris asked. "But they're . . . animals."

"In the beginning perhaps. But consider—the ones that changed on board the Destroyer ten weeks ago don't even bother attacking this shuttle's reinforced durasteel armor with blasters anymore. They've already grasped the fact that it doesn't work. It's the new arrivals, the inmates and prison guards, who are out there shooting at us now . . . and if you listen, you'll see that they've already stopped, too." He snapped his fingers, a brittle *pop*. "That's how quickly their behavior changes."

Sartoris realized he was right. The blasterfire outside the shuttle *had* stopped, just as Gorrister had predicted.

"I think it has something to do with the sickness," the commander said, "the way it was initially designed. They form clusters, tribes . . . swarms. And they communicate with one another. I'm sure you've heard it."

Sartoris thought of the screaming that he'd heard, the weird cyclic quality of it, back-and-forth call-and-response in the hangar.

"And that way they are all able to adapt at the same time," Gorrister said, "as one, like a kind of systemwide upgrade, do you see?"

Sartoris shook his head. "What are you talking about, *designed*? You mean somebody created all this on purpose?"

Gorrister studied him in silence for a moment, with what might have been the tiniest of smirks.

"Naïve, aren't you?" he asked. "I told you we were carrying top-secret weapons. How long have you served the Empire?"

Sartoris didn't bother to provide an answer. He'd noticed something else that bothered him even more than that smirk on the man's face. Throughout the course of their conversation, his fellow soldiers had begun edging slowly closer to him, and they were licking their lips compulsively, over and over.

Sartoris squirmed back a little farther. For the first time his gaze fell on the stack of uniforms folded neatly on the seat in the corner.

"What happened to the rest of your men?" he asked.

"You must understand." Gorrister's voice was soft now, no longer mocking; in fact it was nearly sympathetic. "We had ample water here inside the shuttle but precious little food, and it's been *ten weeks*. It was nothing more than a simple matter of survival. We were *starving*, you see."

Sartoris frowned. The men were getting to their feet now. It suddenly occurred to him that they might have been sitting here saving their strength until this moment.

"Hold it." He stood up, backing away, and felt his shoulders hit the wall behind him. "We're not like them."

"Of course not," Gorrister murmured, dismissing the idea. "We drew lots. To keep things fair. We gave each man a quick, humane death. At first we threw the remains out there . . ." He nodded above, at the emergency hatch. ". . . to those things, as if that might somehow satisfy them. But it only made them come back. So we ate the remains, too. In the end we sucked the marrow from the bones. But none of my men felt any pain, I promise." One emaciated hand slipped into his uniform jacket and produced a small transdermal patch. "And neither will you."

"What is that?"

"Norbutal," Gorrister whispered. "A paralytic. You'll just go to sleep. And when we're rescued, the Emperor will recognize your sacrifice with the highest of honors."

Sartoris started to say something else.

He realized that the commander had told him there were six other men and he only saw four of them.

Then he felt a pair of hands grabbing him from behind, pinning his arms behind his back.

36/Lab Rat

■■■■■▬■■■■▬■■■■■

ZAHARA WASN'T SURE HOW LONG SHE'D BEEN RUN-
ning. Lactic acid cramped her thighs and calves, oxygen debt reaching the point where it cried out, no
longer able to be ignored, and she'd lost track of
where she was—the end of another protracted corridor somewhere deep in the Star Destroyer's main
hangar level, but farther back. With no sense of direction and no destination, she guessed it was just a
matter of time until something caught up with her.

She stopped and leaned against the wall, temples
throbbing, and whooped in a series of deep breaths.
Her throat and lungs ached, and the root of her
tongue had that sprained, dizzy feeling it got when
she'd overtaxed herself. Counting her heartbeats,
she made herself calm down, calm down, just *calm
down*.

She held her breath and listened for screams. Heard
none.

The corridor was absolutely silent.

Up ahead, blocking the way, were what appeared to
be stacks of crates. She started walking toward them,
feeling marginally steadier now that she'd taken a

rest, and stopped at the hatchway on her left, looking at the sign posted over it.

BIO-LAB 242

AUTHORIZED PERSONNEL ONLY

Zahara glanced down at the security pad that someone had pried from the wall, dangling on stalks of variegated wires. With the strong sense that what she was about to do was not at all wise, she put her elbow to the hatch itself and forced it open.

At first the lab was almost reassuringly familiar, a research area, a clinical space designed for the usual flights of emotionally detached observation and interpretation. It was a great gleaming dome, white-walled and blazing with overhead fluorescent lights, the walls honeycombed into dozens of empty, glass-enclosed cells.

Each cell was equipped with its own research and observation workstation—not that any of them seemed to be actually working. The entire chamber smelled powerfully like antiseptic and chemicals, with an undertone of hot copper wiring. Giant ventilation fans stood in the walls, but they were all motionless, which probably explained the stillness of the stagnant air.

Walking forward, Zahara noticed the dead computer terminals, broken doors, and abandoned keyboards, the individual keys scattered across the high-impact durasteel floor like loose teeth. She saw a protocol droid standing in the corner, a 3PO unit, apparently broken, one golden eye flickering spastically, fingers twitching. As she got closer, she heard a low, almost inaudible whine escaping from its vocabulator.

Next to it, an overturned chair lay on top of a de-molished rack of syringes and vials, and she noticed a human-sized bloodstain on the wall, arms upraised, like a spirit painted in red. The workstation in front of it appeared to be operational, however, the screen half filled with lines of text and a blinking cursor awaiting reply. It was the first functional indication she'd seen of possible communications.

Tentatively, she bent forward and tapped a key.

More data washed up instantly over the monitor, skimming past too fast for her to read. Then it stopped again, cursor ticking, and the wall in front of her clicked and peeled open to reveal a thick pane of glass beneath it.

On the other side of the glass was another hive-cell.

But this one wasn't empty.

Inside it, two yellow human corpses dangled in front of her at face level, webbed to the ceiling by thick networks of wires, feeding tubes, and monitor-ing equipment, a pair of hideous puppets. They were both badly decayed, facial features rotted beyond any recognition, eye sockets empty, and Zahara won-dered if she was looking at volunteers who had been abandoned here after whatever happened aboard the Destroyer. What would it have been like, she thought, being trapped in there while everyone on this side of the glass ran away?

Something clicked in front of her and began to whir steadily—one of the big ventilation fans in the wall above the glass. Zahara braced herself for the blast of foul air from inside, then realized that she could feel her clothes and hair actually being sucked away from her skin.

The fan was pumping air *into* the cell . . . and that made more sense. They'd have to deliver oxygen to the research subjects while they were still alive. Those chambers were probably airtight, and without the fans running, they'd suffocate in there, which was probably exactly what happened, she guessed, once the research staff had decided to abandon the lab.

One of the corpses lifted its head.

Zahara felt the room stretching around her, all sense of perspective seeming to elongate on gluey strings. On the other side of the glass the thing gaped up at her with its sagging, grinning face, moving the rotten stumps of its legs, swaying back and forth.

The air that went in, she thought, *it carried my smell in to them and woke them up—*

The other corpse had already awakened next to it. Its face twitched up and down as if sniffing her through whatever remained of its nose. Zahara started backing away as it lifted one tattered arm to grapple with the lines and wires that held it suspended from the ceiling. Sensing her standing there, both of the bodies started to do a jittering, swaying dance. One bumped into the other, and they both swung forward, arms outstretched. Back and forth, higher and higher. Some of the monitoring wires had already pulled off, but there was one particular tube leading straight from their chests that was still connected. The gray liquid oozing inside the tube reminded her of the substance that she'd tried to dig out of Kale Longo's abdomen. She followed the tube with her eyes and saw that it connected to a set of black tanks.

They were collecting it, Zahara thought. *That's*

what this is all about, their bodies actually produce that stuff and—

Behind her, a footstep scraped inside the lab.

She spun around and stared across the white space, the path between dead research workstations, and saw nothing. Her gaze fell to the broken rack of vials and syringes on the floor, only six or seven meters away, close enough that she could probably reach it before—

Before whatever came in here has a chance to get its hands on you? Do you really think so, Zahara? At the rate those things move when they're hungry?

A shape emerged between two of the workstations, a foot crunching something beneath it. Zahara glimpsed it, and then it was gone again. She looked back at the syringes—her only weapon. The muscles in her calves and thighs felt so tight she thought they'd snap, the tension rising upward to grip the bones of her spine.

Wham!

With a cry of fright, she whirled around and looked back. One of the research-subject corpses had managed to slam itself into the glass, leaving a red smear, a streaky imprint of its face and hands. She watched as it arced backward in its harness of monitoring equipment while the other corpse swung forward, smacking the glass hard with its face and hands, then shoving off again.

Get to the syringes and get out of here—now.

She bolted, crossing the distance in what felt like three big leaps. Grabbed a needle in both hands. Started to stand up.

And felt something move in behind her.

A rich smell of decay blew in over her shoulder, like wind from a grave.

She spun around and it grabbed her.

Zahara looked into its face.

The sickness hadn't rotted the researcher away as badly as the corpses in the containment chamber. She could still see some of the features the way they'd looked pre-infection—the silvery gray hair, the aquiline nose, the deep, distinguished creases of the face. A man of science. It wore a blood-grimed lab coat, one sleeve torn away at the wrist. There was a soft click as it opened its mouth and lunged for her.

She rammed the syringe into its eye, and jammed another into the side of its head, depressing both plungers at once.

The thing went rigid, mouth wide open, and screamed. Its legs went out from under it, its entire body collapsing.

As it fell writhing to the floor, Zahara moved for the exit. She was almost there when the screaming dwindled and she heard its voice behind her, a rasping gurgle.

"Frrrng unn ufff . . ."

It was trying to talk.

Hating herself for it, she looked back. The thing in the lab coat was crawling blindly toward her now, both needles still protruding from its head. Somehow the injections had restored some fragile measure of its former humanity, enough for it to try to make contact.

Its mouth moved up and down, making more garbled sounds she couldn't translate—pathetic attempts at speech. It raised one hand beseechingly. It was doing something, trying to tell her—

"What happened here?" she asked. "What did you do?"

The thing in the lab coat produced the same mucilaginous noises, more urgently. Its face worked strenuously, and it swung its arm toward the console behind her.

"Thrggh uff usss . . ."

"What?" she asked.

It made the noises again, swung its hands with evangelical fervor, and fell over. It growled and beat its fists on the floor. Its fingers crawled and prodded, and she realized it was miming the act of writing.

Gradually, with great effort, it reached up and pulled one of the syringes from its eye socket, jammed the spike against the durasteel, and started dragging it back and forth, etching out some crude type of ideograph. It made a high, desperate squealing sound as it did so, grinding the needle's tip harder into the reinforced plating.

The needle snapped and it sat up, no longer looking so weak, or so human.

It was grinning at her again.

Zahara realized whatever she'd done to it with the anti-virus had already run its course.

She looked down at the series of scratches that the thing had scraped into the floor, jagged letters like an erratic brainwave. It didn't make much sense, but had she honestly expected it to?

She was still mulling that over when the thing in the lab coat jumped on her, pinning her down.

She screamed. The thing clamped both hands around her throat and she felt its cold fingers slithering, squeezing, pinching, and choking off her scream at the same time that it lowered its mouth toward her gullet. She tried to push back against it but it was like struggling against iron manacles. The harder she fought to resist, the more constrictive its grip became. She was blacking out. What had her surgeon at Rhinnal always told her about oxygen deprivation? *Time is muscle. Time is brain.* She already felt the heavy penumbra of blackness crowding down on her vision, muffling her hearing, tightening into an indifferent, anesthetized nothing.

It ended with a metallic scraping crack, durasteel on bone, and cold, foul-smelling liquid splashed in her hair. The pressure on her throat went abruptly weak, the dead hands falling slack and sliding off to the side.

Zahara looked up, her vision coming clear. The thing's head was twisted sideways now, a surgical bone saw shoved through its neck, half buried in the gray flesh.

What . . . ?

Hovering behind him was a flat metallic face she couldn't believe she was seeing, even now.

"Waste." Her voice was barely a whisper. "You . . . came back . . . ?"

The 2-1B just looked at her. "I beg your pardon?"

"You saved me."

"Well, yes, of course," the surgical droid said, a bit puzzled. And seeming to remember that it was in the process of sawing the head off the thing in the lab coat, it thrust both the bone saw and the thing aside, dropping them to the floor. "That creature was attempting to injure you. And per my programming at the medical academy in Rhinnal, my prime directive is—"

"To protect life and promote wellness whenever possible," Zahara finished for him. "I know."

The surgical droid continued to look at her expectantly, as if awaiting orders. Zahara could already see that it wasn't *her* 2-1B, *her* Waste . . . but she nonetheless felt a throb of gratitude disproportionate to all reason. Of course a vessel this size would employ such a unit, and this lab would be the perfect place for it. Yet the tears in her eyes were not only tears of gratitude and relief but recognition of a friend she'd lost, but hadn't truly lost after all.

"Is there anything else I can do for you?" the droid asked.

"Can you . . ." She sat up, looking around the lab again with what felt like fresh eyes. "Can you tell me anything else about the research that was going on here?"

"Very little, I'm afraid. In a strictly scientific sense, I do know that my programmers were working on an easily conveyed chemical means of slowing the normal course of decay in living tissue. Ideally the virus would be able to take over nerve receptors and make the muscles fire even after clinical death has resulted."

Zahara thought of the corpses screaming at one another, linking up to form organized armies.

"Were there . . . military applications?"

"Oh, I really couldn't say. It was highly classified, and I'm strictly a surgical and scientific unit, nonpartisan in such matters and certainly not very knowledgeable when it comes to such clandestine weapons operations."

"Then do you know where I could find a workstation that might still be functional?"

"Oh, most certainly." The droid paused, and she could hear its components clicking and whirring busily beneath its torso cowling, a familiar noise that brought back another painful memory of Waste. "My sensors indicate that there seem to be several nondisrupted consoles available in the hangar control center. However, I am obliged to inform you that given the hostile environment, such an exposed area could prove particularly hazardous to you."

"I'm used to it."

"Very well. Would you like me to diagram the most direct route?"

"How about one that I can get to without going into the hangar itself?"

"Right away."

"And Waste?"

It eyed her again. "I'm afraid I'm—"

"Thank you," she said, and resisted the urge to take hold of its cool metal hand and kiss it.

37/Lifter

CRACK!

The next blast that slammed into the hull of the Imperial landing craft was no handheld weapon. Sartoris only realized this fact when the craft jolted suddenly upward and to the side, jerking him free from the two soldiers who'd come out of the cockpit, and launching him across the cabin headfirst into Gorrister.

The X-wing laser cannon, he thought wildly. *Those things out there, they saw me use it—*

And then:

I guess Gorrister was right after all. They can *learn.*

The commander stared up at him with an expression of perfect disorientation, like a man shaken from a particularly vivid dream.

"What . . . what's happening?" Gorrister's full attention was still riveted on Sartoris, then his eyes got even wider and he looked around the cabin at his starved men and the empty, folded uniforms of the ones he'd killed and eaten. For an instant Sartoris thought he glimpsed total self-realization in the commander's expression, a revelation of the depthless depravity to which he'd sunk over the last ten weeks.

Sartoris reached up and punched the button over his head, deactivating the locking mechanism on the emergency hatch. Then, seizing Gorrister by the collar, he swung him straight upward, using his skull as a battering ram. It would never have worked with the lock still armed—there was a reason the transport had been able to keep out the undead for ten weeks—but now that the mechanism was disarmed, both the hatch and Gorrister's skull gave way on impact, the steel flap swinging open. Sartoris hoisted him outward, flung his limp body to the side, and reached down to grab another man at random, plucking him up under his arms. Starvation had made their bodies considerably lighter, and Sartoris managed to wrench him through the hatchway single-handedly.

Outside, the mob of the undead had surrounded the landing craft on all sides, a sea of hungering faces: inmates, guards, and the original crew of the shuttle. As Sartoris had predicted, one of them had already clambered into the X-wing next to the shuttle and was groping desultorily at the controls. The cannons weren't pointed at the shuttle—had the thing inside the cockpit somehow banked a lucky shot off the hangar wall into their hull?

Then he saw the *other* X-wing, forty meters away, pointed straight at him. One of them was inside there, too.

Are they all *climbing into ships?*

Sartoris reached down, plucked another soldier from the transport, and heaved him out into the mob. The things fell on him instantly, grabbing his arms, legs, and head, ripping him to pieces while he was still alive. Despite his attempts to look away, Sartoris caught a glimpse of the man's face stretched wide in a silent scream as one of the undead popped his shoulder cleanly from the socket. The thing next to him took an enormous bite that removed one of the soldier's arms, waving it at the others, wielding it like a club.

Sartoris swung back down through the emergency hatch into the shuttle and grabbed the next man, who had been coming at him with some kind of primitive melee weapon in his fist, some truncheon or knife. Sartoris yanked him through in one thoughtless, adrenaline-fueled gesture. There was a third man behind him, and Sartoris grabbed him as well, under the arm and beneath his scrawny shanks, and hauled him up onto the shuttle's hull, the starved soldier gaping up at him from a place beyond all helplessness.

"Please," he said. "Please, don't."

Something about the voice stopped him and Sartoris looked into his face, and saw that underneath the filth and hunger and fatigue, the soldier was just a boy, an adolescent thrust into service of an Empire whose only enduring purpose was death.

"You don't have to do this."

Looking out on the soulless, shambling things, Sartoris saw them devouring the bodies he'd thrown them, waving severed limbs, fighting over the last ragged bundles of shredded viscera. Then he looked down at the young soldier again, the sunken face and terrified eyes. The boy was watching them, too. He looked like he was about to pass out from sheer horror. Sartoris could hear the air scraping in and out through his throat, the hollows of his lungs. For a moment Sartoris was completely transported back to the last seconds of Van Longo's life, the upturned face, the beseeching eyes peering into him for some trace of mercy.

"What's your name?" Sartoris asked.

"S-sir?"

"Your name. Your parents gave you one, didn't they?"

For an instant the kid seemed to have forgotten it. Then, tentatively:

"White."

"Does this ship still fly, White?"

"The sh-shuttle?" The soldier's head went up and down. "Well, yeah, but that tractor beam—"

"Let me worry about that. I might be back and if I am, you and your buddies—" Sartoris flicked his eyes off in the direction where he'd thrown Gorrister. "—we understand each other, White?"

"Yessir."

"I'm gonna make a break for it, and I recommend you use that opportunity to get this vessel locked down the best you can."

Without waiting to see if the kid got the message, Sartoris released his collar, allowing him to slide back down inside the shuttle, and gazed back across the hangar, his mind instinctively calculating a trajectory between the diversions he'd created when he'd thrown the other bodies out. It was a simple mathematical equation, and he'd always been good at math.

Turning hard, head down, he went pounding down the other direction, toward the bow of the shuttle, leapt off, and hit the ground running. Instantly a throng of the things came slamming toward him, arms outstretched and grasping. Sartoris plowed into one of them, skidded in a pool of blood, and felt an abrupt slash of pain across his left forearm but didn't stop to look at it.

He ran on, making a hard dash for the back of the hangar. The salvaged vessels behind him might be his only way off the Destroyer but they were no good to him unless he could disable the tractor beam, and that would mean getting himself to the command bridge first, and then—

There was a doorway at the far end of the hangar and as he ran through it, he heard an electronic beep go off—probably just a simple light sensor registering traffic through the walkway.

He looked around but didn't see anything. If one of those things had followed him back here, it was hiding from him now, which didn't make sense. At what point, he wondered, did fear itself become so redundant that it atrophied and dropped off entirely like an unnecessary, evolved-away appendage? Or would his species always find a use for fear, no matter how extreme the circumstances?

Sartoris took another look at his empty hands. Never in his life had he wanted a blaster as much as he did right now. The idea of venturing unarmed through the Destroyer was practically unthinkable. But if he stayed here, death was a guarantee.

It is anyway. The only question is when.

Walking backward, trying to see everything at once, he bumped into something hard and felt it recoil against him, jostling on a cushion of air.

Sartoris turned around and looked at it, unable to keep the half smile from spreading over his face.

It was the hoverlifter they'd come across earlier, the

one they'd left here because it couldn't hold all of them.

Maybe my luck's finally starting to turn.

He took a breath and reached up to pull himself aboard the lifter—and noticed the bloody gash just below his right elbow.

That was how he realized he'd been bitten.

38/Bridge

"I DON'T KNOW ABOUT YOU, PAL, BUT I WAS HOPING for better."

That was Han Solo, as he finally set foot inside the command bridge of the Star Destroyer. He'd been around a long time and seen a great deal of strange things, but if he survived this he'd definitely have people buying his drinks for a long time to come.

The catwalk had—well, to be honest, it had almost been more than he could handle. Crossing over had been difficult enough, weaving their way along through open space with nothing to hold on to, the bowel-churning vertigo as his center of gravity whirled like a gyro with a broken ball-and-socket.

He hadn't wanted to look down. But once the things down in the pit started shooting, he didn't have much choice.

They fired randomly, like they hadn't had much experience with blasters, but that was little reassurance when Han saw the sheer number of them. Firing back would have been a waste. There could have been thousands—at this distance it was impossible to say. It occurred to Han that they still seemed to be waking up, roused to consciousness by the presence of fresh meat, and their aim was poor, though by the end it had seemed to be improving. More than once the blasts had come close enough that he'd tasted ozone.

And if he'd lost his footing—if he'd slipped and fallen down into that sea of hungry bodies—

With deliberate effort, he forced himself back into the present moment. They were inside the command bridge, faced with the expanse of low-slung computer modules and navigation equipment with which the entirety of this kilometers-long miracle of interstellar destruction was steered.

It was smashed almost beyond recognition.

The screens had been punched through, banks of circuitry and sophisticated sensor arrays blasted, shattered, or yanked completely loose from their moorings, most of them flattened as if under some unthinkably heavy boot. Every step they took announced itself with the muffled crumple of broken glass.

"Looks like we finally found somebody that hates the Empire more than we do, huh?" Han asked, shaking his head. "You try the navicomputer yet?"

Chewie barked without bothering to look around.

"Okay, I'm just asking. Can't blame a guy for hoping, right?" He sighed and brushed debris from a seat facing one of the less thoroughly demolished consoles, plopping down. "Only thing still running is the tractor beam, huh? What kind of encryption we looking at?" He reached for a working keyboard and punched in a series of keystrokes. "Guys who designed this stuff weren't all that bright. How hard can it be?"

Something in the console chirruped, and crystalline

patterns began to coalesce on the cracked screen, clarifying and sharpening into lines of navigational code.

"Hey, Chewie, I think I got something here—"

Beneath him, in response to his directive, the entire Destroyer tilted slightly on its axis. Han, who'd never flown anything remotely this big in his life, felt a kind of fatalistic good humor taking root in the floorboards of his psyche. What would the Imperial High Command have to say about this, he thought, seeing a lowly smuggler with a price on his head sitting behind the controls of a Star Destroyer?

"See, what did I tell you?" He tapped in another set of instructions, not looking up. "Hey, did you get a chance to look inside those hyperdrive systems?"

Everything jolted hard and Han sat up fast, trying to figure out what he'd done and how to undo it. It felt like the Destroyer was listing slightly, and one of the consoles had begun to emit a low, steady whine. Lines of text were crawling across the broken monitor.

"Chewie?"

The Wookiee was gone. Han stood up, looking across the empty bridge. He listened, holding the blaster he'd found at waist level. The space around him suddenly felt very large, and absolutely silent, except for the faint click of data emerging on the screen. His eyes flicked down to it again with increasing impatience. Whatever encryption had locked the tractor beam into place was still active. It was awaiting a password.

Then, from one of the adjoining spaces, he heard it—a faint growl.

"Chewbacca?"

Finger on the trigger, he crept across the bridge, following the sound, and found himself looking into a subchamber he hadn't noticed until now. It was lined floor-to-ceiling with backup systems, whole panels of pulsating lights. The Destroyer tilted again, not dramatically but enough that Han could definitely feel the shift in equilibrium, and he wondered if he'd done something to destabilize its processing systems. The last thing they needed was for this entire vessel to go belly-up on them in the middle of nowhere.

He looked inside the subchamber. "Chewie? What's going on in there?"

Chewbacca was crouched in the semidarkness, looking at something. When he rose up, Han saw he was holding a small, hairy body—another Wookiee, Han realized, very young. It was wearing a tattered prison uniform.

"How'd he get in here?"

The young Wookiee gave a weak bleating cry. Chewbacca gazed at him and then back up at Han.

"Great." Han sighed. "Anybody else we're supposed to rescue while we're here?"

Chewie uttered a warning grunt.

"Okay, okay, bring him out," Han muttered. "You put yourself on the line once and all of a sudden everybody's got their hand out."

Chewbacca carried the small Wookiee out, and Han got a better look at the youngster's face. His eyes were reddish and cloudy; his throat was swollen so badly that he seemed to be having trouble breathing. The tongue protruded thickly from his throat. "Where's the rest of your family?"

The Wookiee bleated again and Han saw where he

was pointing: to another hatchway on the opposite side of the command bridge.

"They're in there? What are they doing, hiding?"

Chewbacca carried him over, shifted his weight to one arm, and reached out to open the hatchway. As he did so, the Destroyer yawed slightly again. Han saw a trickle of blood come oozing out from underneath the door and across the tilting durasteel floor toward them.

"Whoa," Han said, and nodded down, where the trickle had become a steady stream. "What *is* that?"

Chewbacca made a quizzical grunt and looked back at the young Wookiee, who sat up with a sudden burst of energy and pushed the button himself to open the hatch.

There were three full-grown Wookiees in prison uniforms hunched together in the corner, squatting together, sloshing around in what looked like an entire ocean of blood. Han could see that the fur of their faces was slathered in gobbets of meat, and they were snorting and smacking and breathing heavily as they tore into a pile of human remains sprawled around them. The corpses they were devouring appeared to be wearing Imperial guard uniforms.

Han breathed, "What the . . . ?"

All at once they looked up.

It happened instantaneously—a blur of bloody hair and hot, shaggy musculature jolting toward him faster than his eyes could process. Han's reflexes took over and he opened fire on the closest one, the point-blank assault tearing the Wookiee's chest apart, laying it out flat on the floor where the thing flopped and coughed and tried to right itself. The one behind it went pinioning sideways and landed on its side, scrambling to get up while the third trampled over it. Han shot it in the face, snapping it backward. Then he opened on the one that had been trampled, blasting it until he'd reduced it to a mangled heap of trembling fur.

Next to him, Chewbacca appeared to have frozen, as if utterly detached from the situation. As Han took a step backward, he felt small sharp hands hooking into the hollow of his neck and looked around to see the young one's mouth snapping at him. He tried to shove it off, but the thing had attached itself to him with its arms and legs, its frantic, overheated body squirming against him like a giant rat.

A deafening explosion went off next to him and the young Wookiee's head burst apart. As it slumped off him and hit the floor, Han saw Chewbacca lowering his blaster.

"Thanks," Han said. "Nice of you to join in."

Chewie didn't say anything. He was still looking at the body on the floor.

"Let's get out of here, huh? Check the hyperdrive."

Eventually, with what seemed like great difficulty, Chewie turned away.

39/Stop

━━━ ┉┉ ━━━

THE VENTILATION SHAFT HADN'T BEEN MUCH WIDER than Trig's body when he'd first entered it, and now it seemed to be constricting as he squeezed through. Every few seconds a thick blast of humid air came roaring over him, buffeting his clothes and hair, and he heard metal clanking like a broken valve somewhere inside its endless length. How far it would take him, or where it ultimately let out, he didn't know— he could just as easily die inside here, lost and dehydrated, one more speck in the indifferent maw of the universe.

Then, up ahead, he saw the end of the shaft. Dim light from somewhere below cast a pale yellow rectangle on the top of the shaft—he wouldn't be able to go any farther.

Creeping closer, right up to the edge, he stuck out his neck and peered over.

He felt his stomach plummet down to his knees.

The vent emptied out into the same abyss that he'd labored so intensely to avoid earlier, the yawning pit with the long tube of the Destroyer's main engine turbine at its bottom. It looked even bigger from directly overhead. Immediately below him, less than a meter away, was the narrow catwalk where Han and Chewie had crossed, close enough that he could probably lower himself down onto it, if he absolutely had to. It would mean clinging onto the edge of the vent while he swung his legs down, dropping down onto the catwalk without losing his balance, and—

From behind him inside the shaft, something shifted.

Trig looked back.

Froze.

Wanted to scream.

The thing in the stormtrooper helmet was making its way up the vent toward him.

No question about what was happening now. It was groping its way forward and looking at him intently through the soulless lenses of the helmet.

"No," Trig whispered. *"Don't."*

It kept coming, the oversized helmet wobbling on its head as it crept forward. Trig looked back over the edge of the vent again. He could feel his entire body shaking helplessly, his heart racing so fast and hard that he thought it might burst inside his chest.

You have to go down there, a voice said inside his head. *You have to go to the catwalk. It's the only way, or else that thing, that thing—*

I don't want to! I can't!

He glanced back at the thing crawling toward him. It ducked its head and started crawling faster.

That was when the helmet fell off.

Trig blinked, momentarily undone by shock and dismay so disorienting that he actually forgot where he was and what he was doing. In that second he could only stare at the face that had been revealed under the helmet, his brother's ruined grin, one entire side of his face destroyed beyond recognition, the gleaming socket and smashed bone.

And then he heard himself trying to speak, his voice rusty, scarcely a whisper:

"Kale?"

The thing looked at him and just kept coming.

"Kale. It's me—it's Trig."

It showed no sign of hearing him. Trig could see it salivating now, the drool mixing with runnels of blood dried to its face. He could hear it breathing, and the noise reminded him of the sound the air made as it whooshed through the vent. This was too much. It wasn't happening, and if it was, then it meant he'd gone mad, in which case—

It pounced forward, smashing him down against the vent at the very edge of the outflow lip. Trig opened his mouth to say something and burst into tears. This time he let them come out all they wanted, tears and snot and sobs and bawling, and why not? What possible difference could any of it make now?

Kale's mouth opened and closed, and Trig could smell the death that was locked in there, the death that had been dealt to his brother, the death that his brother was about to deal to him. Kale wasn't going to answer him, and he wasn't going to stop. Trig had loved his big brother more than anything else in the galaxy, and it didn't matter now.

"Kale?"

It gave a snarl and lowered its face to Trig's neck, the teeth and tongue sweeping over his throat, dripping hot breath that smelled like some ghastly, poisonous moss. Kale's hands felt both hot and cold at the same time, the dead flesh moist, sticky, and clutching. He'd climbed on top of Trig now, pressing down on him with his full weight.

With a cry of pain, Trig shoved him back. A white-hot spark of something he'd never felt before went sizzling across the pit of his stomach and landed on his heart, and a light went out inside him, followed by a dismal realization of what was about to happen. It was like a story he'd already heard, the ending written long before he ever got a chance to do anything about it.

Look after your brother.

"Kale, I'm sorry."

As Kale pushed in on him again, more hungrily now, Trig straightened his knee under his brother's torso and rammed it upward, momentarily lifting his brother's body off him. Throwing Kale to the side, Trig twisted around, grappled with his wrists, and levered his brother backward to the edge of the vent.

Then he pushed him over.

40/Awakening

KALE FELL WITHOUT A SOUND.

Trig watched him drop, growing smaller, a teardrop against the expanse. As the semidarkness swallowed him up, the silhouette only partially illuminated by the faint lights surrounding the engine turbine, Trig saw what he hadn't seen earlier, down below.

Upturned faces.

Thousands of them.

They were—as they always must have been—clustered down at the bottom, on either side of the turbine, as if drawn to the ghost of its now absent hum. Even through his veil of shock, the delayed reaction to what had just occurred, Trig knew what he was looking at.

It was the original crew of the Star Destroyer.

They were screaming up at him as one.

At that same second Kale's body hit the turbine and bounced, flopping off the side and disappearing into the teeming morass of bodies. The resulting sound was an even louder scream, like a single entity awakening and achieving a kind of brute mass-consciousness, awareness that hardly progressed beyond the immediate physical needs. Their breathing wafted up toward him in invisible gradations of damp warmth, their hunger seeping through the air like thermals rising before a storm.

They see me.

Already they began to reach up toward him, the moaning noise becoming more aggressive, rising in pitch and volume to find that steady, now familiar waveform. Shifting and swaying, some of them began attempting to climb up the sides of the turbine itself, in an effort to get closer to him. Some appeared to be holding things, but at first Trig didn't know what the objects were.

Just as he started pulling himself back into the vent, thinking he could at least backtrack far enough to evaluate his options, the blasters started firing.

They were shooting at him, and their aim was deadly accurate. Before he could start crawling inside, Trig felt the vent shaft jerk and burst open in front of him, squealing free of its soldered housing and dumping him straight out. He toppled out the end without being able to grab on to anything, and for a moment he was falling through space, one final trajectory echo of his big brother.

He hit the catwalk hard and it doubled him up upon impact, chiseling shards of pain up through his ankles and legs. Trig grabbed it and held on, fingers curled into the cold latticework, clamping down on it with his entire body. He could both hear and feel the blaster bolts resonating through space around him. One of them was going to hit him, and he could only hope the blaster killed him before he fell into that far-off mass of outstretched hands and gnashing mouths.

He wanted to be dead before that happened.

All around him the catwalk shook and bonged with the impact of the blasters. Chips of durasteel streaked past his cheek, tiny cold specks of pure velocity. He wasn't thinking clearly at all anymore, and that might have explained why he didn't react immediately when he saw Han and Chewie at the far end of the catwalk, staring back at him.

They must have just come back down from the command bridge, Trig's mind droned dazedly. *I guess things didn't work out so well up there, either.*

Han could definitely see him, Trig knew—he was waving at him frantically, either to move forward or stay down, Trig wasn't sure. Meanwhile, what exactly was the plan? Both Han and Chewie had blasters, but two weapons hardly mattered against the blitz of firepower below them—they might as well have been as unarmed as Trig himself. And neither of them appeared willing to venture back out onto the catwalk in the middle of all this, not that Trig blamed them.

Trig narrowed his eyes. Han was gesticulating even more desperately now, shouting at the top of his lungs. He was pointing up, up, and when Trig tilted his head straight up he saw the last section of the vent shaft dangling loose from above, swinging back and forth.

Hands were reaching out of it.

Trig thought of the mountain of corpses on the other end of the shaft, how it had started coming to life as he'd climbed it.

They followed me down the shaft.

He watched in mute and suffocating terror as the owner of the hands slithered out. It was an Imperial soldier, its dead face lit with urgency. Clamoring for

Trig, it rocked back and forth inside the dangling vent, lost its balance, and then fell out, hands scrabbling furiously as it fell past him, plummeting down into the blackness. Three more Imperials squirmed free after that, spilling out like hideous, fully formed offspring from some unthinkably fertile ovipositor.

The vent section swung back again, and this time Trig realized that whatever was inside it was actually waiting for the vent to arc forward before it jumped, so it could use that last ounce of forward momentum to grab him as it sprang free from it. The corpse launched itself at him, too fast for Trig to see its face, and he plastered himself to the wall, feeling claw-like fingers scrape and smear across his torso.

The thing snapped its fist around his leg.

And this time, it held on.

Trig looked down. For an instant the only thing he could see was the limp sac of bruise-colored flesh that had once been its face, staring up at him, the place where the piercings had been ripped out, the gaping, leech-maw of its mouth. When the mouth opened Trig could still see the glint of steel piercing up through his gullet, the blade that Kale had shoved up through there, what felt like a thousand years ago.

It was Aur Myss.

41/Blackwing

ZAHARA TRIED THREE KEYBOARDS BEFORE SHE FOUND one that worked. Fingers trembling, she jacked it into the secondary workstation and held her breath, waiting to see if they were compatible.

The 2-1B had declined to accompany her up to the hangar control room, electing instead to stay in the bio-lab, "in case I'm needed." But the droid's directions had been flawless. He had sent her through a Byzantine maze of walkways that delivered her to a service lift, and she'd taken it straight up to the pilots' ready room, through another set of doors that opened on hangar control itself.

The large enclosed booth stood at least thirty meters off the docking floor. From her current vantage point she could see everything—the six or so random ships that the Destroyer's tractor beam had sucked in on one end, and on the other, the half-destroyed docking shaft that had brought them up here from the barge.

The things were down there, too.

Hundreds of them, or perhaps thousands, swarmed the different damaged ships, teeming so thickly that Zahara couldn't begin to estimate their numbers.

More were pouring in constantly through various hatchways and doors, a nonstop flood of bodies crawling over one another toward the different vessels. Every few seconds they screamed together, that same sonic waveform, and that only seemed to accelerate the arrival of others.

How was she going to get down there? And if she did, how could she possibly hope to get inside one of those captured spacecraft without—

First things first.

The screen in front of her blinked obediently on, awaiting the password. Her fingers hovered over the keyboard for a moment, and then she typed in the word she'd read scrawled across the floor of the bio-lab:

`blackwing`

There was a long pause, and the screen went completely blank. Then, abruptly, across the top:

`Password accepted.`
`Enter command?`

Zahara let herself exhale a sigh that seemed to loosen every muscle in her chest, shoulders, and back. She typed in:

`Access master control to Star Destroyer`
`tractor beam.`

After a split second the response came back:

`Master control to tractor beam is accessed.`

She typed:

> Disable tractor beam.

For a moment, nothing happened. Then the computer responded:

> Unable to complete command.

Zahara scowled.

> Explain inability to complete command.

Immediately:

> Tractor beam has already been disabled.

She sat back and looked at the screen with a slight frown remaining on her forehead. Had Han and Chewie actually managed to switch the thing off from the command deck? If so, then they should be on their way back now, assuming the plan was still to get out of here on one of the scuttled ships.

She looked back down at the heaving mass of bodies that filled the hangar floor. Hopefully Han and the Wookiee had found some more firepower along the way.

Leaning forward, she typed:

> What is blackwing?

The system replied:

Blackwing:

Imperial bioweapons project I71A. Galactic virus
dissemination and distribution algorithm.
CLASSIFIED: TOP SECRET.

Project status: In progress.

"*Distribution* algorithm?" She looked back out at the bodies in the hangar, now packed so densely that in many places she couldn't even see the floor. Every few seconds, they released another version of that ringing, rhythmic scream, and when she listened she could hear the other scream reverberating back from somewhere in the Destroyer. It only made them move more urgently.

But they weren't just milling around anymore.

The corpses were climbing into the different spacecraft, the X-wings, the landing shuttles and transports, the freighter in the far corner of the hangar. Still others were streaming back into the half-blasted docking shaft leading back down to the prison barge. Zahara saw that they were lugging something on their backs.

She looked more closely.

Black metal tanks.

She glanced back at all the different vessels in the hangar, thinking again about the distribution algorithm, a coordinated means by which the Empire could spread the virus everywhere it wanted across the entire galaxy. Distractedly, she watched a group of the things lined up alongside an X-wing, working together to turn it around, pointing it up toward where she was standing.

Her mind went back to what Waste had told her about quorum sensing, the way the disease worked.

They don't do anything until they can all do it together—when it's too late for the host organism to fight it—but why?

Then it hit her, and she spoke aloud without realizing it.

"They're leaving."

Down below, the X-wing was aimed straight up at her. What had that other 2-1B said about being exposed up here?

A blinding column of flame tore across the hangar, hurtling straight for her.

42/River

THE KID STOOD NO CHANCE.

Even from here, Han could see how it was going to play out, and if he and Chewie went out on the catwalk to try to help him, it would just mean all three of them would die together. It was a miserable thing to realize, yet there it was—a rock-solid certainty.

Chewie gave a long, mournful howl.

"Yeah, I know," Han shot back, hating himself all the more for having to say it out loud. "You got any better suggestions?"

Out on the catwalk, the kid was slipping off, the thing dangling stubbornly from his ankle, dragging him down. He might be able to hang on for another five seconds, certainly no more. In an act of pure desperation, Han leveled his blaster, knowing he had no shot—he could just as easily hit Trig from this distance, or miss altogether. But what else was he supposed to do?

Are you really going to sit this one out? Cash it in, go down without a fight?

Chewbacca was looking at him, awaiting the decision. At last Han nodded and lowered the blaster.

"Okay," he muttered, "on my signal, we go out, just try to grab him—"

Chewie gave another howl, this one more startled, and Han saw what he was looking at.

It was too late.

The kid had let go.

The kid was falling.

From the moment his fingers finally slipped off, some part of Trig felt nothing but pure weightless relief: after everything that had happened, just to give up and surrender himself to gravity and the void. As he fell, Myss still clinging to his legs, he looked down into the screaming faces coming closer and felt the full intensity of their wrath swallowing him up. He remembered hoping that he'd be dead by the time he hit, and guessed that probably wouldn't happen either, unless—

Something swooped underneath him, and he smashed into it, connecting with his right hip and shoulder and rolling backward, arms and legs flopping with the leftover momentum. A heartbeat later and his forehead ricocheted off the smoothness of cold prefabricated resin. He propped himself up, felt the speed accumulating around his face, pushing forward. He wasn't falling anymore—

But he *was* moving.

He realized that he'd landed inside some kind of hovercraft, a utility lifter, shooting across the empty space above the main engine turbine, still twenty meters above the deathscape of screaming faces.

Trig turned his head and glanced forward. There was a figure perched up at the steering console. He couldn't see who it was—

Except that the man seemed to be wearing an Imperial prison guard uniform.

The lifter tilted, arcing sideways over the abyss, and when the driver shot a glance back around, Trig got a look at his face. Not that it made any sense, but after two and a half months aboard the prison barge, he would have recognized Jareth Sartoris anywhere.

Sartoris banked hard and swung the lifter around toward the far side of the catwalk where Han and Chewie stood staring at it with a look of disbelief that matched Trig's own. The guard's voice was a hoarse croak above the screams and blasterfire.

"You coming?"

Han and Chewie dived in without a word. The lifter sank under the new weight, and Sartoris rammed the stick forward and up. Watching him wrestle with it, Trig noticed the deep bite on his forearm, the way the underlying tissue had already started to bulge and pucker from some gray squirming necrosis deep inside.

Sartoris was fighting more than just the throttle, he realized.

The lifter rocked sideways, straining to hold them above the mob below, faces lit up by steady, strafing blasterfire. Han and Chewie had already taken their positions over either side, shooting back.

"You're that pilot, right?" Sartoris shouted, not looking over. "Can you fly this?"

Han blinked at him. "You're gonna let me—"

"See this?" Sartoris held up his bitten arm, the exposed tissue squirming visibly now as though it had a series of small, electrically charged serpents writhing just below the flesh, trying to find a way out. "I don't have much time."

"Yeah, well—" Han leaned over and squeezed off another round of fire into the masses. "Chewie and I are a little busy right now."

Sartoris looked over his opposite shoulder. "What about you?"

"Me?" Trig squeaked.

"We're overloaded." Sartoris gestured over at the pitch and yaw alarms that had already started flashing faster on the main console, and Trig realized with horror that they were still going down, descending slowly but steadily into the shrieking morass below. Within seconds they'd be feeling the clutching hands thumping the underside of the lifter, yanking themselves on board. "The hover won't take the weight."

"I don't think I can—"

"Time to learn." Sartoris took hold of the boy's arm and steered him forward past Han, planting him in front of the console. "Got it?"

"Where are we going?"

"There's an Imperial shuttle down in the hangar with some soldiers aboard. Look for a kid named White." Trig realized the captain of the guards was holding on to his shoulder, looking at him; the man's eyes burned through clear and bright. "You understand what I'm telling you?"

"But—"

Sartoris squinted, the vertical lines deepening on either side of his mouth, furrows that you could fall through if you weren't careful. "There's something you should know about your father."

"You knew him?"

"He was a good man," Sartoris said. "Unlike me."

Trig stared at him.

"He would've been proud of you. You ought to know that."

"How—" Trig started. He was still talking when Sartoris swung his legs over the lifter's side rail and jumped.

"Kid!" Han cried out. "Are you flying this thing or what?"

Trig leaned forward, grappling clammy-palmed with the throttle, barely keeping them from colliding with the wall. The turbine and its abyss were behind them now, shearing off at some unlikely angle. Everything in front of him was coming at him too fast, a smear of reckless velocity.

Twenty meters below, in the concourse leading forward, the original inhabitants of the Destroyer were still shooting, and climbing the walls trying to get them. They were packed together, thousands of them, a solid river of reeking and deteriorated flesh. As one, they threw back their heads and let out another group scream. It was answered by another scream from far away.

"You know where you're going?" Han shouted.

Trig glanced down at the layout on the lifter's navigational screen, the blip showing where they were among the labyrinth of midlevel passageways. He felt sweat dripping under his armpits and over his ribs.

You can do this.

The lifter jerked. Something was climbing up from

the underside. He could feel the lifter tipping. Han leaned over, trying to see what it was, and shook his head.

"I can't get a shot!"

Trig looked forward again. He brought the throttle down as low as he dared, until he saw the exhaust manifold rising up from the corrugated floor. Holding his breath, he nudged the stick forward, dropping them another fraction of a millimeter. It was pure seat-of-your-pants speculation—the sort of thing his father and his brother would have excelled at, but he was the only one left to do it.

"Trig, what—"

Wham!

The corpse underneath the lifter slammed into the manifold, scraped off, and went pinwheeling sideways, headless now, down into the masses that had spawned it. Han threw him an appreciative glance.

"That's more like it."

Careering around a corner, Trig steered them down the slightly wider throughway, dull yellow lights whickering past like his own wildly careering thoughts. He kept going back to what Sartoris had said just before jumping off the lifter.

He was a good man. I'm not.

It had been a generality, spoken by a man who knew he was going to his death. Why had it sounded like he'd been confessing to killing Von Longo?

A burst of static broke from the lifter's comlink, a voice rising from its speaker.

"Hello, is anyone there?"

Han's arm shot past his face to grab the link, flicking it on. "Who's this?"

"—Cody—" the voice cut in. "—hangar control—"

"We're on our way now," Han said.

"—*no*—stay away—"

"Say again."

"Under attack—"

The comlink sputtered, Zahara's voice reduced to a warble. Trig thought he heard blasters in the background, the twang and crash of catastrophic wreckage. He watched as Han changed frequencies, trying to home in on the signal.

"I'm losing you, Doc," Han said. "Just hang on, okay?"

". . . too many of them . . ." Zahara's voice was drifting, lost between clouds of heavier static. Trig thought he heard the words "laser cannon," and then the link broke off entirely. Han dropped the comlink and checked the lifter's digitized schematic.

"It's okay, we're almost there, right?" he said. "That's the entryway straight ahead."

Trig eased the stick back and then let it go forward, getting a feel for it at last, now that the trip was all but over. The lifter blurred through the end of the corridor, toward the hatchway where Han was pointing. Despite the fact that they were almost there, Trig felt an odd tug of apprehension, a sense of having made the wrong decision about something so long ago that there was no way to correct it now.

Chewie growled, and Han's nostrils flared. He looked worried.

"Yeah," he said. "I smell it, too."

Trig glanced over. "What?"

"Smoke."

*   *   *

The hangar wall was on fire.

Through the smoke Trig could see the army of the dead pouring through, headed to the far end of the hangar. The X-wing that had evidently attacked the wall was still pointed at it, its laser cannons tilted upward with random blocks of salvaged equipment. Trig glanced back up where flames had overtaken the west end of the hangar, obscuring everything in a wall of thick, oily smoke that smelled like burning copper wires and charred durasteel.

"Where did Dr. Cody say she was?" he shouted.

"Main hangar control," Han said.

"Which is . . . ?"

Han pointed directly into the flames. Trig pulled back on the stick, angling the lifter up into the choking black wall. Instantly his eyes, nose, and throat started stinging, tears streaming down his face. He could hear Han shouting at him, and Chewbacca let out a loud, angry roar that broke off in a burst of deep coughs.

"What are you doing?" Han said. "You want to get us killed?"

"I'm not leaving her."

"If she's up here she's already dead!"

Trig brought the lifter upward until he was staring through the flames into what was left of the main hangar command. Melted computers and consoles lay bubbling across the warped durasteel floorboards like a surrealist nightmare of Imperial technology.

She's not in there, he thought. *She made it out. Maybe—*

The thought snapped off cleanly in his mind.

It was a small shape, dwarfed by the oblong slab of charred components that had toppled over to crush it. Trig looked at the slender hand protruding out-ward from underneath the pile, remembered how it had looked resting on his father's shoulder in the in-firmary. He felt the last of his breath evaporate from his lungs, leaving him absolutely still.

"Kid." Han's voice was far-off, and from the sound of it, Trig knew he'd seen her, too. "We have to go."

Trig opened his mouth to speak but nothing came out. He turned the lifter away, and down.

43/Death and All His Friends

IN THE FINAL MOMENTS BEFORE LEAVING THE STAR DEstroyer, Trig Longo saw things he knew he'd never forget, no matter how much he wanted to. Later, when he tried to put the pieces together and make sense of it, the words weren't there, and he found himself sifting through jumbled images, raw memories and feelings that still frightened him as badly as they had when he'd first experienced them.

He was still reeling with shock over what he'd seen up above. After losing Kale, he'd figured his capacity for grief and pain had been exceeded—but the knowledge that Dr. Cody was gone, too, was almost more than he could stand. It left him grief-stricken and miserably nauseated, as though he might vomit up some small bitter piece of his own heart.

Down below, on the hangar floor, the things inside the hangar had stopped screaming and were focused only on packing every remaining spacecraft. Watching them, Trig saw that there was no longer any question of priorities. They wanted off the Destroyer as badly as Trig, Han, and Chewie did.

He hated them.

Hated them worse than he'd ever hated Sartoris or Aur Myss or anything in his life. Hated them with an intensity he'd never imagined himself capable of. It was as if all the molten fear he'd suffered up till now had hardened into glassy black peaks of pure rage.

His eyes flicked forward. The landing shuttle that Sartoris told him about was already airborne. Hardly thinking, Trig swung the lifter alongside it. He saw the emergency hatch pop open and Han looked around at him hesitantly.

"You sure about this? That's an Imperial shuttle."

Trig pointed. "Look."

A skeletal arm waved from the hatch, gesturing them inside, and Trig didn't wait around to argue. He brought the lifter up, flipped it into auto-hover, and climbed over the transom.

It was darker inside the shuttle's cabin but easier to breathe without the smoke. The Imperial soldier standing in front of them had a pale, starved expression that immediately made Trig ill at ease; when the soldier smiled it was like watching a skull stretching through a thinly knit web of yellow flesh.

"You're White?" Trig asked.

"Tanner." The skeleton shook its head. "White didn't make it. It's just me and Pauling, up in the cockpit."

"Yeah, well," Han said, and cleared his throat. "We planning on leaving now, or are we taking up permanent residence?"

"As soon as—"

The whole world started shaking.

* * *

"What's going on?" Trig asked.

Han shot a glance up to the shuttle's cockpit, where another cadaverous Imperial soldier—Pauling, he assumed—was fumbling with the controls, hands dangling from his emaciated, stick-like wrists, all of which seemed to be under the control of some ridiculously inept puppeteer.

"What is that?" Pauling croaked, head jerking from side to side. *"What's happening down there?"*

"Hangar bay's opening," Han said. "I figured you boys were doing it."

"Negative." Pauling jerked one crooked thumb out the canopy. "I think they are."

Down below, Han could see the bottom of the Star Destroyer sliding open to reveal the void of space. Off to the right he thought he glimpsed the bow of the Prison Barge *Purge,* appearing very small at the end of its docking shaft, a tiny footnote dangling from the bulk of the saga of Imperial dominance.

As the bay came wide open, the captured ships began flying out—a pair of TIE fighters, the freighter, an Imperial shuttle, and the X-wings—spewing outward in all directions, scattering into space like flies off a corpse. As one of the smaller craft flew past them on its way out, Han glimpsed the sallow faces of the dead peering out at him from the cockpits, crammed in so tightly that their rotted flesh was pressed against the glass. Were some of them actually *licking* it?

"Let's go," Han said. "What are we waiting for?"

Pauling punched in a series of commands and the shuttle started vibrating, then jolted hard to port and stopped moving.

"What's wrong?"

"I don't know," Pauling stammered, "the thrusters . . ."

"Get up," Han said, practically jerking the Imperial soldier from his seat and shoving him back toward the cabin. "Chewie, we're gonna have to do this ourselves." He looked around. "Chewie?"

No answer came back, and Han didn't have time to go looking for him. He reset the navigational systems to manual and brought the throttle straight up, nosing the shuttle around and angling down until he saw the open bay below him. The galaxy was out there, wide open, just where he'd left it.

He punched it.

The shuttle shot downward from the Star Destroyer's hangar, rocketing past the prison barge and into space, and for that moment, Han Solo felt the surge of adrenaline he always got when whatever ship he was piloting began living up to her potential.

He didn't want to think about the lady doctor, what it must have been like for her in the end when those things had opened up on her with the X-wing's laser cannon.

But he knew he would eventually.

Couldn't be helped.

Concentrate on what you're doing. Don't get stupid now. We're not out of this yet.

He was starting to recalibrate the hyperspace navigation system when he first heard the screams.

"What's happening back there?"

There was a thump, and Pauling came staggering back into the cockpit. Deep red arterial spray was jetting from the stump where his arm had once been.

His face had gone an even paler shade of gray, his mouth gawping open in amazement.

"Those things . . ."

Then his voice stopped. The screams back in the cabin were only getting louder, and Han stared as Pauling did a weird, wandering pirouette back around and flung his remaining arm in that direction, as if to tell Han about what was going on.

Then something grabbed him and jerked him away.

Han flicked the guidance systems on remote and groped instinctively for his blaster. What had he done with it? Laid it aside when he'd taken the throttle, but where had it gone?

Standing up slowly, he peered around the corner.

One of the things from the Destroyer's hangar was standing in the cabin. It had removed its broken stormtrooper helmet to eat. How it had managed to get inside the shuttle before takeoff, Han didn't know, and it didn't matter—its mouth was buried in Pauling's throat and it was busily slurping his blood, ripping off huge gobbets of his flesh. Han looked down and saw its white-booted foot planted on the chest of the other Imperial soldier, Tanner, or what was left of him—not much more than a heap of bloody refuse, a black uniform packed with seeping meat, one eye rolled completely backward.

Han's gaze swept the cabin. On the other side he saw Chewbacca and Trig crouched at the end of the row of seats, staring back at him. Han mimed the word *blaster,* and both of them shook their heads.

What am I supposed to do here? he wondered. *I'm not the hero. How many more miracles do these people expect from me anyw—*

He stopped.

The trooper-thing was looking up at him.

And grinning.

Strands of Pauling's flesh were dangling from its teeth. It lurched for him, arms outstretched, howling loud enough that, inside the confines of the cabin, it made Han's ears ring.

He tried to dodge backward into the cabin, but his foot caught on something—Pauling's severed arm. As his legs went out from under him and he fell, the last thing he saw was the thing in the stormtrooper uniform dropping on him with his full weight.

And then only darkness.

44/Freebird

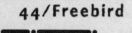

TRIG HEARD THE BLASTER GO OFF BEFORE HE SAW IT. Hunched next to Chewie, he'd been looking around the cabin for anything he could use as a weapon when the air suddenly came alive with a now familiar jolt. When he swung his head up, the thing in the stormtrooper uniform was already flailing sideways, away from Han.

Chewbacca was on his feet, running toward the thing, picking it up—smoke still pouring from the hole blasted in its back—and smashing it down into the cabin floor.

Trig looked back in the direction where the shooting had come from. What he saw was enough of a shock to render him momentarily speechless.

"Dr. Cody?"

Zahara leaned in the rear of the cabin with Han's blaster in both hands, upraised and ready. Her voice was low, not much more than a whisper. "Careful, Chewbacca. I think I'd better hit him again. Just to be sure."

Han—still on his hands and knees—scrambled backward, searching himself frantically for signs of bites or infection. When he saw Zahara standing there he gaped at her. "Where did you come from?"

She didn't respond, just kept her attention fixed on the thing in the trooper armor. It was seizing now, arms and legs flailing, head flung backward as sluggish grayish fluid pulsed up from its lips to pool behind its head. As they stared at it, more of the fluid started leaking from its nose and ears and finally from the corners of its eyes like sticky infected tears running down either side of its face.

"They never did that before," Han said.

"They've never been this far from the source before."

Han looked at her, bewildered.

"There's probably a heavy contamination residual spread throughout the Destroyer from all those tanks. Maybe it's what helped sustain them—slows down the decay process and keeps the muscle receptors firing."

"How do you know all this?"

Zahara gave him a sidelong glance. "I get my information from a droid, remember?"

"Hey, I didn't mean—"

"It's all right," she said. "Look." She pointed out the glass at the other ships that had left the Destroyer ahead of them. At first Han couldn't see what she was trying to show him, but after a moment he realized what was happening. The escaped ships had stopped moving—they were drifting aimlessly into the depths of space. As he watched, one of the TIE fighters listed drunkenly sideways, swiveling directly into the path of another TIE, and they slammed into each other, exploding on impact.

"That was Blackwing's flaw," Zahara said. "It's going to keep them from spreading it any farther than this."

"Blackwing?"

"That gray liquid in those tanks was a highly refined

version of the virus. The whole operation was set up
to create an unlimited supply of it, probably so that the
Empire could manipulate its behavior wherever they
wanted."

"So all those zombies down there," Han said, "they
were just the middlemen? Like a means to an end?"

Zahara nodded. "I think so. Their resurrected bodies were probably intended to be the suppliers and
distributors. But without constant and direct exposure to the virus, they can't function."

Han scratched his chin. "I still don't get how *you're*
here. We saw your body up in the main hangar control."

"That was White," Zahara said. "He picked up my
distress call. He came out looking for me—got me out
of there. But he wasn't fast enough to get out himself."

"Some random stranger sacrificed himself to save
you?" Han asked. "No offense, that doesn't make a
whole lot of sense."

Zahara's smile was a pale, wan line.

"He said a stranger did the same thing for him."

They traveled for a long time without talking. Chewie
helped Han fly for a while and then went back into
the cabin to nap, leaving Han alone. Sometimes he
thought the galaxy was better observed that way, in
silence, when you could sit and look at it and wait for
things to make sense—not that they always did.

After a while the kid came into the cockpit and sat
down where Chewie had been. Han didn't say anything, giving him time until he was ready to talk.

"Where are we headed?" Trig asked finally.

Han shrugged. "A better place."

"So there's no plan?"

"There's always a plan. Sometimes it just takes a while to see what it is."

Trig looked at him.

"What?" Han asked.

"Nothing. That sounds like something my dad used to say, that's all."

"Your old man, huh?"

"You would've liked him." Trig sat back, gazing far out into the depths of space at all those stars. "Were you ever scared back there?"

"Me? Pfft." Han cocked an eyebrow. "Not that I'm looking for an excuse to go back, mind you."

"How do you like the shuttle?"

"This thing? It's okay. I mean, if you want to see fast, you should see mine—or should've, before the Imperials impounded it, that is. Not much to look at, but . . ." He was aware of the kid staring at the instrumentation panel and navicomputer feeding itself coordinates in a steady chain of silent dialogue. "You want to give it a try?"

"You serious?"

"You flew that hover like a champ. Seems to me like you're ready for something bigger."

"I couldn't."

"Sure you could." Han handed him a headset. "Here, put these on. I'll show you how this works."

Trig blinked at him, a hesitant smile finding its way around the corners of his mouth.

"You know, Dr. Cody said before that guy White died, he told her about the shuttle."

Han nodded. "Right."

"White said his guys had a name for it."

"Oh yeah?"

"Yeah," Trig said. *"Freebird."* He glanced at Han tentatively. "I like that."

"Freebird, huh?" Han considered. "I guess that sounds about right." Han pushed back from the controls so Trig could get a closer look. "Come on over, I'll show you how it's done."

Two days later they sold the transport to a group of Black Hammer pirates on Galantos, in a city called Gal'fian'deprisi.

"The sooner I get out of here," Han groaned, "the less I'll have to try to say the name."

They were sitting in a tapcaf outside the starport, Trig looking up from his side of the table, Han and Chewie on one side, he and Zahara on the other. "Where are you headed?"

"With our half of what we got for that transport?" Han grinned. "Buy my ship back."

"I thought you said it was confiscated by the Imperials."

"Are you kidding? As corrupt as those local bureaucrats are, they probably had the *Falcon* at auction before we were even loaded on that prison barge. It's just a matter of tracking her down."

"You're not sticking around?"

"Nah." Han stood up and extended a hand across the table. "Be seeing you, Doc." He glanced at Trig. "Kid, take care, huh?"

"You, too."

"What about you guys, anyway? You got big plans?" Zahara thought for a moment and nodded.

"Unfinished business."

Epilogue

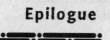

EVERYONE IN HANNA CITY ASSUMED THE TEENAGE BOY and the woman were brother and sister. Although she was significantly older, they both carried themselves with the same hard-won grace, as if they'd both come through the same fire together. Something in their manner was humble, almost common, and when they traveled, as they did endlessly now, they had little trouble avoiding any difficulties with the Imperials.

The morning that they arrived on Chandrila, they spent hours walking through the planet's rolling hills, along the shore of Lake Sah'ot. The air here was cool and almost supernaturally clear, crisp enough that they could smell the lush green land far in the distance. It was the kind of place that Trig Longo could imagine settling down in someday, and when he said that to Zahara Cody, she just smiled.

Along the eastern shore they came across a small community of local people, fishermen and farmers. They knew of the family that Zahara asked about, and it wasn't hard to find the small ranch a kilometer away, perched at the edge of a pasture overlooking the water.

When they got there, she approached the door and knocked.

The woman who answered was darkly beautiful, haunted and haunting at the same time, her eyes deeper than space. At her feet, three young children clung to the hem of her frock, gazing fearfully at the two strangers on her doorstep.

"Yes?" she said. "May I help you?"

"Are you Kai?" Zahara asked.

"Yes, that's right."

"My name's Zahara Cody. I worked with your husband aboard the Prison Barge *Purge*."

"I'm sorry, I don't understand." The woman stared at them nervously. "I already spoke to the Empire about this."

"We're not here as representatives of the Empire," Trig said.

The woman didn't say anything, but her look of wariness grew deeper.

"Your husband had something he meant to pass on to you," Zahara said. "I just wanted to make sure that you got it." Reaching into her pocket, she handed the woman a single tattered sheet of flimsi.

The children all gathered closer, craning their necks to watch as Kai opened it up. The smallest of them, too young to read, looked at up his mother. "What is it, Mommy?"

The woman didn't answer for a long time. Her eyes moved back and forth across the page, and Trig saw tears glimmering there, rising up and spilling over. Then she looked back up at Zahara.

"Thank you."

Zahara and Trig waited while she read it silently to

herself a second time. By the time she finished, the tears were running down her cheeks. She didn't bother wiping them away, and the oldest child had slipped his arm around her, as if he could somehow protect her from her own sadness.

"Thank you for this," she said. "Would you . . . would you like to come inside? I was just making some tea."

"That sounds good," Zahara said, and she and Trig stepped inside to the clamor of children and the smell of tea.

Read on for an exciting preview of

STAR WARS: RED HARVEST

by Joe Schreiber

Published by Del Rey

Header

On the other side of the academy, fresh snow had begun drifting up outside the dormitory where Scopique had recently returned from his afternoon workout. The Zabrak was finishing his shower—it was his routine to wash up at this time of the day, when he had a rare moment of privacy—and stepped out of the foggy stall with a towel wrapped around his waist, when he noticed a trail of blood across the floor.

Scopique stopped and looked down at it. The blood hadn't been there a moment before, when he'd gotten in the shower. The splatters were fresh and bright, streaking across the floor in the direction of the bunks.

Scopique felt his defense mechanisms tensing, going into a state of vigilant readiness, his natural aggression already ramping up to the next level. Easing his way silently the rest of the way out of the shower, he dressed quickly in his uniform and followed the blood-trail to the right. He could smell something now, the rancid smell of meat that had started to decay. It seemed to be growing worse with every second.

That was when he saw the body lying on his bunk.

It was dressed in a tattered academy uniform, its limbs and back contorted at unnatural angles so that the head lolled sideways from the obviously broken neck. Staring at it, Scopique murmured a whispered childhood curse in his native language. The possibility that this might be a trick, some kind of poorly conceived prank, never crossed his mind. Someone had beaten a Sith academy student to death and abandoned the corpse here on his bunk—as a warning or threat he didn't know which.

He edged closer, hoping he might be able to recognize the victim from what remained of its face. There wasn't much left to identify. The skull was badly crushed, half the face swollen and purple, the other half grotesquely pancaked so that one corner of the mouth peeled upward in a hideous parody of a smile.

Scopique took another step, leaning forward, reaching down to the turn the head over.

The corpse swung itself up and lunged at him.

It was Jura Ostrogoth.

Scopique sprung back, instincts taking over, as the thing charged at him in a ragged, flopping blur. He flew across the dorm floor, used a Force leap and jumped straight up, grabbing the ventilation fixture that hung five meters above the beds, legs dangling, using the vent's beveled surface for purchase while he scanned the room below for any kind of weapon.

Below, the corpse snarled and lunged at him, every leap taking it closer to where Scopique hung on.

Thick ropy spit swung from the half-pulverized jaw. From above, the Zabrak thought he could actually see colonies of maggots squirming in the thing's lacerated scalp. No doubt about it: Death had come for Jura Ostrogoth, but it hadn't finished the job.

The Zabrak stared down at the corpse, heart pounding, killing instincts fully engaged. On some level, from that first moment when he'd made the tape of Jura on his bunk, he'd always known there would be an hour of reckoning between them. Now that the moment had arrived, couched in terms that he never could have expected, Scopique was filled with a wild, adrenalized bloodlust and he actually felt himself grinning a crazy grin. Was he actually *enjoying* this?

Yeah, he thought. *Yeah, I guess I am.*

Drawing on the Force, gathering it inside as he'd been taught during hundreds of hours of training, he jerked the vent fixture from its housing. It came loose with a hollow metallic pop, bolts rattling free, opening a rectangle of cold space that fed into an open air-shaft above. Still dangling from the open shaft, Scopique turned the vent fixture over in his free hand, evaluating its immediate utility as a weapon. It was thin and aerodynamic, with sharp edges—it would serve the purpose well enough.

He looked down at the thing.

"Whatever you are," Scopique muttered, "say goodbye to your head."

Swinging himself around, he flung the vent housing as hard as he could at Jura's corpse.

The makeshift discus whistled down through the air and found its target perfectly, shearing Jura's head from its shoulders and sending it tumbling forward across the floor. Thick, half-clotted blood spurted from the stump of the corpse's neck. The decapitated body took another shambling step, tilted sideways and fell to its knees, then down on its belly.

Still dangling from the open vent—he was taking no chances—Scopique stared down at the thing in frank fascination. Nothing he'd learned at the academy even came close to what he was looking at right now. When he told the others—

Thumping noises from below: the headless monstrosity was still moving. In fact, it was leaning forward, groping around the floor until it found its severed head, sitting back up again and holding the head face-forward in front of its chest, tilting it up in Scopique's direction, so that those runny black eyes were staring straight up at Scopique, mouth working up and down as if it were chewing on something.

The mouth opened, and it screamed.

Scopique saw the decapitated corpse of Jura Ostrogoth haul back and fling its own head straight at him, its mouth still wide open. Without thinking, the Zabrack swung his free hand in front of his face, and felt teeth clamp into the tender flesh of his forearm, ripping through the skin and muscle, right down to the bone. The pain was unbelievable, chemical somehow, as if the incisors were coated in some kind of fast-acting acid. Agony shot up through Scopique's arm to his clavicle, and he let go of the vent and fell, the head still affixed to his arm, and hit the floor hard. Blurrily, he looked down at the head. It was making little gurgling sounds now, its jaw tightening and releasing, the eyes still gleaming.

"Get off me!" Scopique shouted, trying to shake his arm but unable to muster much strength. Was the arm broken? *"Get off!"* He grabbed a hank of the thing's hair and pulled as hard as he could, but it still wouldn't release. *"Get off my arm!"*

For several horrible seconds, he tried slamming it against the floor, pounding it as hard as he could, but nothing seemed to affect it. It was locked on tight, the burning liquid pain continuing to drip through the wound in his forearm.

Scopique stood up. The floor felt crooked under his feet. Staggering toward the bed, he underestimated the distance and crashed to the floor a second time, this time landing on his face. Blackness was crowding up through his vision, eclipsing the light, and he realized now that the pain in his arm had basically stopped, overwhelmed by a cool numbness that had begun spreading through his entire body.

Scopique fell utterly still.

All sound faded.

The numb feeling deepened, bringing with a kind of near euphoria that swept through his entire consciousness in one solid black wave.

This isn't so bad, was his final, fleeting thought. *This isn't so bad at all.*

Sometime in the next thirty minutes, a group of students came back to the dorms to find the room in disarray. They didn't see what was left of Scopique—he had crawled under the bed—but they did find Jura Ostrogoth's severed head.

And by the time they heard the noises coming from behind them, under the bunk, it was far too late.

Subzero

IN THE FIRST HOUR THAT TRACE PASSED THROUGH the collapsed walls and stone temples of the academy, the blizzard around him only worsened. It was as if the planet itself had read his arrival as a kind of infection on the cellular level and was fighting him off however it could. The temperature, already freezing, continued to plunge until his throat and lungs burned with every breath. The wind roared between the massive boxy shapes of the buildings and substructures, the great slabs and half-submerged corridors. Its scream was wraithlike, endless, the cry of something hungry for more than simple meat. Even the pellets of snow themselves felt sharper, jagging into his skin like tiny bits of shrapnel from an endlessly recurring explosion.

In his peripheral vision, a shadow twitched and slithered.

Trace stopped, hand reaching back for his lightsaber, and that was when he saw the man stepping out of the arched doorway to his left. Even before Trace saw the man's face, he sensed the thin, bitter smile twisted over his lips, the threat of violence in those half-lidded eyes. The man's tunic and cloak blew out behind him, snapping whip-like in the irregular gusts of wind, and his voice, when it came across the broken landscape between them, was a low snarl.

"You landed on the wrong world, Jedi."

Trace turned and faced him directly. The man was a Sith Master; that much was readily apparent—perhaps an instructor at the academy.

"I am Shak'Weth, Blademaster here on Odacer-Faustin. I can only assume that you came here seeking humiliation and an unpleasant death."

"I'm here on other matters."

"Ah?" The Blademaster cocked his head slightly, looking marginally intrigued. "But you've found me instead."

Trace nodded. Actually it was only stillness that had found him, clarity of thought, and it came as a blessing. The cold, the darkness, the stinging wind—all of these outside factors had simply ceased to exist. His entire world had shrunken to the exact distance between him and the man who stood before him, an obstacle in the way of finding Mestizo. Trace felt everything inside him beginning to relax and flow smoothly as the Force extended through his nerves and muscles, generating a kind of weightless balance between action and intent. He drew his own lightsaber, felt it blaze to life in his grasp, a perfect extension of himself.

The Sith Master's response was immediate. With a harsh grunt of fury, he flew at Trace, vaulting upward in the wind and angling the blade down with both hands, ripping through the ground where Trace had just been standing. The execution was flawless, a thing of almost organic brutality, as if the Blademaster had become a force of nature, another component of the blizzard that roared around them.

Yet he was still too slow.

Leaping sideways, Trace had already caught himself and spun around with his own lightsaber extended in front of him in a sweeping blow. The Sith Master was already there, deflecting the attack and charging him again, hammering him backward with a vicious series of piercing thrusts and jabs, offering no quarter. Twice the blade came close enough to Trace's face that he could smell the scorched stubble on his cheek; the third slash came within millimeters of taking off his head.

Trace realized that regardless of what Shak'Weth had said a moment earlier, the Blademaster didn't intend to humiliate him, to toy with him or prolong the duel any longer than was necessary. At this point the Sith Master was attacking for the most primitive reason imaginable—to slaughter Trace and leave his steaming carcass in the snow. In that split-second Trace saw the rest of the duel playing out in two distinct ways, neither of which would last long. Death was hovering over them now like a scavenger, close and claustrophobic—he saw it reflected in the Sith Master's eyes.

When the red blade came at him again, Trace jumped upward. He put everything he knew about Form V's Djem So variation into that jump, leaping over Shak'Weith, spiraling through the flying snow, landing on the other side, and twisting around instantly, keeping his lightsaber at throat level with the intention of finishing the duel in a single stroke.

Shak'Weth laughed—a bone-dry chuckle—and deflected the maneuver with mocking ease. He swung at Trace and this time the Jedi felt a hot, bright stab of pain as the lightsaber seared through his cloak and tunic, slashing into the flesh along his ribcage. Drops of blood fell into the snow, disappearing as they melted.

"Too easy, Jedi." Now the Blademaster's shoulders and back were braced against the slouching stone wall behind him, its outer surface cracked and half-collapsed, and he tensed to spring forward. "Now I shall finish you."

As he arched forward, Trace saw a pair of hands shoot out from the broken wall behind him, gripping the Blademaster by the throat and jerking him backward. Shak'Weth slammed into the cracked stone hard enough to drop his lightsaber, and Trace saw a ghastly white face burst up through the open hole in the wall, a screaming face, suctioning down on the Sith Master's right cheek and eye, teeth bared, gouging into his face.

Trace took a step back, still holding his own lightsaber up, watching the thing that hauled Shak'Weth through the hole in the wall where it could more easily devour him. Great arterial eruptions spurted up from the ragged perforation in the Sith Master's throat, spraying up over the wall and down into the snow and ice, painting the whole world red. Inside the wall, the thing lifted its face up and Trace saw its eyes—flat and without the slightest spark of life—yet they had once been human, even youthful. A Sith student, he realized— a teenager. What had happened to it?

The thing shoved its mouth back down into the ragged red cup that had once been Shak'Weth's right eye socket, slurping noisily. When it paused a moment later, the noise that it made was a high-pitched, ululating scream, and Trace realized that there were other screams, countless screams, a threnody of them rising up along with it, coming from every direction at once.

The night was full of them.